Main

DIRTY WORK
Part One

Melodrama Publishing
www.MelodramaPublishing.com

This is a work of fiction. All of the characters, organizations, and events portrayed in this novel are either products of the author's imagination or are used fictitiously.

www.melodramapublishing.com

Library of Congress Control Number: 2017909509
ISBN-13: 978-1620780862
First Edition: September 2017

Printed in Canada

BOOKS BY

Erica Hilton

10 Crack Commandments
Bad Girl Blvd
Bad Girl Blvd 2
Bad Girl Blvd 3
The Diamond Syndicate
Dirty Little Angel
Dirty Money Honey
Wifey: From Mistress to Wifey (Part 1)
Wifey: I Am Wifey (Part 2)
Dirty Work (Part 1)
Dirty Work (Part 2)

DIRTY WORK

Part One

Erica Hilton

PROLOGUE

ESPN played on the 32-inch flat-screen in the bedroom, and Stephen A. Smith and Skip Bayless could be heard commentating on tonight's basketball game on First Take. The Nets were playing the Atlanta Hawks at the Barclays Center in downtown Brooklyn. Both men were going back and forth, expressing their outlook on tonight's game, the playoffs looming. The Nets were potential playoff contenders, but the Hawks were a powerful team to beat, especially with Jeff Teague having the best season of his career. Skip Bayless mentioned Nets player Jason Miller, a talented small forward from Georgetown who was dominating the game with his three-pointers and strong inside game. He was the leading scorer on the Nets. Bayless compared Miller to Ray Allen, another fierce three-point shooter. Smith had his doubts about Miller, criticizing his lack of defense. They also mentioned the four-year multi-million-dollar deal he had recently signed with the Nets, making him one of the wealthiest players in the NBA.

The noise from the television woke up Kip Kane. Kip stretched and yawned and lifted himself from his bed. He was shirtless, his chiseled physique covered with tattoos and battle scars. He stared at ESPN and listened to Smith and Bayless talk about Jason Miller's multi-million-dollar contract with the Nets. It was a lot of money—twenty-five million guaranteed, and he was expected to earn ninety-five million dollars.

"Ninety-five million! Shit!" Kip muttered to himself. *A hood nigga from Brooklyn earning that much money to dribble and dunk a ball?* Kip felt he was in the wrong profession.

He stood up and went to the bedroom window. The morning sunlight percolated through, indicating another sunny spring day. He pulled back the blinds and gazed at his city. Harlem was alive this morning, buzzing with people, cars, and his beloved projects—Manhattanville Houses in West Harlem, between Broadway and Amsterdam. From his eleventh-floor window, he had a picturesque view of the city that stretched from Harlem to the George Washington Bridge.

Kip wiped the cold from his eyes. He'd heard what he needed to hear, so he turned off the television. He lit a Black & Mild, picked up his cell phone, and sat at the foot of his bed. It was eleven a.m. There was a lot to do today. It was time to get that money.

He puffed on the Black as he dialed a number. It rang three times until someone picked up. "Where y'all niggas at?" he asked.

"We on the block," Devon said.

"A'ight, come get a nigga by noon."

"A'ight."

Kip tossed his cell phone on the bed and stood up. He walked toward the closet mirror and gazed at himself. He had a rough image, but he was handsome. He was twenty-two years old with a low-cut Caesar, his waves were always spinning, and he had a growing mustache. He had dark skin with an athletic build, and his eyes were cold—it was like he had a blizzard in his spirit. He had seen a lot and been through a lot in life.

Kip Kane saw himself as a survivor. Harlem was a battleground, and he was a warrior—a thoroughbred from the mean streets. He had a lot of pressure on his young shoulders, but he refused to be weighed down by poverty and lack of finances. Kip was the moneymaker in his family—if he could call it a family. He only had two people he truly cared for in his life: his younger brother Kid, who sometimes went by "The Kid," and Rhonda, his Nana, who was sixty-five years old and living comfortably in a retirement community upstate. Her apartment came with all the amenities. Nana had her groceries brought to her door three times a week, and staff that came to clean her apartment twice a week. Kip's Nana didn't have to lift a finger. Everything had been taken care of for her, thanks to Kip.

Kip felt that he owed her a lot. She had taken him and his little brother in from abusive foster homes to a real home when he was ten and Kid was seven. She was a single, childless woman in her early fifties at the time. She took care of the boys, fed them, clothed them, and became a grandmother to them. Kip thought the world of her, but Kid thought differently. He wasn't as loving toward Nana as Kip was and always believed she was a fraud, despite what she had done for them.

Kip walked out of his bedroom, moved down the hallway, and knocked on the bedroom door, the master bedroom. He didn't wait for a response. He opened the door and marched into his little brother's room. Kid was lying in bed and absorbed in a game of chess on his tablet. He was beating the computer.

Kip smiled at his little brother and said, "You gonna stay in here and play video games or enjoy the day?"

"Play a game with me."

"You know I don't play like you."

"I can teach you."

"Nah, chess is your thing, little brother, not mine. I move real-life pawns on these streets, and I'm the king." Kip beat his chest. "You goin' down to the park?"

"Yeah. You got your hustle, and I got mine."

Kip smiled. "No doubt, little brother."

Kid ended his game and decided to get dressed. He would need his brother's help. Kip moved Kid's wheelchair closer to the bed, and then he helped him dress for the day.

It was eighty degrees outside, so Kid decided on some black cargo shorts, a T-shirt, and his fresh white Nikes. He was a nineteen-year-old whiz kid, paralyzed from the waist down since he was eleven.

One day, Kid was riding on the handlebars of Kip's BMX bicycle, and the two were horsing around on a construction site, executing tricks and jumping dirt hills like daredevils.

Kip tried to jump a large dirt hill with Kid on the handlebars. He pedaled feverishly, wanting to go airborne to show off for those watching. But he lost his footing and lost control of the bicycle, which abruptly veered right. Kid went flying off the handlebars and tumbled down some nearby concrete stairs, severely injuring his spine. The doctors told him that there was a 99.9 percent chance that he would never walk again. He had become a paraplegic.

Kip felt super guilty and promised to help his brother walk again, or when possible, get him some of the best help and physical therapy money could buy when he was old enough and able. Until then, Kip always stayed glued by Kid's side. Whatever or whenever Kid needed him, he was there.

Being wheelchair-bound didn't stop Kid's enjoyment of life and doing what he loved, chess. Video games were his second love. He spent most of his days in the parks playing chess, and he became the best in the city and the most talked about in the Tri-State area. He was a vibrant chess player, and competitors would travel from far and wide to challenge him to a game. So far, he was undefeated.

Kip rolled his brother, dressed and looking fresh in a pair of gold-rimmed bifocals, into the hallway.

"You want breakfast?" Kip asked him.

"Nah, I'm not really hungry."

"You sure? You know I can make you some grits and eggs real quick."

"I'm good, bro. I just want to get out and about."

"You want me to come with you?"

"Kip, I'm nineteen. I'm a grown man. I don't need you to babysit or escort me everywhere. I can handle myself."

"A'ight."

Kid rolled himself toward the front door and gave his brother the deuces sign before leaving.

Kip watched his brother exit the apartment. Everything in the building was wheelchair accessible. His little brother was growing up fast and becoming independent. Kip wanted to do more for him. He wanted him to walk again. It had been eight years but still no change. The physical therapy treatments he was paying for at one of the top medical facilities in New York City weren't effective. But he wasn't going to stop trying. He was determined and positive that one day Kid would walk again.

Their apartment was well furnished with costly sofas and big fluffy chairs. It was comfortable and spacious. It was the perfect bachelor's pad for the brothers with a 60-inch smart TV in the living room, a high-end stereo system, and tall surround-sound speakers situated throughout the apartment, along with countless consoles and video games everywhere. It was Kid's domain—video games and online gaming—especially when it came to playing Minecraft.

Kip glanced at the time. It was already eleven thirty. He needed to get dressed and start his day. He was a busy man trying to make his cream on the streets or *from* the streets. His illicit hustle was a full-time job. He went into his bedroom to prepare himself. His goons would be there soon.

Kip was a monster on the streets. He had to walk out of his building wearing the right gear. It was all about his image, yes, but it was also about implementing the perfect plan to get money by any means necessary. He had come a long way from being a nobody to a feared and respected man in Harlem.

ONE

The corner of Amsterdam Avenue and 133rd Street was flourishing with springtime activity. Traffic flowed back and forth, with bodegas and the mom-and-pop shops lining the avenue open for business. Don Pedro Albizu Campos School on the corner was filled with students and teachers, and with summer break approaching, the young girls were out in their short skirts, short shorts, and halter tops, their pretty sneakers hammering the urban pavement from block to block. Some of the best eye candy in the city came from Manhattanville Houses.

In the midst of the activity, a black Ford Expedition on 22-inch chrome rims double-parked in front of the towering project building on 133rd Street. The truck was blaring Jay Z's "Dead Presidents," and the two occupants in the front seats nodded to the beat, mouthing the song. They shared a burning blunt while waiting for Kip to exit the building.

Devon looked ominous behind the wheel of the Expedition in his dark army fatigues and his small Afro. His eyes shifted everywhere as he sat parked on the block, smoking weed in public. He scanned potential victims closely and from afar. Everyone was a target to him. He didn't care who they were or who they were connected to. It was a dog-eat-dog world in Harlem and everywhere else, and he was the bigger dog with the sharper teeth, more bite than bark. His eyes were always threatening.

Devon had dark skin and a yuck mouth, and everyone, especially the girls, was afraid of him. They called him "Devil" behind his back.

Twenty-four and a mental case, he was as grimy as they came in Harlem. He had grown up eating out of trash cans to survive. His mother would buy drugs instead of food with the welfare checks and whatever cash she earned selling sex. Devon's father had abandoned them since birth. Though Devon would see his deadbeat dad in the neighborhood, his pops had never claimed him or ever said a word to him.

Growing up, Devon's peers made fun of him, poked at him, and kicked him when he was down. Society was a cruel place, so Devon decided to become an even crueler man. He was a man with dirty fingernails, ashy skin, and dirty clothes, but his character was a lot filthier. He and his friends made money from robberies, burglaries, and stick-ups.

Devon took a pull from the weed and passed it to Papa John in the passenger's seat. Papa John took a long pull and exhaled. He sat back and chilled. The kush had him feeling nice. His eyes were faded while waiting for Kip to come down from his apartment.

Papa John was nineteen and Kip's right-hand man. He had also grown up in a single-parent household. His father Darryl, a renowned detective at the 75th Precinct, had raised him. Darryl was forty-nine years old with a twenty-two-year-old girlfriend, and though he was a detective, he had no clue about his son's illicit activities in the streets.

Papa John had no recollection of his mother. There were only pictures of her around the house, and his father spoke about her vaguely. When he was just two years old, Papa John's mother left the family and ran off with his father's best friend Anthony. The two had fled Harlem and headed south to Miami, but they never made it. Anthony had fallen asleep behind the wheel, and they both were killed instantly on I-95.

Papa John was the opposite of Devon. Where Devon was the critter of the crew, Papa John and Kip were the smooth-talking, handsome bad boys in the neighborhood. Papa John was meticulous about his wardrobe and his appearance. He had brown skin with dark, soft, curly hair that he kept cut low and the brightest brown eyes. He also carried a small scar on his right cheek courtesy of a nightclub brawl several years earlier. He hadn't seen it coming but felt the razor peel his skin back like a banana, coating his face with blood. The culprit was a jealous boyfriend who attacked because Papa John was fucking his girlfriend.

Papa John took a few more pulls from the blunt and handed it back to Devon. Just then his eyes became hooked on a young cutie walking across the street. She was light-skinned with long black hair, a small waist, and thick thighs underneath a short skirt. She was definitely his type. He tapped Devon and pointed her out. "That's nice right there," he said.

Devon smiled.

"Hey, beautiful," Papa John catcalled her way. "How you doin' today?"

She glanced his way and kept things moving, not looking interested in what he had to say. In fact, she had an attitude. Papa John had never seen her around before, so she was probably new to the neighborhood. He loved new things, especially the ladies.

"You can't speak, beautiful?" he continued.

Ignoring him completely, she walked like she had somewhere important to be.

Papa John was mesmerized by her curvy physique, and when she walked by, his eyes stayed glued to her butt. It was all put together perfectly.

"Damn, beautiful, you're definitely workin' that body," he hollered. "Can I have a picture of you so I can show Santa what I want for Christmas?"

Devon laughed.

Papa John was relentless. If he didn't get her attention today, he would try tomorrow, and the next day, and the day after that. Eventually, he would get what he wanted. He was funny and cute. He was a ladies' man. The hood had named John "Papa John" because he was promiscuous with the ladies. He had six kids with six baby mamas at his young age, and all of the women were gorgeous and completely in love with him. Word around the hood was that Papa John carried a ten-inch penis and was adept at using it. Ever since his mother walked out on him when he was a baby, he had "mommy issues." He couldn't get close to women, so he couldn't stay in relationships.

As the woman walked by, Papa John sat back, taking her in. Then he muttered, "What the fuck is takin' Kip so long?"

"Y'all pretty boys always take forever getting dressed," Devon said.

"It's called flavor, nigga. You should try it out once in a while."

"Fuck you, nigga!"

"You still my nigga, *D*. We gonna get you some pussy tonight."

"I'm no charity fuckin' case, Papa John. I get mine."

"I know you do. How much the bitch charge by the hour?"

"Your mama never charges me. She gets down on her knees for free."

Papa John's easygoing attitude quickly transitioned into anger. He frowned at his friend. "Nigga, don't ever talk about Mama!" He was serious.

"What? I hit a sore spot?"

"Just don't talk about her."

"A'ight, nigga. My bad," Devon apologized feebly.

Papa John put the blunt to his lips and inhaled. He continued to frown. "Where is this nigga Kip?"

***

Kip stepped out of the lobby looking like a superstar. He was dressed in beige cargo shorts and a white V-neck T-shirt, highlighting his athletic body and showing off his long white gold chain and diamond encrusted TEC-9 pendant, along with his white-and-blue Jordans fresh out of the box. His waves were spinning in the sunlight as he trotted toward his homeboys in the Expedition. He was the prince of the projects—well known and well liked by many, but not by all. He was an Adonis and a bad boy mixed into one.

Kip moved with authority and pride in the Harlem projects. He could see Devon and Papa John in the truck smoking weed. He frowned at their stupidity. Today was a special day, or it was going to be a special night— and his crew was on board wholeheartedly. They were about their money, and if tonight's score went down as planned, then they would come off like kings swimming in the money pit.

Kip's chain swung as he walked—he had a tiger's stride in the concrete jungle. As he approached the truck, he was greeted by two thots with long weaves, wearing tight jeans, tight shirts that accentuated their balloon tits, and bright smiles aimed his way.

"Hey, Kip," the girls greeted simultaneously.

"Hey," he replied nonchalantly.

"Kip, you comin' to the party tonight?" Judy asked.

"What party?"

"We can make it a party, Kip," Cindy chimed in with an inviting smile. "But we gonna do our thang at Cream tonight, and we want you there."

Kip smiled, knowing the type of parties the girls would throw. It was known in the hood that Judy and Cindy were both strippers and thots of the year—easy pussy for the right price, sometimes maybe no price. They were into drug dealers and bad boys and could suck a dick so good, they could deflate a rock with their porn-style talents.

Cindy was up close and personal on Kip, patting at his chest, admiring his style, and talking into his ear. It was obvious that she wanted him. Judy too. But Cindy was into him more, though they'd never fucked.

Cindy licked her lips and asked him again, "So, you comin' tonight?"

"I'm busy tonight," Kip announced.

"Aaaah, too bad, we could have had some fun. You know . . . we still can." Cindy bit her bottom lip, toying with her long hair and eyeing his crotch.

Kip chuckled.

Making her way toward Kip and the dynamic whores of Harlem was Eshon. She marched toward Kip with a frown, seeing Judy and Cindy talking to her ex-boyfriend. Even though they weren't together at the moment, she wasn't about to let Kip fuck either one of the girls. Dressed in a short skirt that showed off her toned thighs and her long, defined legs and a Swarovski crystal top that glimmered like diamonds on her chest, she strutted their way, her high heels thumping against the pavement. Eshon was a truly beautiful woman. Twenty years old with rich, brown skin, a straight weave, and round chestnut-colored eyes, her body was thick in all the right places. Along with her looks, she had a voice like Jennifer Hudson's, singing wherever she went.

"Um, excuse me," Eshon exclaimed to Cindy and Judy. "Do y'all bitches have someplace to be, besides up in my man's face?"

The two thots looked at Eshon with a matching attitude.

Cindy said, "I thought y'all weren't together anymore."

"Bitch, you thought wrong. Y'all two bitches need to walk off now before I snatch y'all weaves and leave both y'all bitches fuckin' baldheaded."

Cindy sucked her teeth and rolled her eyes, but she didn't want any part of Eshon, who was both a beauty and a beast. Eshon was hood-certified and had a reputation for roughly snatching out hair weaves and leaving bitches bloody and dazed. She ran with Brandy and Jessica, and they were down for whatever. The ghetto had started to call the girls the "E and J Brandy bitches." They worked hustlers like they were magic tricks, wore the best clothes, and dealt only with prize niggas. They got respect in Harlem.

Cindy and Judy got the message. Both girls pivoted and walked away.

Eshon stood there with her arms across her chest, looking at Kip like he owed her an apology.

Kip barked, "Bitch, what the fuck is up wit' you?"

"What's up wit' me? What the fuck is up wit' *you*? Really, them two thots, Kip? Cindy and Judy? I know you weren't about to fuck wit' them."

"And if I was?"

"Them some nasty hoes."

"Yo, you ain't my bitch anymore, so you need to stay the fuck out my business!"

"So you just gonna do me like that, like you ain't never loved me? Like I didn't do everything for your ass?"

"We ain't together anymore, Eshon. You need to get that in your fuckin' head!"

Eshon sucked her teeth and glowered. "So you rather go from classy like this"—She gestured toward her nice and well-dressed figure—"to them ashy and nasty bitches?"

Kip shook his head and sighed.

Eshon and Kip had fucked around for years, but Kip was tired of the drama and Eshon's jealousy and petty ways. He liked being a single man and wanted to fuck who he wanted without Eshon hating on him. But she was having a hard time getting over him.

"Did you prank-call me last night?"

"What the fuck I look like, Eshon? Huh? I ain't got time for games. I ain't on no childish bullshit. I'm tryin' to get money on these streets."

"I'm just sayin' Kip, somebody's been calling me and hanging up."

"Bitch, it ain't me. Step off wit' that drama." Kip nudged her out of his way and proceeded toward the truck, leaving her there looking dejected.

She watched Kip walk toward Devon and Papa John, who were laughing. She marched off upset.

Papa John climbed out of the passenger seat, so Kip could ride shotgun.

Once inside, Kip barked, "Y'all are two stupid muthafuckas! Y'all smoking weed in public. I could see y'all asses a mile away puffing. What if I was five-*O* driving by? Huh? Y'all niggas tryin' to get locked up before we do this shit tonight?"

"Yo, my bad, Kip, you right," Devon said.

Papa John extinguished the weed. "I guess you ain't smoking then."

"Yo, Papa John, it ain't no time for your jokes," Kip told him.

"Yeah, you right."

"Y'all ready to do this thing tonight?"

Devon answered, "Nigga, you know we ready." He was itching to get this money. "We always ready."

Papa John reached down in his seat and slyly handed Kip some new burners for the night's task—Glock 19s. Everyone received new guns because their old ones had too many bodies on them.

Kip quickly inspected the Glock with the extended clip. It felt great in his hands. "Yeah, these are nice. I like 'em," he said.

"I'm glad you do," Papa John said.

"We good for the night? Is everything set straight?" Devon asked as he navigated the truck toward the Henry Hudson Parkway.

Kip replied, "Yeah, we gonna pick up the tickets right now. Shorty on point."

"Cool." Devon smiled, his yuck mouth showing in the rearview mirror.

They headed toward the Bronx, moving through the neighborhoods of Washington Heights and Inwood, and crossing over the Broadway Bridge.

TWO

Kip Kane climbed out of the Expedition on West 225th Street in the Bronx. He told his crew to wait there and walked alone into the Marble Hill Housing Projects. With the shopping center and Applebee's right across the street, the road was swamped with afternoon traffic and pedestrians. Kip wasn't worried entering an unfamiliar housing project. Leaving his pistol in the truck, he showed no trepidation as he walked toward his destination with his head held high. The area was flooded with local goons and police. Kip couldn't risk having a stop-and-frisk implemented on him. NYPD patrolled the area heavily because it was close to a shopping area and a few eateries.

He entered the building lobby, stepped into the pissy elevator, and pushed for the eighth floor. He ascended alone. The bell soon chimed, and the doors opened. Kip stepped out into the narrow hallway and made his way toward apartment 8E. He knocked twice and waited coolly. Soon, the apartment door opened, and a woman appeared. She was in her early forties with tan skin and blonde dreadlocks. She was dressed conservatively for the spring weather, wearing a vibrant, printed maxi-dress and some embellished thong sandals. Stepping to the side, she invited Kip inside.

Kip entered the large, neatly furnished apartment. The woman was living large in the projects, with a 90-inch TV, Italian furniture, and high-end stereo system. Kip removed a bulging white envelope filled with hundred-dollar bills from his pocket and handed it to her. In return, she handed him an envelope, but it was thinner than his.

Kip checked the contents and was satisfied. He had three tickets to the Nets against the Hawks that night. The seats were only a few rows behind the floor seats at the Barclays Center, Section 24. It was a costly area. She came correct for him.

"We okay?" she asked him.

"Oh, we good. These will do," he said.

His business completed, Kip turned and marched out of the woman's apartment.

He soon climbed back into the truck with his boys and said, "We're good tonight. We in the house." He showed them the tickets, and each man smiled. The game started at 8:30, and they wanted to get there early.

To kill some time, the men went to eat at Junior's on Flatbush Avenue and went over their plan for the night. Kip had gotten good intel that a lot of NBA players were going to frequent a certain nightclub in the city. He wanted to know the name of the club. The trio ate and enjoyed themselves at Junior's and ordered their famous cheesecake.

While dining on dessert, Papa John suddenly said, "Yo, you remember when Puffy made them fools from *Making the Band* walk from Manhattan to Brooklyn for some fuckin' cheesecake?"

"I ain't watch that stupid shit," Devon said quickly.

"Yeah, fuckin' idiots! And for that faggot! Yo, Puffy would have gotten got for that stunt, fo' real," Kip said. "He got too much money to keep it all for himself."

Papa John added, "They probably sucked his dick for a record deal."

They all laughed.

Soon, it was going to be time for them to get down to business.

✳✳✳

It was the second quarter of the game, and the Barclays Center was erupting in cheers and boos as the Nets battled it out with the Hawks in a fast-paced game. The crowd at the Barclays Center was loud and fierce. Almost everyone was standing from their seats, their attention held by the game. The Nets were down by four, but it was a good game and a close game. Jason Miller was in control and dominating Lamar Patterson on the court, and the arena was screaming out his name. He was worth the millions he was being paid. The spectators watched as the Nets applied full-court pressure on the Hawks.

Seated in Section 24, only a few rows behind the floor seats, were Kip, Devon, and Papa John. They watched the game and cheered for the Nets, but they were really watching certain players intently. It was amazing—nothing but millionaires dribbling a basketball up and down the court and entertaining the large crowd.

Kip thought about these players' endorsement deals, million-dollar contracts, and the exotic cars they drove. He wanted that same wealth for himself. He wasn't born with talent and towering height like most of these players. He had to rely on his wits and bravado to get paid. The boys politicked with a few people in the crowd, especially the moneymakers, and pretended to be like them—sheep—when they were really wolves lurking for their next big score.

The arena erupted in a thunderous roar as Jason Miller executed a 360-degree dunk over a lone Hawks player, tying the game before halftime.

Kip and his cronies lifted themselves from their seats and followed the crowd toward the concession stands. It would be fifteen minutes before the next half started. After spending a small fortune on hot dogs, chips, and sodas, they returned to their seats and were ready for the next half to start. Kip had what he needed: information on tonight's after-party and the location where most of the NBA players were going to be partying. Club Revolt in midtown Manhattan was the place to be after the game.

The fourth quarter was winding down, the Nets trailing by four points again. The Nets had possession with twenty seconds left on the playing clock. Their point guard Donald Sloan brought the ball up court and attempted a three-pointer but missed. Jason Miller grabbed the rebound and followed up with a slam dunk.

The crowd went wild.

There was now ten seconds left in the game, and Atlanta had the ball. Jeff Teague threw a chest pass to Kyle Korver, but Jason Miller came out of nowhere and intercepted the pass and threw up a hasty three-pointer, sinking it just before the buzzer sounded.

Barclays Center erupted with deafening cheers. The Nets had won, and the team went berserk, and so did every fan in the building. It was a great game and a needed win for the Nets to keep their playoff hopes alive.

Kip and his crew didn't stick around for the celebration. They left right after the final seconds and headed toward the Expedition. Kip wanted to get to the club early. He didn't want his victims to see him coming.

***

Club Revolt in midtown Manhattan was a vibrant and fashionable club filled with sexy women, ballers, and shot-callers. The expansive nightclub featured a public party lounge with a large-scale dance floor as well as several intimate suites. It was a sleek place with a full bar and bedecked with 46-inch LCD flat-screens throughout. Club Revolt exemplified elegance through its rich and polished décor.

"Work" by Rihanna and Drake blared throughout the club, and the floor was packed with dancers. VIP was in full swing and occupied completely with the celebrities and ballers popping bottles and even pills, and keeping companionship with the sexily dressed females.

In the mix of the party were Kip and his crew. They stood right by each other at the bar and were watching everything, Kip being the most vigilant.

DIRTY WORK - PART ONE

Security was tight with bouncers everywhere inside the club. Each bouncer was dressed in black with "Club Security" stamped across their shirts, and each one stood over six feet tall. They were looking to prevent trouble inside and outside before it started since Club Revolt had a reputation to uphold. Club Revolt was a place where the celebrities, rappers, and athletes felt safe to show off their wealth. There was bling shining everywhere. Club hostesses with their short black shorts and sexy tops regularly moved through the crowd with expensive bottles of champagne with sparklers to serve the VIP.

Kip found his mark. In fact, he found a few marks inside the club. He steadily watched three ballplayers from a distance. They were living it up in VIP with the sexily dressed ladies and downing champagne like it was water. The two Atlanta Hawks players he watched were wearing six figures on their wrists, hands, and necks, giving "icy" a whole new definition, but they were heavily guarded by security. Though there were some fine black females in Club Revolt, the two players seemed mostly interested in the white girls with their shorts dresses, blonde hair, and petite figures.

The third player Kip watched was Jason Miller from the Nets. He stood solo in the club with no bodyguards and no entourage, a bold move on his part. He thought he was secure with his street credibility and hood upbringing. He was a multi-millionaire with his new NBA contract and endorsement deals, but he also had a reputation for being a thug and a hothead, on and off the basketball court. Jason Miller was a product of Brownsville, Brooklyn and very proud of it. Basketball had taken him out of the ghetto and a life of crime to a life of luxury.

Jason stood in the club ice-grilling anyone that stared at him for too long. Completely standoffish, he was a mean fucker with monstrous height, standing six seven and muscular. He clutched a Moët bottle and drank straight from it like a goon.

Kip looked Jason's way. He was definitely the prize; his jewelry alone was worth hundreds of thousands of dollars. Kip hated him already.

"Who we on tonight?" Papa John asked.

"Yeah, Jason Miller and them two Hawks players in VIP," Kip replied in a low voice in Papa's ear.

Papa John wasn't expecting to hear three. "What? You want to get all three of them fools?"

Kip nodded.

That wasn't the plan originally. They were to single out one fool in the club and set him up for a robbery, take everything he had, and leave. But Kip was being greedy. How were they going to rob three NBA players at the same time, especially when the two Hawks players had security?

Devon was with Kip. He felt it could be done. He needed the money too, and the more of it, the merrier.

Kip looked at a skeptical Papa John and said into his ear, "Look, nigga, we need the money, and this is our one moment to get paid from these rich niggas."

Kip needed the cash for his Nana. Her rent was due, and it was ten thousand dollars a month to keep her comfortable in the opulent retirement home upstate. Plus, he had other expenses to take care of. Tonight, Jason Miller and the two Hawks players were going to get got. Kip was certain of that.

"Look, I'll be on Jason, and y'all two niggas stay on them fools." He motioned his head toward the Hawks player. "I'm sure y'all can get them niggas despite security around. We done hit fools like them before."

They both nodded.

The night was still young, so the party at Club Revolt wasn't ending anytime soon. For the trio, it was about blending in and playing things cool until it was time to light the fireworks and get on with the show.

Kip was focused, but his two counterparts decided to order champagne

DIRTY WORK - PART ONE

and keep up with the Joneses inside the club. They gazed at the lovely ladies, especially Papa John, who thought he had seen a number of future baby mamas roaming around that he wanted to sex down and make lucky number seven. And Devon threw back drink after drink.

Kip didn't indulge in drinking. He wanted to stay focused and clearheaded. He said sternly, "Y'all niggas really need to chill wit' the drinks."

Papa John said, "Nigga, we just having some fun."

"We ain't here to have fun, we here to get paid tonight. Don't forget that shit! You think we got room to fuck this up?"

Papa John and Devon knew Kip was right. A drunk or tipsy stick-up kid was an arrest or murder waiting to happen, so they cut back on the alcohol.

"Y'all niggas keep an eye on them," Kip said. "I gotta make a call."

Devon nodded.

Kip turned around and walked toward the bathrooms. He pulled out his cell phone and looked for her number. He found an empty stall to occupy and called her. Though he had shunned her earlier today, there was no doubt in his mind that she would be there for him. Three rings later, she picked up.

"Now you call me?" she answered. "You got some fuckin' nerve, Kip."

"I need you tonight," he murmured, getting straight to the point.

"Why? Where are you?"

"I'm at Revolt in the city, me and my crew."

"You doin' a lick?"

"Yeah. So I'm gonna need you and your friends' help on this one."

Eshon sighed. Though she was hesitant in answering, she had already made up her mind. She was coming to help him. She loved him, and she wanted to be his everything, even if it meant breaking the law. "A'ight, give us about two hours."

28

"Two?"

"You want us lookin' right, right? So don't rush perfection, Kip. And you owe me." Eshon hung up.

In Kip's profession, two hours felt like a lifetime. But what could he do but wait for his backup to arrive? He walked out of the bathroom and connected back with the nightlife.

Devon and Papa John were still at the bar. Papa John was flirting with a woman with red hair and a black dress. Being a playboy, he couldn't keep his dick in his pants for one night.

Kip frowned at Papa John. He marched their way and immediately had Papa John dismiss the bitch. "Focus, nigga," he reminded them.

Papa John smiled. "I already got her number anyway."

The ballers in the club were blowing through money and consuming expensive champagne like bottled water during a heat wave. Lines of groupies and whores were a mile long inside the nightclub. Eager to snatch up a baller or athlete, all the girls came in their best dresses and with their best game.

The inside of Kip's palm began to itch while he studied Jason. He watched as the man looked down on people, even bullied those around him. He had a smug attitude, and Kip disliked him more and more as the night wore on. He couldn't wait to rob that arrogant muthafucka and get himself a nice piece of his million-dollar contract.

THREE

The gypsy cab came to a stop in front of Club Revolt. Traffic was a nightmare, and the sidewalk was swamped with people. Eshon looked at the chaotic scene outside of the club and took a deep breath. Kip was depending on her tonight, and she wasn't going to let him down. She was with Jessica and Brandy. Eshon paid the driver his forty-dollar fee, and all three girls climbed out of the backseat and strutted toward the club. There was a line and a list. Eshon stood erect in her silver high heels looking fabulous in a purple Jason Wu dress with the neckline that plunged to just below her belly button. The dress left folks in awe, but Eshon had the body to pull it off.

Eshon had her ways despite the line outside and the list in the bouncer's hands. Flanked by Jessica and Brandy, she was confident they would all get inside.

"Damn, your boo was right," Jessica said. "It is sick out here."

Jessica was a stunning twenty-two-year-old Hispanic *mamacita* with long legs and more curves than the letter *S*. She had long, black hair, light hazel eyes that lit up, and long eyelashes. She wore a body-hugging Bebe dress with spaghetti straps and a plunging neckline.

Jessica had come from L.A., where her family showed loyalty to the Latin Kings. She always felt she had something to prove. No stranger to tragedy, her father, her uncles, and her brothers had all been killed in L.A., either through gang violence or by the police. The deaths started to take a toll on her and her mother.

Then there was the confrontation with the Mexican Mafia and the threats against her family. So her mother decided to move what family they had left in L.A. to Harlem, where it was supposed to be a whole new start inside their small two-bedroom apartment on West 134th Street.

Brandy was a twenty-two-year-old wildcat with dark skin, a blonde weave, and hazel contacts, which irritated her eyes. The only reason she wore the contacts and the blonde wig was to keep up with Jessica and Eshon. Though she was a beauty too, Brandy always felt like the runt of the group. She couldn't sing like Eshon, and she wasn't light-skinned with real hazel eyes and long hair like Jessica. They would always catch the attention of men first, and then she came last. Brandy had always been insecure about her complexion and was envious of both her friends. Sometimes she would spew hate, but Jessica and Eshon didn't take it seriously. Brandy was still their bitch, a friend to them, and though she was a hater, they loved her anyway.

Brandy strutted behind her friends wearing the raunchiest outfit of the three—a sheer mini dress with a halter neckline. Twenty-one inches in length, the dress exposed the gold rhinestone G-string she wore underneath. She moved her perfect body seductively in her stilettos as she followed Eshon's lead.

Eshon walked toward the main bouncer at the door. He looked at her, and she looked at him. It was about an hour's wait to enter the club, and with the club's capacity reaching its limit very soon, the wait was looking even longer. But Eshon didn't do lines.

Jessica and Brandy stood on the sidelines and watched Eshon do her thing. The bouncer was hypnotized by her confidence and beauty. They didn't have any doubt that she would get them inside without having to wait; she always got them in. She always knew what to say or do to get her way.

Eshon started to converse with the tall, black, mean-looking hunk of beef. The other bitches standing on line looked at Eshon with questionable stares; they didn't believe she had what it took to persuade him. But they were wrong. It only took a minute until he started to waver. Then he smiled and shook his head. Eshon passed him something. The exchange was quick, and before they knew it, she was waving her girls to come inside. Jessica and Brandy strutted toward the entrance as the bouncer unhooked the velvet rope, allowing the ladies to slide right through and leave the other patrons waiting on line. Eshon moved through the crowd like she was a boss bitch, her friends right behind her.

Club Revolt was the place to be tonight. The renowned DJ was an expert at getting the party hyped with his mixes. The music was thunderously loud and on point with "Diced Pineapples" by Rick Ross and Meek Mill as bodies gyrated on the dance floor. And there was so much money in the place.

The girls found Kip, Devon, and Papa John by the bar. Eshon smiled at Kip then threw her arms around him and kissed his lips.

Kip allowed the public display of affection. They all had a part to play tonight, and with the girls around they would look less suspicious. Eshon, however, was loving every moment of it, taking full advantage of the time she got to spend with Kip, who looked good and smelled great.

Papa John had had his eyes on Jessica for a long time, but he knew how Kid felt about her. But she was tempting tonight, with legs and cleavage showing.

"So where are they?" Eshon asked.

"Jason Miller, across the room, and to my right, the two ballers seated in VIP," Kip said, discreetly pointing out the two Hawks players surrounded by women.

Eshon glanced their way. "They're cute."

Kip snapped, "Fuck that cute shit!"

"Aah, you jealous, baby?"

"I want you to stay on point. The competition is fierce right now in their area," he said, signifying the sexy, blonde-haired white girls the players were taking interest in.

"You let me worry about the competition; we got this, boo."

"Then go do you," he said seriously.

"Give me another kiss first."

Kip looked reluctant, but he kissed her anyway. She and her girls were needed tonight, so he did whatever it took to keep her happy.

Eshon gave her girls the signal. It was time to put in work tonight and flaunt their sex appeal and their bodies. Yes, Kip was pimping them out, but it was worth it. The bigger the score, the larger their percentage.

They migrated toward the NBA players that were surrounded by beauties. The girls pushed their way through the crowd and made it closer to VIP. Two bouncers stood guard near the players, and there was a bevy of girls that wanted a piece of the pie.

Eshon knew it was going to take more than beauty and a tight, short dress to get close to the players. She locked eyes with the bouncer that separated her and her crew from payday. He stood in the club dressed in black and looking like a skyscraper.

Eshon boldly strutted his way and demanded his attention. He leaned into her while Jessica and Brandy watched and waited. Whatever Eshon was saying to him, it seemed to be working. His stretched frown leisurely transitioned into a smile, and she slyly slipped him three hundred dollars. He took the money and moved to the side, allowing the girls to pass through.

Immediately, the girls had hate on them like President Obama at a Republican Convention. Once in the area, Jessica immediately caught the attention of one of the players. With her Spanish roots, long black hair, light eyes, and cleavage showing like a sneak peek, she was the showstopper.

She worked her way toward him, and the hate around her was glowing brighter. She succeeded in capturing his attention. He was riveted by her just that quickly. She introduced herself and took a seat on his lap.

One down, two to go.

Eshon made her way toward Hawks power forward, Kennan Thompson. His jewelry was blinding, and his physique was impressive. He had twin blonde snowflakes against him, one on his lap and the other to his right, and everybody was all touchy-feely. It looked like a sure thing for him tonight. Eshon knew she had her hands full with the twin white girls that each had a body like Pamela Anderson in her prime. Kennan looked like he wasn't ready to let them go anytime soon.

Eshon had to rethink her strategy. Jessica already had the small forward, Mike Blackmon, eating out of her hands. Now there was Jason Miller to worry about. She and Brandy headed Jason's way. He was accompanied by a voluptuous white girl with brunette hair. Her dress was so short, her pussy was showing.

Eshon frowned at the white bitch on Jason's lap. These white girls were winning tonight, and the sisters in the club were looking left out. Now it wasn't just about business, it was about her pride. She approached Jason Miller and exclaimed to the white girl, "Why you sitting on my man's lap?"

Both of them looked up at Eshon with bewilderment.

"What?" the white girl sputtered. She turned and looked at Jason. "You know this bitch?"

"Nah, I don't know that bitch," Jason replied.

The brunette turned to face Eshon with a smug look and sharply said, "Step off, bitch!"

"You need to get you some color in your life, Jason, and stop fuckin' wit' these white whores."

"Bitch, you don't fuckin' know me," the white girl exclaimed.

Jason glared at her and returned, "Yo, I don't know you, and I don't do black bitches—y'all fuckin' drama—like you, bitch. So get the fuck away from me!"

Eshon scowled. She wasn't about to let him disrespect her, especially in front of his white tramp. She screamed, "Nigga, you better watch who you're talking to like that! Nigga, you don't fuckin' know me!"

Eshon's plan was unraveling. Now it was personal. He was an asshole.

Brandy stood beside her friend and was ready for war.

Jason pushed the brunette off his lap and stood up abruptly. His face was stretched out into a heated scowl.

Eshon was up in his face, ready to throw punches.

They got into a heated argument.

Kip stood in the distance watching it all fall apart. "Damn!"

"You a clown-ass nigga! Wannabe Michael Jordan, no-ring-ass-having scrub!"

Jason had heard enough. "Fuck you, bitch!" and suddenly, a drink was tossed into Eshon's face.

Eshon and Brandy went for blood. They attacked Jason with blows, and a fight ensued.

Jason wasn't afraid to hit back. He tossed Brandy to the floor effortlessly and kicked her while she was down.

Eshon tried to break a champagne bottle over his head, but her attack was halted by security rushing to the fight and grabbing her from behind.

"Get the fuck off me!" she screamed. "I'm gonna fuck him up!"

Eshon was angry and wanted to see bloodshed. How dare he put his hands on her and Brandy? She didn't care who he was, who he played for, or how much money he had, she wanted him fucked up.

Security was roughly dragging her and Brandy out of the club, kicking and screaming. Their highs heels were scuffed, their weaves twisted, and their sexy outfits disheveled. Brandy even had a nipple showing.

Kip frowned at the minor brawl between his ex and Jason Miller. He had to bite down hard on the inside of his lip to prevent himself from bum-rushing the Nets player. Jessica wanted to intervene and come to her friends' aid, but she knew Kip would want her to stick with the program.

After Eshon and Brandy were thrown out of the club, things calmed down, and the party continued. Eshon and Brandy called Kip and told him they were going to wait outside.

Later on that night, Jessica finally left with her mark, his arm securely around her. He looked eager to get her into his bed for some fun.

Kip nodded his head proudly. Jessica had worked her magic, and his plan was still going forward, despite the distraction earlier.

The second Hawks player started to make his exit from the party with his groupies and his bodyguard.

Kip wanted Devon and Papa John on him quickly. They knew what to do and knew how to handle their business. Stick-ups and robberies were nothing new to them.

Papa John looked reluctant at first, saying, "You ain't coming?"

"Nah, I got plans for someone else," Kip said.

"Jason Miller?"

"I'm on him."

"Alone? But how? We got the ride?"

"I got my ways, my nigga. I want all three tonight. I repeat. . . I want all three tonight."

Papa John nodded. When Kip was determined to do something, no matter what obstacles were thrown in front of him, he always found some way to conquer them.

Devon and Papa John left the club with the intent to rob Kennan Thompson.

Kip watched Jason Miller like a hawk from a distance. He was determined to make him pay seriously for what he had done to Eshon and

Brandy. The man was an asshole that needed to be taught a lesson. Now, it became personal for Kip. He was patient and he was poised, like a cobra ready to strike and spread its venom.

FOUR

Though separated, the crew kept in communication with each other via text message. Jessica cunningly hit Kip with a text saying that she was on her way to Mike Blackmon's hotel room in the city. He was staying at the Gansevoort Hotel, a lavish place on Ninth Avenue in midtown.

And, so far, Jessica had him eating out of the palm of her hands. Mike couldn't control himself. His hands were all over her body while they rode in the backseat of a black Escalade. He couldn't resist her L.A. accent, Spanish heritage, and stunning beauty.

"Shit, I might fuck around and get you pregnant tonight because you so damn fine and sexy," he joked, cupping her breast forcibly and kissing on her neck.

He unzipped his jeans and pulled out his snake-looking penis, wanting a quick blowjob in the backseat. "C'mon, sexy, give me a sneak peek of what I'm gonna get from you tonight," he said with a perverted smile.

Jessica was nonchalant toward the comments. She didn't cringe or become offended. She eyed his watch and his jewelry, and in due time, she was going to pick him clean. So she had to open her legs and let him fondle her pussy, grab her tits, kiss him passionately, suck his dick in the backseat. If push came to shove, she would have to fuck him too to get her way. So what? She was a big girl with an agenda.

She leaned into his lap and wrapped her lips around his thick penis and bobbed her head up and down. He moaned and rested his head against the headrest, becoming utterly blissed out by her full lips and adept tongue.

***

Devon and Papa John followed behind Kennan's black-on-black Range Rover, their guns on their laps, loaded and ready for action. They remained two or three cars behind Keenan's Range Rover, and where he went, they went—left turn, right turn—south on Eighth Avenue. It was early morning, so the city streets weren't crowded with traffic, but it was still alive with people and businesses. The Big Apple never sleeps.

Devon was keen on moving, but Papa John knew it was going to be difficult. They couldn't go back to Kip empty-handed. Kennan was too much money to lose. They continued to follow the vehicle, trying to remain inconspicuous. The windows to the Range Rover were tinted, but they speculated only five were inside—Kennan and his groupies in the backseat, the bodyguard, and the driver.

"We gonna have to smash and grab on this muthafucka," Papa John said.

Devon agreed. He loved violence. Impatient to see his payday, he didn't see the robbery happening any other way.

Finally, the Range Rover came to a stop in front of Brazil Grill, an all-night diner nestled between other open businesses on Eighth Avenue. The late-night hour meant the eatery was almost unoccupied, but there were a few customers inside. The Range Rover parked, and the doors opened. All five occupants climbed out and stepped onto the street. Kennan Thompson looked like a movie star with his darks shades, expensive gear, and blinding bling. He had his arms around both his blonde-haired groupies and was ready to get his eat on.

Kennan's bodyguard soon spotted Papa John walking their way, dressed in a dark hoodie with his head lowered toward the ground, his hands in the front pockets of his hoodie. Kennan noticed Papa John too, but he was sure that his six-foot-three bodyguard had everything under control. He didn't think anybody would be stupid enough to try to rob him on a busy city block.

Papa John stayed focused. He walked toward the group undaunted. He quickly locked his eyes on the group and shouted, "Is that Kennan Thompson in New York?"

"Yo, my man, he's busy right now if you're looking for a selfie," the bodyguard said.

Papa John dismissed the comment and looked at the man like he was stupid. "Fuck a picture—I'm here to collect his city tax."

"City tax?" the bodyguard repeated with bewilderment.

"Yeah, city tax, nigga!" Papa John swiftly pulled a .45 from his hoodie pocket and thrust it into the bodyguard's face.

The group was suddenly taken aback and in awe. One groupie with Kennan attempted to scream, but Papa John warned her to shut the fuck up.

While they were distracted by Papa John, Devon came from behind the group and struck the bodyguard in the head repeatedly with his gun. The large man fell to his knees, hurt badly.

"You know what this is, nigga—Run ya shit, muthafucka!" Papa John ordered, pointing the barrel of his gun at him, while Devon held the bodyguard at bay.

The driver was a coward, and the bitches were useless. They didn't want to die. So Kennan found himself a victim of a stick-up.

Devon snatched the platinum chains off his neck and forcibly removed his rings and his expensive watch. Devon was burning to implement more violence upon the basketball player, but Papa John kept things cool and kept him under control.

They had his jewelry and his dignity. It was time to go.

Before they left, Devon glared at him and suddenly cold-cocked him with a right hook, sending the millionaire ballplayer stumbling backward and leaving him with a bloody lip. Devon shouted, "That's for beating my Knicks last time," and the men ran off, leaving everyone stunned and shaken up.

Smash-and-grab, it was one way they operated.

***

Finally, Jason left the club with the white groupie with the brunette curls under his arm. He had his prize for the night and was ready to enjoy himself. He deserved to be happy. He'd won the game for the Nets and was their golden boy—their Michael Jordan. His groupie was all over him as they left the nightclub, and he was all over her. He was a bit tipsy but still alert. This was his town, New York City, though he was from Brooklyn. Jason Miller was that goon in the NBA, the epitome of that old saying, "You can take a boy out of the ghetto, but you can never take the ghetto out of the boy."

Jason walked toward his burgundy Bentley coupe that cost $250,000. He hit the alarm button, and it deactivated. The area around Club Revolt was busy with people, cars, and the nightlife. He crossed the busy city street and was nearing his car.

His white groupie was full of laughter and perversion. She was ready to please him anywhere at any time. If he had asked her to suck his dick in the middle of the street, she wouldn't have hesitated in doing it. She was open for anything tonight. He knew he had picked the right one to take home. He was a few feet from his luxury coupe when, suddenly, out of the shadows, the threat came.

Kip was cunning when it came to executing the element of surprise. Jason didn't see him coming until it was too late.

Kip hurried behind them, thrust the gun into Jason's back, and said into his ear, "You already know what this is, playboy—Run ya shit!" Kip was so close to him, he could feel the man's heartbeat. And he wasn't intimidated by the athlete's imposing height and his size. He had the gun and he had the wits.

Jason scowled. "Nigga, you know who the fuck I am?"

"Yeah, muthafucka," Kip sardonically replied. "Why you think I'm robbing you?"

The groupie was suddenly frightened and ready to scream.

Kip said, "Tell ya bitch to chill."

Jason grabbed her and roughed her up and warned her to chill and be quiet.

Kip then ordered him to take it all off. He wanted everything.

"You really gonna do this?"

"You think I'm a fuckin' joke, nigga?" Kip pushed the barrel of the gun into Jason's back harder, ready to blow his spine out. "Fuck around with me and catch yourself having an early retirement."

Jason Miller shook his head. If this had been back in the day, things would have gone differently. Jason used to be the one with the gun and doing the stick-ups. He knew the underworld very well and never thought he would become the victim.

Slowly, he removed his watch and his jewelry and handed it over to Kip. "I'm gonna find you, muthafucka. I'll bet everything on that, you clown-ass nigga."

Kip didn't respond to his threats. In his line of work, it came with the business. Kip then told him to take off his diamond earrings. They were big and pricey.

Jason had to take his time unscrewing them from his ear, the barrel of the gun pushed into his back.

All this was happening on a city street in a busy area, and no one around was any wiser.

"You got balls, nigga, doing this shit here like that. I'll give you that, nigga. But I know plenty of niggas that had balls and were bold, and you know where they at now? Fuckin' dead, nigga! Like you gonna be soon, you clown-ass, stupid muthafucka!"

Kip responded, "You know, there's a way to kill a nigga and still leave him alive. And you know how that happens? You take everything he has."

Kip quickly glanced around his surroundings and saw his opening. He then pointed the gun downwards and deliberately shot Jason in both of his ankles.

Bak! Bak!

Jason hollered from the pain and collapsed to the pavement, clutching at his bleeding ankles.

Kip backed away slowly and then took off in a slow jog. That was for Eshon and Brandy.

Kip reconnected with his crew, along with Eshon and Brandy. They had all done well so far tonight. Two down and one to go.

***

Devon parked the truck across the street from the Gansevoort Hotel and left it idling. Kip had texted Jessica earlier and learned that she was in the hotel room still working Mike Blackmon.

***

Inside the lavish hotel room, Jessica little by little removed her naked frame from the unconscious athlete's arms. He was sleeping heavily and wouldn't be awake for hours. Jessica had drugged his drink with rohypnol while he wasn't looking. She didn't even have to fuck him.

With Mike out cold, she had plenty of time to go through his pockets and pick him clean of all his valuables. He had ten thousand dollars cash on him. His cash was now hers, and she took all of his jewelry and crammed it into her clutch and some into a pillow case she'd transformed into a carrying bag.

Dressed and pleased, she smoothly strutted out of the hotel suite before dawn, made her way down to the lobby, and coolly made her exit from the opulent hotel and onto the city streets, where she found her friends waiting.

Jessica climbed into the Expedition. As Devon drove off and headed back uptown, toward Harlem, she boasted about her score.

Kip was pleased too. They had done it—They hit all three players at once and stole countless jewelry and cash from them. He couldn't wait to tally it up and see how well they'd done.

FIVE

Feeling relaxed and mellow, Kip lit his Black & Mild and stared at today's news on his flat-screen in his bedroom. Last night was a risk, but he needed the money. He needed to live. He had shocked the world with his bold robberies on three NBA players and the shooting of Jason Miller. It was breaking news that morning on every channel, and Club Revolt was under heavy criticism.

The major story was this: Jason Miller was shot twice and had been rushed to the nearest hospital. He was expected to live, but his playing days in the NBA looked bleak. His season was over, leaving almost no hope for the Nets to make the playoffs.

The news told Kip NYPD had no leads and no suspects. It was limited information, but it was still information. Having heard enough of his work broadcast on TV, he turned it off and stood up. His bedroom was quiet.

He walked to his window and peered out, and it was another sunny, spring day in the projects. No one knew that he and his crew had done the robbery the night before.

Kip did fifty push-ups and fifty sit-ups. He needed to keep his body in shape. He had to always stay fit and ready. Being frail and weak was a death sentence to him.

He broke a little sweat while working out and then guzzled down a full bottle of water.

Subsequently, he went into his little brother's bedroom and saw Kid already in his wheelchair, fully dressed and playing *Call of Duty* online on his Xbox. Kid was the wholehearted gamer. He sat in front of his plasma TV with his headset and remote control, communicating with other gamers from all over the world.

"You up and dressed, huh?" Kip said.

"Yeah," Kid replied, not looking at his brother but focusing on the game.

Kip walked farther into the bedroom and noticed several hundred-dollar bills on the dresser. He picked it up and counted six hundred dollars. He looked shocked. "You won all this playing chess yesterday?" he asked.

Kid glanced at him and smiled. "Like I said, you got your hustle, and I got mines."

"Damn! You definitely hustlin', little brother."

"You can't be the only one bringing income into this home," Kid replied.

Kip chuckled. He was impressed. "Do you."

Kip sat on the foot of Kid's bed and watched *Call of Duty* on the 50-inch flat-screen. It was an intense game of guns and soldiers, not to mention it was loud and busy.

Kid moved his avatar like a professional gamer and took on all enemies with a fierce machine gun.

Kip couldn't keep up with what was going on. It almost matched his real life. He then looked at Kid and said, "Look, I'm thinking about going to see Nana this weekend. You wanna roll?"

The mention of Nana's name put a frown on Kid's face. "I think I'll pass," he said.

"Again, Kid . . . you know she misses you."

"That old woman doesn't miss us. The only thing she misses is the checks she used to get for keeping us," Kid replied dryly.

"Nana is a sweet lady. She has always been good to us."

"Because she got paid to care, Kip. And you keep her dolled up and living a lifestyle that she doesn't deserve."

"Why you resent her so much, huh? If it wasn't for her, they would have separated us," Kip reminded Kid.

Kid continued to frown. "But they didn't. There was something about her that I never liked. She used us, and she's still using you. She uses people, Kip."

"She's a good woman."

"Good to herself."

Kid wanted to fart on her name. He had always believed that when he had gotten seriously hurt and paralyzed, she was elated. A crippled child would bring her a bigger paycheck from the state.

"You're supposed to be the kind and forgiving one," Kip joked.

"And you're supposed to be the one who thinks several steps ahead and could see a setup coming a mile away. Too bad you didn't see Nana coming."

Kip managed to chuckle. "Oh, you got jokes now."

"Anyway, go see the wicked witch of the west and give her my hate."

"I'll give her your love," Kip said.

"Don't go lying on me now."

The machine guns on the video game exploded louder. It seemed like Kid had turned the volume up, and his thumbs moved rapidly against the buttons on the controller. He didn't even blink.

Kip asked him, "You going down to the park today?"

Kid nodded. "You coming to see me play?"

"If I got time."

"It's been a minute since you saw me play."

"I know. I'll make the time."

"I would appreciate it, big bro."

Kip felt a tinge of guilt. He hadn't seen Kid play a chess match in weeks. The streets mainly occupied his attention. But his brother was important, and chess was his love. Kip had been around and had been supportive of his baby brother, but he'd also been distant, doing capers and building a violent reputation.

"I gotta go, but I love you, Kid," Kip declared genuinely.

"I love you too. Be safe out there."

Kip wasn't afraid to kiss his brother on the cheek and show affection. After he did, he walked out his bedroom.

Kip loved and respected his brother. They were both hustlers in the city, but Kip's riskier hustle paid off a lot more. Kid was so good, he was making his own profit from playing numerous games with some of the best players. He was the master chess player, and there was a long line of challengers ready to try and beat him at the game. For so many, it was embarrassing to be beaten by a wheelchair-bound ghetto kid who played video games in his spare time.

Kip took the elevator down to the lobby while clutching his bag full of goodies. Last night's stick-up was lucrative, and he had a lot of merchandise to move. He and his crew had come off with three big-faced watches—one a platinum diamond Cartier and two gold Rolexes; three platinum chains; several diamond rings; a pair of diamond earrings; and over twenty-five thousand dollars in cash. Their total take could be in the hundreds of thousands, depending on how Kip moved the stolen merchandise. He was wise not to pawn off any of the athlete's jewelry at any shops in town, knowing everything could be traced and that dealing with pawn shops left behind too many fingerprints. It would be the first place the cops would look for the stuff.

Kip had a better way to fence the stolen goods. He had a guy named Maserati Meek who would probably want to buy it all from him. The first call Kip made that day was to him.

The phone rang twice then Meek picked up with, "My favorite friend. How are you, Kip?"

"I'm good, Meek."

"This call must be about business then, my friend." Maserati Meek had a strong Middle Eastern accent. He sounded nasal and spoke from his throat.

"Of course. When can we meet?"

"Eh, today, my friend. Four this afternoon."

"I'll be there." Kip hung up.

Kip didn't like to prolong phone conversations or discuss business over the phone. There was no telling who was listening and who was watching. He was certain that Maserati Meek would buy the jewelry from him at a reasonable price, where he wouldn't feel cheated. The stolen cash had already been divided up, with Eshon and her girls getting their percentage.

With over seven thousand dollars in his pockets on another sunny and warm spring day, Kip took a deep breath of fresh Harlem air and exhaled. He had time to chill and think. Besides, after last night's stick-up, they needed to keep a low profile. He was confident that they had escaped arrest. Surveillance cameras were in the area, but Kip had made sure to cover all angles, remaining covert and unseen, and Midtown was a busy place with many people. He was sure that Devon and Papa John were careful too. They didn't need anything coming back on them.

His meeting with Maserati Meek was in five hours.

SIX

Eshon walked around her apartment in her panties and bra singing her heart out. Thinking about Kip, she belted out Jennifer Hudson's "If This Isn't Love." She continued as she walked into her kitchen, matching Jennifer Hudson's stellar voice.

It was a sunny day, and the only thing or person she could think about was Kip. She wanted to spend the day with him. She wanted to nestle inside his arms and make love to him. Last night was eventful, despite the incident with Jason Miller. Once again, she showed Kip that she was there for him always. He paid her and her girls three grand from the cash they took off the athletes. Eshon was ready to go shopping with her cut.

In the kitchen, she made herself French toast and scrambled eggs for breakfast. Her attention shifted from Jennifer to Fantasia, when she started to sing "When I See U." While she stood over the stove, her voice traveled throughout the apartment.

Eshon had the place to herself. Her mother was at work, her father wasn't around, and she didn't have any brothers or sisters. The only sisters she had in her life were Jessica and Brandy. She'd grown up with Brandy, knowing her since the fifth grade, and Jessica came around when she was fourteen years old, bringing that L.A. swag and gang attitude to Harlem.

At first the girls were skeptical of Jessica with her West Coast demeanor and pretty features. Brandy, in particular, was extremely envious of the girl. Jessica proved to everyone that she wasn't just a pretty face and a stuck-up bitch. Jessica was a pit bull in a skirt and a fighter, and she planned on making her bones in Harlem just like she had in L.A. It took a while for Jessica to fit in and adapt to Harlem, but once she did, she became one of the girls.

With breakfast made, Eshon turned on the television to NY1, a twenty-four-hour news channel that aired only in the five boroughs. She stopped short in what she was doing when she saw Jason Miller's mug displayed on the television. She searched for the remote and increased the volume. Right away, she heard the news of Jason Miller being shot twice last night, but he was in stable condition. The news anchor went on to inform the public that two other NBA players were robbed last night but weren't harmed.

Eshon's eyes were glued to the TV. She had no idea that Kip had shot him. He didn't say a word about it. She was shocked. Did he do it for her? Was he protecting her honor? Eshon was floored. She was happy that he had done it. She hated that muthafucka and felt he had it coming. He was arrogant and disrespectful to women—especially black women.

She smiled. She wanted to have Kip's baby. She knew he cared and it would only be a matter of time before they got back together.

***

Eshon met up with Jessica and Brandy on West 133rd Street. She wanted to enjoy the sunny spring day and hit 125th Street with them to do some shopping.

"Hey, girl," Brandy greeted with a smile and a hug.

"You looking special today," Jessica said.

"Thanks."

Eshon felt special. Her smile was white and she was glowing. She was hoping to run into Kip today. She was always thinking about him and trying to look pretty for him.

DIRTY WORK - PART ONE

The girls climbed into Brandy's old gray Chevrolet Malibu and headed toward the shopping area. Though Brandy schemed and robbed with her crew from time to time, she still held down a job, making ten dollars an hour at a cafeteria in the city to occupy some of her time and give her some pocket change on the side.

"Y'all heard about Jason Miller?" Eshon started with the talk.

"Yeah, he got shot last night," Brandy said.

"He was a bitch-ass nigga fo' real," Jessica added. "Homes deserved that S.O.S."

Brandy and Eshon looked at each other and asked, "S.O.S.?"

"Shoot on sight," Jessica informed them.

The girls laughed.

"Eight years in Harlem and still that L.A. shit comes outta you."

"I'm never gon' forget where I come from."

"We all won't," Eshon said.

"Kip did that for you?" Brandy asked her.

"Maybe," Eshon said.

"That's love right there, Eshon," Jessica said.

Eshon sat in the front seat feeling like she was voted prom queen. She broke out into a Fantasia song right there. Lyrics from "Truth Is" spilled out.

Brandy rolled her eyes and sucked her teeth. Eshon was always singing and showing off, no matter where they were. She had to let everyone know that she could sing.

"Okay, Whitney Houston, this isn't a concert hall, and we ain't an audience of seventy thousand."

"Don't hate, Brandy," Eshon replied.

Brandy continued driving while Eshon continued to sing different songs.

***

The girls came out of the H&M store clutching several shopping bags. It was the fifth store they had been to on 125th Street. They felt like queens as they tried on different outfits and paid cash for the best. One Hundred Twenty-Fifth was always active and fun. They had a girls' day out, laughing and clowning around, piquing the fellows they came across. Three beautiful girls smiling and dressed nicely—they were a girl group in the public.

After they were done shopping, the girls wanted to show off their new clothes right away and do it someplace crowded. They thought about the park—St. Nicholas Park. It was late afternoon and the perfect time to stunt and shine. So, they hurried back to the buildings, changed clothes, did make-up and hair, and then climbed back into Brandy's old gray Chevrolet Malibu and headed toward the park.

***

St. Nicholas Park was crowded with sweaty Negros playing a pickup game while girlfriends and admiring ladies watched from the sidelines. The crowd was screaming and playing children occupied the playgrounds while their parents sat nearby and talked amongst themselves.

There was a slight breeze in the park, and it was a welcoming one for those exhausting themselves with activity.

But the place to be was where the men played chess. Some of the smartest people in the city came to play on the stone chess tables in the park. There would be crowds of people around, watching move for move. It sometimes looked like a basketball tournament was happening, or like observers quietly witnessing a golf tournament. Like golf, chess was a quiet game, and lots of money was involved.

Eshon and her girls strutted into the park and made their way toward the playground, where the men were seated playing chess at the stone tables.

Immediately, the girls received catcalls and lingering stares. They showed off skin and cleavage, but not too much, wanting to leave something to the imagination. Their sneakers were Nikes, white and clean. Their hair was long and silky, even if some of them were wearing weaves. But they all felt good and sexy. The boys were watching them, hungry for their attention, and they ate it up like it was a good scoop of ice cream on a hot summer day.

From a short distance, Eshon saw Kid in his wheelchair, playing a game. He looked pensive. The men around were all ages, and a few were drinking jasmine tea and eating muffins made by Mr. Harry Walker, a regular at the park. Kid was playing against a guy with a white beard reminiscent of Santa Claus. He was mostly jolly and cheery—when he wasn't losing—and he was a great player. The men were playing for a hundred dollars a game, and already The Kid had won four hundred dollars.

Eshon and her girls approached.

Kid was always focused on his games, scrutinizing every move and continuing to win, but there was one person that could distract him from an intense match, and that person was Jessica. When he saw her standing nearby, looking sexy in a white tennis skirt and sleeveless shirt, his concentration broke. He looked at her and smiled far and wide. He had a serious crush on the L.A. native.

"You know he likes you, girl," Eshon whispered in Jessica's ear.

"And what I'm supposed to do with a cripple?"

"You can get creative," Eshon quipped.

"Ha-ha, you funny, bitch. You take him then."

"I want his brother. You know that."

"And I want a man that can walk, not some crippled *hombre* with dead legs and a dead dick," Jessica said seriously.

"You foul, Jessica."

"No, you foul, *muchacha*. I know what I like, and that's a *hombre* that can please me good. Why we here anyway? I wanna see some real niggas in this park."

"Do you then," Eshon said, defeated.

Brandy just stood to the side, listening to them talk and not bothering to put in her two cents.

Kid was happy that his dream girl Jessica was finally watching him play a game. Now he had to show off for her and win another one. He waved her way, a simple hi, but she didn't wave back. She stood there, deadpan and not interested in men playing chess.

Kid didn't take any offense at it. He put his focus back into playing his game. He was thinking five to six moves ahead.

Before he knew it, Jessica had walked away. Brandy too.

Eshon remained behind. She found chess somewhat interesting. Besides, she didn't mind getting closer to Kip's brother. Maybe he could tell her where he was today.

Half an hour later, Kid won the match by controlling the center of the board. It was a strategy that consisted of placing pieces so they could attack the central four squares. He also had his bishop controlling the center from afar. His opponent wasn't happy, but he paid Kid the hundred dollars he owed. Kid was undefeated. He did a spin in his wheelchair and boasted.

Eshon laughed. He couldn't walk, but he had an upbeat attitude.

"I want a rematch. Make it two hundred this time," the white-bearded man said.

"One moment." Kid wheeled himself from the table and rolled toward Eshon. "Hey, where's your friend?" he asked, speaking about Jessica.

"She went to the basketball courts."

"Oh, I guess the game became too intense for her, huh?" he joked.

Eshon laughed. "I guess so. But you are nice with them chess pieces. How long did it take for you to play like that?"

"It's natural, I guess. The game's just in me."

"I see that. You're smart."

Kid shrugged.

Eshon saw that he was a cute guy—smart, humorous and very charming. His only fault was his handicap. She was itching to ask him about Kip.

Kid knew how bad she had it for his older brother. It was hard for her to hide it. He wasn't a fool. The main reason she hung around to watch him play was that she wanted to know about Kip. Besides the few words they exchanged, their conversation was mostly dry. Meanwhile, Kid's attention and heart were on Jessica, if she ever gave him the time of day.

"You're looking for my brother, right?" he asked.

"Is he around?"

"Haven't seen him since this morning. I think he had to take care of some business on Long Island."

"Oh," Eshon uttered, looking disappointed.

"You really like him, don't you?"

"I'm in love with him. Does he talk about me?"

"I hated that y'all two broke up. Y'all were really good together."

His comment made her smile. If he was avoiding her question, she couldn't tell. "He takes me for granted."

"He takes everyone for granted. Don't take it personally."

"I'd do anything for him, and he knows it. I don't want to lose him."

"You won't." Kid said it like he could foretell the future. "Hey, let's do each other a favor."

She smiled. "And what's that?"

"You put in a good word for me with Jessica, and hook me up, and I'll make sure to speak highly of you to my brother."

Eshon smiled down at Kid and extended her right hand. "Deal!" She loved his positive attitude. Jessica was missing out by not giving him a chance.

SEVEN

Kip navigated his Nissan Quest minivan through the winding roads of Long Island, New York. He entered the Great Neck area, an affluent neighborhood in northern Long Island where both sides of the street were lined with pricey homes and nice cars. The neighborhood was posh and majority white, and Kip never felt too comfortable in it.

Papa John rode shotgun, acting as his support, and the two men scoped out the homes with admiration as they made their way toward Maserati Meek's place two miles down the road.

"These fuckin' people live too good," Papa John said.

"They do."

"What you think it would feel like living out here?"

Kip chortled. "Like these white people out here would accept us into their community. We too hood for these crackers."

"It would definitely be a step up for us."

"I love Harlem."

"I do too, but think about the pussy we would get wit' a crib like one of these."

"You think wit' your dick too much, Papa John."

"I think like a nigga that loves to bust a nut. Like you wouldn't want to fuck a bitch in a million-dollar home."

Kip laughed and shook his head. Leave it to Papa John to soothe the tension with his vulgar humor.

They pulled up to a moderate-sized home with a curved driveway on Middle Neck Road. They were familiar with the address. Kip parked behind two red Ferrari 458s, and he and Papa John climbed out of the minivan, in awe of the sleek, exotic cars.

"Shit!" Papa John said, running his hand across the hood of the car as he passed it by. "Maserati Meek definitely knows how to live it up. Imagine it, Kip—getting your dick sucked in one of these things while doin' a hundred miles an hour on the highway."

"Nigga, you better have control first."

"Oh, I'm gonna have control, over the car and my bitch. But I like this. Damn! You think he would let me take it for a test drive?"

"We're here on business, Papa," Kip reminded him.

"Yeah, yeah, business . . . then pleasure."

The two men walked toward the solid mahogany double doors with rain glass. The property was tastefully decorated with trimmed shrubberies and blossoming flowers, surveillance cameras everywhere.

Kip pushed the doorbell, and they waited. In Kip's hand was a bag full of goodies—the stolen watches and jewelry from the basketball players. The contents inside weighed the bag down, so Kip was sure he would get a good price for everything from Maserati Meek.

Soon, the doors opened, and standing in front of the men was one of Meek's goons. The man recognized the Harlem thugs, but that didn't stop him from thoroughly searching them in the large foyer for any weapons. Once cleared, the goon stepped aside and allowed them farther into the home. From the foyer, they entered a great room dominated by a huge, honed, black granite-topped island. The room doubled as a kitchen and living room.

Maserati Meek was in the kitchen, cooking. He turned around and greeted Kip and Papa John happily. "My friends, once again, I welcome you to my paradise."

From the smell in the kitchen, it seemed like he was a good cook. Whatever he had brewing, it enticed Kip and Papa John's nostrils.

Maserati Meek was all smiles and animated, like a child with ADHD. Dressed in beige shorts exposing his hairy legs, a T-shirt, and a white apron, he walked toward the two men like he was ready to go outside and play. He hugged them, but they were standoffish to his warm greeting. It was awkward. But he was weird.

Maserati Meek's eyes moved down to the bag in Kip's hand. He already had an idea what was inside. "You brought gifts for me, eh, my friend?"

"Came here to do some business," Kip said.

"You guys, you hungry? You stay for dinner? You want a taste of some good Middle Eastern chow?"

"Not hungry," Kip replied nonchalantly.

"You sure? I'm making some smoking baba ghanoush with oil-cured black olives. It's a very tasty dish. It is de shit, my friend."

"Smoking *baba ghan*-what?" Kip couldn't even pronounce it, and he definitely didn't have any desire to taste it. He just wanted to show Maserati Meek the jewelry, make a deal, and leave.

Though Maserati Meek was animated and friendly toward the two of them, Kip was well aware of his notorious reputation that carried from state to state. Behind that smile and the hospitality, he was a violent, murderous drug kingpin. His iron fists ruled from the Tri-State to Detroit, Baltimore, and Chicago, and had become a huge blip on the FBI's radar. His organization was under federal investigation, but there wasn't enough evidence to build a case yet.

"We'll pass this time," Kip said coolly.

Maserati Meek pivoted and went back to the large stove to tend to his meal.

Kip and Papa John stood in the kitchen knowing it wasn't wise to rush the man into conducting business.

DIRTY WORK - PART ONE

✳✳✳

Maserati Meek, born Akar Mudada, could be eccentric at times, but he was fair and he was smart. Business was in his blood, and so was bloodshed and carnage. His parents were from Egypt, and his family was no stranger to aggression, oppression, and death. When he was ten, his uncles were killed by drone attacks. They were blown to pieces in the bunker they'd taken refuge inside. Maserati Meek had witnessed the family remove body after body after the attack. Nearly half a dozen dead and bloody men were laid out on the rubble for him to see. They said that his uncles were linked to Al-Qaeda.

Maserati Meek was a handsome, tall man with shiny, long black hair that he sported in different styles from time to time, either pulled back into a bun, cornrows, or two braids. He had dark skin and his accent was slightly urban, sometimes *Black*-ish. He emulated the urban culture, fell in love with the lifestyle and the people.

This was a punch in the face to his parents, who believed in the unity of their own people and race. Maserati Meek contradicted their beliefs, indulging himself in the black lifestyle and in a life of crime.

He ran his criminal organization like a terrorist. He had committed soldiers who were ready to die for what they believed in—his organization and never-ending praise to Allah. When his organization went to war with another, it was like Iraq, Beirut, or Afghanistan on an urban street with deadly bombings and AK-47 gunfire. Though most of his family had disowned him, Maserati Meek continued to send lots of money back home to his family in Egypt to help support their terrorist regimes, and for food and a decent living.

He had come to America on a work visa from his employer when he was nineteen years old. He was a gifted engineer and computer programmer who had caught the attention of a fledgling software company called Sillicus, which was willing to sponsor him. He did extraordinary work for

Sillicus until he became infatuated with the ghetto lifestyle. His attitude started to change, and his career in engineering and software design began to suffer.

It didn't take long before he started dabbling in the drug world. He covertly helped fund several kilos of cocaine for a Texas crew he'd befriended. He rose fast in the underworld, and twelve years later, he was the boss.

Maserati Meek farmed out murder contracts to Kip and his crew when he didn't want to get his hands dirty or involve his organization. Kip had a success rate of 100 percent, and a level of trust had been built between the two men.

***

"Sit and let's talk," Meek said finally. "I'm ready to see what my two players got for me today . . . something nice, I know."

The two men sat at the island. Kip removed the contents from the bag and spread it across the island. Everything gleamed brightly. It all looked very expensive—diamonds, gold, and platinum, a black man's glory.

Maserati Meek stared at the jewelry and the watches and he lit up like a lightbulb. "Whoa! Whoa! We done hit payday, I see," he exclaimed. "Damn, muthafuckas, I love it already."

"Everything you see here is from NBA ballplayers," Kip informed him.

"Eh, that thing on the news, that was you and your crew?"

Kip nodded proudly.

"I'm impressed, my friend. I am."

He picked up the Rolex and inspected it. Off the bat, he knew the worth of the watch. He loved the fact that the jewelry in his kitchen belonged to ballplayers. There was a certain bravado in owning jewelry stolen from NBA players.

"I want it all," he proclaimed loudly. "Yes, I love it! Oh, these muthafuckas definitely had good taste." He threw on one of the platinum chains and struck a pose in front of his men standing in the kitchen.

Kip and Papa John smiled widely. They could see the dollar signs dancing around in the air and falling all around them, drenching them with a shitload of money.

"I'm gonna give the earrings to my girl, and this watch, I'm gonna keep this watch for myself." Maserati Meek so happened to pick up Jason Miller's diamond-encrusted watch for himself.

"Big Sean and Jay P, y'all niggas, c'mere. Let's enjoy this together." Maserati Meek called two of his goons to the kitchen island covered with jewelry.

They stepped toward the jewelry with an expressionless look.

Meek said, "Pick something out for yourselves."

Their stone-faced looks turned into bright and wide smiles. Jay P picked out the gold Rolex, and Big Sean helped himself to a big-faced diamond watch, both costing sixty grand apiece.

"What we owe you, my niggas?" Maserati Meek asked.

No one was offended by his use of the word *nigga*, which he used frequently, and they didn't care. He was the boss. You didn't challenge Maserati Meek.

Kip did the math in his head and came to a price. "Two hundred K," he threw out there, thinking everything had to be in the 1.5 million mark. He felt that two hundred thousand was a fair price for it all.

Maserati Meek nodded. "Okay."

Kip and Papa John smiled. It was payday.

Meek instructed one of his men to get the cash. "Can we talk alone?" he asked Kip.

Kip nodded. They made their way onto the patio in the backyard overlooking the in-ground pool.

Maserati Meek lit a cigar and took a few pulls. The pool held his gaze. He puffed out smoke and without looking at Kip, he said, "I need another job done."

"Who, and how soon?"

Maserati Meek kept his gaze fixed on the calm water in the pool as he smoked his cigar. He then answered, "The contract is on Big Sean, and I need this done right away."

If Kip was shocked, he didn't show it. He remained dispassionate and continued to listen. He had just witnessed Maserati Meek give Big Sean a diamond watch. Kip wasn't one to ask any questions. He needed the work. He needed the cash to keep coming in.

"I'll pay twenty large for the contract."

"I can't do it for anything less than fifty grand," Kip counter-offered. "My peoples gotta eat too."

Maserati Meek nodded in agreement to the fifty grand. It was a deal. "When it's done, I want the watch removed from his body. Keep it for yourself as a bonus, eh, my friend."

Just like that, Kip was once again a hired killer. If the man wanted one of his own lieutenants killed, then so be it. For Kip, it was just business, nothing personal. It wasn't the first time Maserati Meek had one of his men killed by Kip and his crew.

Lately, Maserati Meek had become a bit paranoid, maybe super paranoid. There was no talking over the phone unless it was a burner phone, and even that had its limitations. Everyone was searched, and he constantly had his home, businesses, and cars checked for wires, bugs, or any kind of electronic frequency.

Maserati Meek had been viewing Big Sean with suspicion and started to think he was snitching. Big Sean gave lame excuses for his disappearances, he couldn't look his boss in the eyes, and there were times when he would get really nervous around Maserati Meek. Maserati Meek was trained to pick up on body language. He'd taught himself the art of finding a snitch. It was crazy, but he believed that he was a human lie detector.

Maserati Meek wasn't aware there was another explanation for Big Sean's odd behavior. He was having a covert affair with Nia, the woman he loved.

Kip turned and walked back into the house. He glanced at Big Sean, who was all smiles, enjoying the new watch he'd received, and he felt nothing at all. Big Sean was laughing it up with the other henchmen inside the house. He didn't even know what was about to come his way.

Maserati Meek rejoined his men in the kitchen. Two hundred thousand dollars was handed over to Kip in a small black duffel. Kip took it, opened it, and quickly inspected the loot. The stacks of ten thousand dollars crowded over each other were joy in his hands.

Maserati Meek disappeared from the kitchen. He didn't say a word to anyone. Everyone thought he needed his alone-time. It was usual with him.

Suddenly, he reemerged gripping a big black gun—a Heckler & Koch G36C, a high-powered gun that was meant to destroy whatever, absolutely.

Everyone stood around in shock. The room became tense.

He pointed the weapon at Big Sean and exclaimed, "You my bitch, nigga?"

Big Sean stood frozen in fear and wide-eyed. "Boss? What-what's up?" he asked in a shaky voice.

Kip and Papa John thought they were about to see a man's head get blown off right there.

All of a sudden, Maserati Meek cracked a smile and started laughing, subsequently exclaiming, "I'm just fuckin' with you, my nigga! Lighten up, have some fun. I just wanted to show off my new toy to Kip."

Big Sean released a nervous smile. He damn near pissed on himself. He sighed with relief. His boss had one twisted sense of humor. He didn't get mad, and even if he had, there wasn't anything he could do about it.

Along with drugs, Maserati Meek was heavily into the selling of guns, and not the average firearms. He had access to high-grade, high-powered weapons that he shipped overseas and kept some goodies for himself and his crew. He had the type of guns that Kip and his crew had never heard of. The Feds, ATF, and the DEA all wanted him with a hard-on, but Maserati Meek had always been one step ahead of the alphabet boys. It was one of the reasons he'd been farming out a lot of murders—to lessen the risk of anything connecting back to him.

Kip felt it was time to go. He had his money, and he had a contract to execute. "We're gone," he said.

"So soon, my friend? You don't want to party tonight?"

"We good," Kip replied.

"Okay, until next time then, my niggas," Maserati Meek said. "And I appreciate what you do for me."

Kip and Papa John turned away and made their way out from the home and away from the eccentric kingpin.

While they walked toward the car, Papa John looked at Kip and asked, "What he wanted to talk to you about?"

"I'll tell you later, but it's another payday for us."

"A'ight, I see," Papa John replied, already picking up on the hint.

Before he climbed into the car, Papa John took one last look at the Ferrari 458 and once again imagined getting his dick sucked in the front seat while doing over a hundred miles per hour on the freeway. He looked at Kip and said, "One day, I'm gonna get me one of these, and I'm gonna have an orgasm in it while speeding on the highway."

Kip laughed. "You crazy, nigga."

"I'm just fun. You know you have the same fantasy. Don't front, nigga."

Kip continued to laugh.

They both climbed inside the Nissan Quest and sped away. Another day, another dollar.

EIGHT

Oh shit, this is my song right here!" Eshon and Jessica both shouted out simultaneously, as "The Worst" by Jhené Aiko blared through the large club speakers.

The girls jumped to their feet from the bar and started to dance and sing the lyrics to the song with their cups of Alizé in their hands.

Club Rose in the Village was booming with dozens and dozens of partygoers, from heterosexual males to flaming homosexuals, to well-dressed transgenders, to some of the sexiest ladies in town. The large nightclub on Morton Street was a haven for those especially comfortable with their sexuality. The club boasted of a ten-thousand-square-foot space, two full bars, a giant disco ball, go-go dancers, and colored lights. The regal entryway was only the beginning to stepping into a marvelous party.

The dance floor was crowded, and in some private areas, people were snorting lines of coke and swallowing ecstasy. Everyone was super hyped.

The girls lingered by the bar, mingling with some cuties and partying, but they were also searching for another possible mark for Kip. Working for Kip was their primary income, and so far the money was good. There were a lot of players and ballers as well as flashy homosexuals partying in Rose. A certain song came on, and two men started vogue-dancing in the middle of the dance floor. It was very entertaining.

Eshon laughed and downed her drink. Brandy beamed with excitement, and Jessica was the eye candy for the night. The girls didn't have to pay for their own drinks; they were complimentary from the men admiring their beauty, especially Jessica's.

From the bar, they saw Maserati Meek in attendance. He had his own VIP area, and he was with his main lady, Nia, and his entourage of goons. Their area was cluttered with champagne, women, and drug use, and Meek was in the middle of it all, having a good time and looking like a foreign prince in his expensive jewelry and long hair styled into a ponytail. The girls had never met Meek personally, but they knew he was off-limits because he worked with Kip.

Maserati Meek was a very dangerous man, though sometimes he didn't look like it. The interesting man transfixed Jessica. He seemed to have it all, and he seemed to be a fun guy. The woman he was with couldn't hold a candle to her, but she was living the good life, looking like she could walk a red carpet in her designer dress, her diamonds costing more than an average house.

The night continued with the girls inching their way toward the VIP section. They wanted to catch a nigga's attention. Whether for pleasure or profit, it didn't matter to them.

Eshon and Brandy went off to have a good time on the dance floor when "Part II (On the Run)" by Jay Z and Beyoncé played throughout the club. They danced together, leaving Jessica alone at the bar.

Once more, Jessica glanced Maserati Meek's way and admired his flavor. He was a handsome man. For a fleeting moment, they locked eyes, but he suddenly turned away from the Spanish beauty in the striking tight dress.

Not too much later, she heard a man say to her, "You're looking good tonight in that dress, ma. What's your name?"

Jessica glanced his way and gave him the once-over. Definitely not her type. He was too black, too short, and he didn't look important at all.

"Fuck off, *cabrón!*"

He chuckled. "Damn, ma, don't kill the messenger." He continued with, "You definitely caught my boss's attention with your pretty face and your dress. He would love to get to know you better."

"And who's your boss?"

The man motioned toward Maserati Meek in VIP. "If you know how to keep your mouth shut, then my boss thinks that you and he can have a beautiful time together." Then he passed a number to her on the sly.

Jessica was no fool. She took the small piece of paper and placed it into her decorated clutch bag. From the outside looking in, it looked like Meek's goon was the one hollering at Jessica. It was like a dream come true for her because, damn it, she was just admiring the man from afar and yearning to be in Nia's position. She needed a baller in her life, the type to whisk her away on exotic vacations and finance outrageous shopping sprees in foreign countries.

His job done, the man walked away.

It was hard for Jessica to keep her composure. She wanted to do cartwheels inside the club. She planned on calling him soon and throwing her sexiness, beauty, and good pussy his way to get him sprung. She looked at Nia and felt confident that she could strip a good man like Maserati Meek away from that plain-looking bitch.

Brandy and Eshon rejoined Jessica by the bar after a long moment of dancing.

Brandy asked her, "Girl, who was that nigga hollering at you?"

"You know, some *hombre* interested in this good, good *coño*," she said jokingly.

"He was cute," Eshon said.

"He was corny. And it's getting wack in here. Y'all ready to go?"

"So soon?" Eshon said.

"I'm tired, girl, and ain't nothing really happening tonight."

"Whatever," Eshon said in a considerate fashion. "Let's go."

Brandy looked like she had an attitude. Here was Jessica receiving all of the attention and shooing away cute guys, while she felt like the fat, black bitch. Though she had dark skin, she wasn't fat or ugly. Dark-skinned females always had a hard time finding love or attention, or so she felt. It sucked being the blackest female in the group, and her blonde weave and hazel contacts weren't doing their job tonight. Besides, the contacts started to irritate her eyes like always, but she liked wearing them because she felt that they made her stand out. Once again Brandy became envious because Jessica got attention from what appeared to be a baller. Feeling like the third wheel, spinning nowhere, she followed her friends to the exit.

Jessica's smile was radiant. Something was up, but she wasn't telling anyone. She kept the number exchange to herself, not wanting them to mess anything up. Though they hadn't officially met yet, Maserati Meek was the perfect catch. There was no way she was throwing him back.

NINE

Kip Kane did seventy miles per hour on the I-87 expressway. He was alone, cruising like a city pimp, headed upstate in his cool Nissan Quest, tricked out with the best that money could buy. With the moonroof slid back and the windows down, with a spring breeze blowing inside his car, he listened to Drake's album, *Nothing Was the Same*.

"Started from the Bottom" blared inside his car. He felt the words, no question, as he nodded to the tune. He was a man that started from the bottom and was making his way to the top. He had over sixty grand on him, his cut from the two hundred thousand from Maserati Meek. The money was blowing away fast, going toward luxuries and bills, including the monthly rent for Nana's nursing home. Being the primary breadwinner in his family and taking care of a disabled brother was overwhelming at times, but Kip was holding things down and making things happen.

It was early afternoon on a warm, sunny Saturday. The traffic was light, and Kip was in a good mood. He was on his way to see Nana in her upstate retirement home. He welcomed the trip to see Nana, although his brother didn't come with him. He crossed over the Tappan Zee Bridge and was two hours away from his destination.

Before four p.m., he arrived at Green Grove Retirement Community. The place was nestled in a tranquil suburb of Poughkeepsie, near the Hudson River, giving certain residents a sweeping view of the river and the two bridges from their rooms, along with green rolling mountains.

The building almost resembled the White House. It was two stories high, long, and had four white pillars over the building's entrance. Kip was glad that his Nana had settled there. He parked and exited his minivan with a bouquet of roses and walked toward the entrance.

Inside, he signed in, and before he went to see Nana, he took care of her monthly bill. He met with the director in his office and dropped ten thousand dollars cash on his desk.

"I want my receipt," he told the director.

With her rent taken care of, Kip felt like a good son, though not her biological. It was worth it. He needed to make enough bank, so Nana could continue to live out her golden years comfortably.

The nursing home almost resembled an opulent hotel, with its fine furnishing and classy décor. For the residents, there was fine dining and fine entertainment. The staff took very good care of the people for the price their families were paying to keep their loved ones comfortable; the place delivered nothing but the best.

Kip took the elevator to the second floor and walked to his Nana's room. He knocked on her door, and a moment later, Nana opened it with the biggest, warmest smile on her face. She was always happy to see Kip.

Immediately, she threw her arms around him and gave him a strong and welcoming hug. "There's my favorite man," she said to Kip.

"How you doing, Nana?"

"I'm doing fine. Even finer, now that you're here. Come in."

Kip walked into her room, a large suite with a queen-size bed, a kitchenette, orderly furnishing, and tasteful artwork hanging on her walls. She also had a few pictures of Kip and Kid scattered around the room, mostly in their younger years. Her smart TV was the most recent gift from Kip. She loved her new TV and bragged about it to the other residents. She always talked about Kip and told everyone how good a son he was and how much he loved his Nana.

Nana was a bubbly, stylish woman. She had a lot to be happy about. She stood in front of Kip dressed in a blue silk housecoat, her thick grayish hair recently done by the beautician a few blocks from the place.

"I took care of the expenses this month, Nana."

Nana smiled. "What would I do without you?"

"It's the least I could do for you, Nana. You took me and Kid in when nobody else would. What would we have done wit' out you?"

"You and your brother have always been my joy. It was a pleasure raising y'all. Y'all have grown to become two fine young men."

"Kid couldn't make it. He sends his love, though."

Nana knew Kip was exaggerating. She was aware of Kid's bitterness toward her for some reason. She felt that she had been nothing but good and kind to him since he came into her home. She had supported them and loved them in her own way. At least she had Kip. But Kid treated her like she was the Antichrist.

"You hungry? I can make you something," Nana said.

"I'm good, Nana. I already ate. I only came to see you and take care of your bill for the month."

"You're not leaving so soon. You know I'm an old woman that adores her son's company. Besides, it gets lonely here sometimes."

Kip took a seat in her cushy chair. "How you been feeling, Nana?"

Nana sighed heavily, "Oh, on and off. Lately, my old bones been aching me. I think it might be arthritis. You know this old lady isn't getting any younger." She took a seat at the foot of her bed and looked like she had just walked a mile.

"Oh hush, Nana. You're still young as ever. You look good for your age."

Nana smiled. She moved around her apartment like she was crippled and hurting when, in reality, she was in perfect health. It was all a show for Kip. If he felt sorry for a sick and hurting old woman, then the more he would give to help out, the more he would be there for her. Nana's biggest fear was being alone and not being taken care of. One out of two wasn't bad odds. She thanked God for Kip.

"When is your next doctor's appointment?"

"Next week Thursday."

"I'll take you there."

"Oh, I can manage. I know you're a busy man, and it's a long trip here."

"You sure, Nana? Because it's no thang for me to drive up and chauffeur you where you need to go. I got you."

Nana smiled at his generous offer. "We have transportation already for doctor's appointments and other things, Kip. It's where the money goes— some of it anyway. They do a good job here taking me back and forth to my doctor's appointments."

Kip was glad to hear it.

Nana looked happily at Kip and asked, "So, no new girlfriend?"

"Nah, Nana, I'm a single man."

"I would love to have some grandchildren someday."

"Grandchildren?" Kip chuckled.

"Yes, grandchildren. I'm sixty-five, Kip. My time is winding down, and it would be great to hold a newborn child in my arms and love him the same as I did you and your brother."

Kip didn't want to speak about family. He didn't see any children in his future—not even a girlfriend. He was a playboy and a gangster first. His lifestyle didn't permit him to settle down and become a family man. The bitches in his life weren't the perfect candidates to become his baby mama. Kip gave his Nana whatever she wanted, but this was the one request he couldn't provide her.

He simply said, "I'll think about it, but no promises, Nana."

"That's all an old lady like me can ask for."

An hour went by as the two talked, and though Kip said he wasn't hungry, Nana still made him a small meal. That was her, cooking and enjoying her life with her adopted son when he visited. He was her only family, so she did whatever to make him happy, or to keep him happy.

By seven p.m., Kip had had a full belly and a delightful conversation. It was getting late, and he needed to head back home. It was a two-and-a-half-hour drive back to the city. He lifted himself from the table and readied himself to go. Nana was right behind him, wishing he could stay longer, but knowing his time was valuable.

"Next time, Nana."

"Drive safe, baby."

Before he left, he reached into his pocket and pulled out a wad of bills—mostly hundreds and fifties. He peeled off a few thousand from his giant stack and handed it to Nana.

At first, she was reluctant to take it, saying, "Kip, you already did enough."

"I can't ever do enough, Nana. Take it. Treat yourself to something nice."

Nana was just being pretentious. She had never been known to walk away from cash. She'd always loved material things. She took the money and placed it into her housecoat. She was really grateful. It was more than she needed, and if he would've given more, she would have taken more. Tomorrow, she planned on getting a manicure and pedicure, and there was this outfit she'd seen in the store the other day. It was pricey, but that never stopped her. Kip was her goldmine, and he was spoiling her rotten.

Nana was well aware of where the money came from. Kip wasn't a choirboy, nor was he a nine-to-five working man. He was a proprietor of the streets. His funds were illegal capital and probably blood money, but when it reached her hands, his sins were forgotten.

Kip hugged his Nana goodbye and left the building. He got back into his car and drove to the city with his pockets almost fifteen thousand dollars lighter.

***

Kip sat shirtless on his bed in the early morning, watching NY1 to see if there were any updates on the Jason Miller shooting. He wanted to know if the cops had any leads in the case. The news anchor mentioned that there was surveillance in the area, and they showed surveillance footage of a man leaving the crime scene, but the footage was grainy and unclear. There was no telling it was him. If this was the only thing the NYPD was working with, then Kip felt like he was in the clear. He had been robbing and killing people for a long time. He knew how to rob and when to rob, and how to kill and get away with it.

Now that he had another job to do, he started to prepare himself for it. Big Sean had to be taken out by week's end. The fifty thousand dollars was needed. Papa John and Devon were already aware of the job. He trusted no one but them. It was just when and how.

Satisfied that he had gotten away with the robbery of three NBA players, Kip turned off the TV and stood up. Like clockwork, he started to exercise in his bedroom. He did fifty push-ups and fifty sit-ups. He flexed his muscles in the mirror and was satisfied with his image. He downed some bottled water and then lit a Black & Mild.

He then took a look out of his bedroom window. It was another sunny day with clear skies. *Weather on the Ones* said temperatures would reach eighty degrees today. This year's spring was warmer than last year's, but who was complaining? It was time to take advantage of the warm weather after a brutal winter with several blizzards.

With some time on his hands, Kip decided to get dressed and head over to St. Nicholas Park to watch his little brother play chess. They were having an impromptu chess tournament today in the park. Though chess wasn't everybody's favorite game, it still brought out the ballers and a nice-size crowd to watch some of the best of the best play the game for money. Kip checked his bedroom, and his brother was already gone. He didn't want to miss his brother playing and winning. It was already reaching noon, so Kip hurried to get dressed. He looked handsome in black cargo shorts with white-and-black Nikes and a wife-beater.

The park was swamped with people on a sunny afternoon. It was starting to look like Rucker Park during a celebrity basketball game. Harlem was alive with people everywhere, and a lot of get-money niggas were at the park betting big money on the chess games. It was unique to see the betting frenzy. Kid was at the center of it all, with a long line of competitors ready to dethrone him.

It was loitering at its finest. There was music blaring from various cars parked on the city street, where it looked like a car show with people trying to outdo each other with flashy rims, tinted windows, candy paint jobs, and sound systems, and, of course, liquor and champagne. Women strutted around everywhere, some dressed like they were in the club.

Eshon, Brandy, and Jessica were there too, taking in the excitement and looking good in their sexy attire, matching beauty and style with the other sexy girls in the park.

Kip arrived with Papa John and Devon. Kip was looking for Kid.

When Eshon noticed Kip in the park, she beamed with excitement. Damn, if he didn't look good with his muscles showing through the white tank top he wore, his chain gleaming and swinging. Eshon felt Kip was a fine-ass thug. He damn sure was her paradise. She was eager to approach him and say hello. Maybe they could go somewhere private and talk.

But she wasn't the only girl with eyes for Kip. Several ladies came at Kip with wide smiles and flirty attitudes. He even gave a few ladies a hug.

Eshon frowned. These hoes were becoming a little too friendly with her ex-boyfriend, and she didn't like it at all.

But Kip was being Kip. He was like the Kobe Bryant of Harlem.

Kid noticed Kip watching him play from the sidelines. He smiled at his older brother and gave him a head nod. Kid was playing a guy named

Panasonic from Washington Heights in his second game. He was giving Kid a run for his money, but Kid soon figured out his strategy and was playing possum, pretending to be dead on the chess board with his timid movements. Then, out of nowhere, he executed a move that Panasonic didn't see coming, using the Sicilian Defense. His opening was an odd one, but Kid saw his closing. He felt amped with Kip watching him play.

Eshon marched toward Kip. She wanted a hug from him too. In fact, she wanted more than a hug. She wanted to show these bitches that were sweating him that she was more to him than some regular bitch.

"Hey, Kip," Eshon called out eagerly.

Kip looked her way and managed to smile.

Eshon wrapped her arms around him tightly and passionately. His physique in her hold was refreshing for her. She attempted to kiss him on the lips, yearning for a deep, long French kiss, but Kip pulled away from her. He knew what she was doing, and he wasn't having any parts of it.

"You ain't my girl anymore, Eshon. You need to chill wit' all that affection shit," he said roughly.

His statement damn near broke her heart into two pieces. She felt stupid and played. She noticed smirks on a few bitches' faces, and she wanted to scratch the smug looks off their stupid grills.

Kip stepped away from her and went to be with his little brother. Brandy offered words of encouragement. "He's just being an ass, Eshon. You're too good for him. If he can't see that you're a good thing in his life—that you truly got his back—then fuck him. You can have any nigga out here, girl."

Brandy's words were easier said than done. She didn't want any nigga out there. She wanted Kip. Eshon couldn't get over him. She didn't know if she could ever move on from him. If he ever got with someone else and entered into a serious relationship or, even worse, got the next bitch pregnant, Eshon felt that she would truly die.

Eshon wanted to cry, but she kept her composure and sucked it up. It was a nice day, and she wanted to enjoy it. Kip remained distant from her.

Kid's third match was with a guy named Junior, presumed to be one of the best players in the Tri-State area. He'd even won a few major chess tournaments nationwide and had the trophies to prove it. Junior, an old head from Brooklyn, was highly skilled at the game.

Kid and Junior were locked tight into a concentrated game. It was like Tyson against Muhammad Ali, with big money placed on them both.

Mark Spark, a major drug dealer from Brooklyn, was watching the game from the sidelines. It was his Uncle Junior up against The Kid, and he had placed ten thousand dollars on his uncle to win.

Kip and his crew went up the block for a moment, while The Kid had the tournament on lockdown. Though Kip liked watching his brother play, the game didn't hold his interest. So he found something more intriguing to capture his attention—some pretty girls with big booties and easygoing attitudes.

After an hour of playing, The Kid saw his advantage and went in for the kill against Junior. Junior moved his rook to 5G, trying to entrap The Kid's knight. The Kid saw the move three miles ahead. The old man was good, but Kid countered the move with Queen to C3 and then exclaimed, "Checkmate!"

Uncle Junior and his nephew were stunned by the move. Uncle Junior had lost, and Mark Spark was out ten grand. Mark Spark stormed toward the table and shouted, "Yo, that crippled nigga is fuckin' cheating!"

"What? I'm not a cheater," The Kid said, defending his reputation. He adjusted his wire-rimmed glasses and looked his accuser in the eyes.

"Fuck that! My uncle don't lose," Mark Spark hollered, "especially to no fuckin' cripple."

"It was a good match, but he lost. I give your uncle much respect. He was good, but it's just a game," The Kid said coolly. "I don't want any trouble."

"Nigga, we want a fuckin' rematch."

"He lost. Why can't y'all just move on?"

Mark Spark had his Brooklyn goons behind him to intimidate The Kid, who wasn't trying to spark off anything. The look in the man's eyes told him that the fuse had already been lit, and the man was ready to explode.

Mark Spark looked wildly at The Kid. He wasn't about to lose ten grand to some Harlem niggas.

Meanwhile, Kip and his crew lingered on the street corner laughing and mingling with a few lovely ladies. Being the alpha male, he had first dibs on the best one in the group. He took a few pulls from his Black & Mild.

Papa John had his eyes on the light-skinned cutie with the light eyes and long curls. Meanwhile, Devon, AKA the Devil, tried desperately to impress the friend who looked uninterested in him and kept avoiding his eye contact. She hated his weak game, yuck mouth, and stinky smell.

Suddenly, a young girl came running their way with urgent news. "Kip! Kip!" she hollered, quickly trying to get his attention.

Kip turned around, looking at the fifteen-year-old girl. She looked like a track star running his way.

"Kip, you need to come quick," she said, huffing and puffing. "Your brother is in trouble."

Without hesitation, Kip and his friends took off running toward the park and toward the chess games. Who had the audacity to mess with his little brother—his disabled little brother? Whoever it was, they were looking to die. They sprinted in the direction and hurried to where Mark Spark and his goons were shouting at The Kid. Immediately, Kip, Papa John, and Devon wanted to knock Mark's head off and put him into the ground.

Kid quickly wheeled himself between the two angry crews. "It was just a misunderstanding, Kip. We cool! Just chill!"

"Fuck that! Who this nigga coming at you like that, Kid?" Kip shouted.

Mark Spark retorted, "Y'all Harlem niggas better step the fuck off!"

Kip, Devon, and Papa John were ready to detonate with violence. They glared at these Brooklyn niggas encroaching on their territory, and it was about to be World War III.

Kip suddenly started having second thoughts. He didn't want his brother in the middle of a beef, especially a shootout, if it came to that. His first priority was getting his brother home and out of harm's way.

Mark Spark had a lot of mouth. "Fuck y'all Harlem niggas!" he shouted. "I'll lay all y'all niggas down!"

"Yo, we ain't got no beef wit' y'all niggas," Kip said. "Just go on back home, and we gonna forget this ever happened."

"Or what, nigga? Huh? What the fuck y'all niggas gonna do?" Mark lifted his T-shirt and brandished a .9mm in his waistband. "I want my fuckin' money back from y'all Harlem crooks!"

There was no getting around it. Everyone felt that violence was inevitable.

Kip shot Eshon a stern look, and right away, she was on point. She went over to Kid and grabbed the push bars on the back of his wheelchair and started to wheel him out of harm's way. Kid was reluctant to leave his brother behind, but he didn't have a choice.

Arguing and threats started to fly back and forth between both groups with Kip in the center of the commotion. The arguing escalated into pushing and shoving among the group of men. Kip struck Mark in the face, and a full-blown fight broke out, punches flying everywhere.

It was chaos. Innocent bystanders watched the skirmish play out like it was a movie. It was Brooklyn against Harlem, and over a dozen men were fighting.

Mark Sparks didn't even see it coming. Devon walked right behind him in a sneak attack and blew his brains out with a .45 handgun. Mark went flying forward and crashed against the concrete—dead!

More gunfire erupted, sending everyone scurrying for safety. It looked like everybody was shooting.

Bak! Bak! Bak!
Bac! Bac! Bac!

TEN

Three Brooklyn men were murdered, but two got away, including Junior. The cops flooded the park, with homicide detectives probing everywhere, searching for evidence, and looking for any information on the shooter or shooters involved. The men involved in the deadly shooting were dangerous, so no one was talking. They didn't want to be labeled as a snitch and catch any heat.

Kip and his crew had no remorse about the dead men; their only concern was how sloppy and carelessly it had gone down.

"Fuckin' Devon! Man, how can he be so fuckin' stupid! How could he shoot the nigga in public like that, and with Kid still in the park?" Kip hollered in his living room to Papa John. He was also upset that two men had gotten away, including Uncle Junior, who would surely be seeking retribution for his nephew's murder.

"You know he don't give a fuck," Papa John said.

"I know. It's what I love about him but what I also hate. He needs to start fuckin' thinkin' and stop being so fuckin' stupid and sloppy." Kip clapped his hands together repeatedly in a frenzy.

"Fuck those Brooklyn niggas anyway," Papa John said. "I'm glad they're dead."

They could still hear the police sirens screaming through the night in Harlem, the after-effects of a triple homicide. Papa John took comfort on the couch and was about to ready a blunt to be smoked.

Kip went into his brother's room where Kid and Eshon were conversing. She remained by his side the entire time. "Y'all good?" he asked them.

"Yeah, we okay," Kid answered.

"And you?" He looked at Eshon.

"I'll live," she said nonchalantly.

Eshon and Kip locked eyes. Even after his rudeness earlier, she was still there for him and his family.

"I bought you some Chinese food. You hungry?" he asked Kid.

"Nah, not really."

"Look, I'm sorry about today. Shit just got out of hand, ya know? That nigga had no right disrespecting you like that."

"It wasn't about me. It was about you, Kip. You could have just walked away and let it be," Kid griped.

"Seriously? Walk away after that nigga accuses you of being a cheater and threatening your life? Fuck that nigga!"

"I don't care about someone calling me a cheater because I know I'm not. And what if something was to happen to you, huh? Then what? You all I got, Kip. I have no one else in my life. And if anything was to ever happen to you, then where would I be? What is gonna happen to me?" He just wanted Kip to be extra-extra careful when he was in the streets.

"I'm not going anywhere, Kid. I'm gonna always be around to help and support you."

"I hope so."

Eshon stood up. "It's getting late. I need to go." She walked toward the hallway.

Kip suddenly grabbed her forearm and stopped her. He looked at her compassionately and said, "Thanks for today."

She managed to smile. "I'm always going to be there, Kip."

Her heart fluttered with nervousness and excitement. Once again, his touch made her body flutter. She exhaled. Would he kiss her this time? What did he want? She knew what she wanted.

"I'll call you," he said.

"Do that." She continued to smile, but she felt her heart weakening more and more. She left the room.

The brothers continued to talk. They had such a deep bond, sometimes they could tell what the other was thinking about. Kip treated his brother like a child out of guilt. Kip tucked Kid into bed and wished him a good night. He promised that there would be no more incidents and once again said, "I'm here to stay, bro. I got you for life. You feel me? Get some sleep, and don't worry. We'll talk tomorrow."

Kip walked out of the room and closed the door. He rejoined Papa John in the living room.

"Your brother okay?" Papa John asked him.

"Yeah, he a'ight. Just a little shaken up, that's all."

The two shared a blunt and started to talk business. They had a murder to plot, and Devon had nearly risked capture with his stupidity.

Papa John inhaled the smoke and sat back. "That shit was crazy today."

"It was. That's why we gotta be smarter than that." Kip wanted to forget about Brooklyn and focus on how to get at Big Sean. Today's stupid and deadly stunt wasn't about to stop them from a fifty-thousand-dollar payday.

"How we gonna do this?" Papa John asked him.

"Careful and quick, nigga—You act like we strangers to the murder game."

"Nigga, you know my gunplay is fierce, but this Big Sean we talking about. You know he a killer too."

"I know, but he ain't gonna see us coming," Kip said.

They continued to smoke and plot. It was too bad Devon wasn't there to plot with them. He was staying low at a cousin's place in Queens until things cooled down. They couldn't pull off the job without him.

ELEVEN

Kip's tricked-out minivan came to a rolling stop in front of the two-story home in St. Albans, Queens. The block was quiet and still with the sun long gone and the moon taking its place. The house was decorated with a manicured lawn, and a long driveway led to a single-car garage in the backyard. The place was a far cry from the rough streets of Harlem. Kip and Papa John sat in the car inspecting the neighborhood.

"Fuckin' Brady Bunch, this neighborhood," Papa John joked. "I don't see how Devon was able to function out here."

"Like he had a choice."

"What you think the bitches are like out here?"

Kip shot his friend a look. "Focus, nigga, fo' real," he said sharply.

"I am focused, my nigga. You need to tell Devon the same shit."

"I will, believe me." Kip picked up his cell phone and dialed Devon's number. It rang several times before he answered. "We outside," Kip told him.

"A'ight, I'm out in one minute."

Kip and Papa John sat back and waited. Kip was smoking a Black & Mild, while Papa John toyed with the radio, looking for a good song to listen to. The stillness of the neighborhood was overwhelming to the two men.

"I hope this nigga don't take forever," Papa John said, becoming impatient. "I got things to do and bitches to see."

"He'll be out."

Kip gawked at the quaint house where Dana lived. Devon had grown up with his cousin Dana, who was five years his senior. They were like sister and brother, but over time, he went his way and she went hers, but she still looked out for Devon when he needed help.

Devon's stunt in Harlem was upsetting to Kip. It was a foolish risk, and Kip had reprimanded him severely. But all was forgiven, and they were still good friends.

"I can't believe Dana got her own crib and kids and moved out here," Papa John said. "Damn, she like the soccer mom now, and shit. You remember how wild that bitch used to be?"

Kip remained silent.

"Didn't you fuck her once?" Papa John asked.

"We was cool, that's it."

"Dana always had a thing for you. She was fine, yo. You ain't hit that?"

"Nah, yo," Kip said indifferently.

"Nigga, you should have fucked her. I know if she was throwing the pussy at me, I wouldn't even hesitate. That bitch had the phattest ass and big tits too. I know that pussy had to be good. You know it had to be good, she got some cornball nigga to put three kids in—"

"Just shut the fuck up, Papa John!"

"I was just talkin', nigga. Damn!"

"Don't. I ain't in the mood right now."

Papa John sulked and stared out the window. Kip seemed to be in one of his foul moods—bipolar with a capital *B*. Papa John lit a cigarette. He wanted Devon to hurry outside. Kip was being an asshole. He needed a third party in the car with him.

Moments later, the front door opened, and Devon walked out dressed in a dark hoodie pulled over his face. He was ominous-looking with a heavy frown. He hurried toward Kip's minivan armed with a couple pistols and climbed into the backseat. He gave both men dap and tried to relax, but it was hard for him, knowing he'd committed murder just a few days earlier and the police—and most likely, Brooklyn niggas—were on the hunt for him.

"What's the four-one-one, my nigga?" he asked Kip.

"Still the same shit," Kip told him. "Hot in Harlem like fish grease."

"Yo, I had to do that nigga, man. His mouth was too fuckin' reckless, and you know Kid is like a brother to me too," Devon said with emotion.

"Just chill. I don't feel like talkin' about that right now, or ever. Forget about that shit and let's focus on this job," Kip commanded. "You understand?"

Devon nodded, fully understanding. It was never wise to talk or bring up past murders. What was done was done.

Before Kip pulled away from the house, he glanced at Dana standing in the doorway holding her eighteen-month-old child. She had gained weight and changed her life around. Before Eshon, there was Dana. Though they never had sex and she was a bit older than him, they had feelings for each other. But they both felt that it wasn't meant to be. He went left, and she went right. She wanted a family; he wanted the streets. She chose Queens over Harlem and a relationship with a mechanic over a thug. It had been years since they'd seen each other. Seeing her again, Kip felt something for her, but that ship had sailed.

Devon tapped his shoulder. "You and my cousin would have been good together."

"I ain't thinkin' 'bout your cousin. I'm thinking 'bout this job, nigga. Y'all niggas need to focus. Remember who we goin' after."

Devon nodded.

Papa John stayed quiet. He didn't feel like hearing Kip's mouth.

They headed to a strip club in the Bronx called The Hot Spot, a shady place where the ladies did anything for the right price. Papa John and

Devon followed behind Kip, walking into the badly lit strip club with blaring rap music and over a dozen half-naked hoes walking about. The place had lap dances, wall dances, and several back rooms where sexual favors were performed for cash. The stage was occupied by two butt-naked dancers in stilettos swinging their bodies around the pole and contorting their nakedness on stage in front of many lustful men.

It was a pervert's paradise, and where Big Sean liked to be.

Although they were there for business, Devon and Papa John couldn't take their eyes off the lovely and thick ladies everywhere.

Kip had to remind them that they weren't there to have a good time. They were searching for Big Sean. Kip was determined to find him. The men moved through the crowd like enforcers, and though they weren't armed with guns, since security searched everyone for any weapons before entering, they had a plan to lure him out of the club.

For an hour they searched for Big Sean and waited for him to show up, but there was no sign of him. Devon and Papa John wanted to make the best of their night, since their plan to murder had been put on hold.

But Kip wasn't in any mood for a strip club. "We out," he announced.

"Y'all niggas go 'head. I'm staying," Devon said.

Kip looked at him. "What?"

"Nigga, he ain't here, and lookin' at all this pussy in the room, I'm ready to fuck something tonight. I'm good. I'll catch a cab back to Queens."

"A'ight, be safe, my nigga." Kip gave Devon dap and a manly hug.

"One, my nigga." Papa John gave Devon the same dap and manly hug. He decided to leave with Kip. He didn't like paying for pussy when he always got it for free.

The two men left the club, leaving Devon behind to indulge himself in a sea of pussy. He had a pocket full of money, and he planned on spending it on pleasure. He had a lot on his mind and wanted to escape by busting a nut, squeezing some tits, and smacking some ass cheeks.

Devon walked toward the stage and started to tip the dancers with dollar bills. He had his eyes on two strippers he was eager to take into one of the backrooms and go porno on. One was a light-skinned whore wearing a pink G-string with hearts and clear stilettos. Her long, black hair and tattoos caught his eye as she walked around the club topless.

He approached her and bluntly asked, "How much to fuck you?"

"One fifty."

Devon pulled out his wad of cash to impress the stripper. "C'mon, ma, I wanna fuck tonight." He didn't care about style or etiquette. He didn't care for her name either.

He followed her to the backroom. He handed the bouncer a twenty-dollar bill and walked into a cramped, shadowy room that contained only a bare mattress and evidence of the previous occupants.

Devon paid her the fee and went straight to work on her. There wasn't much for her to remove. Her G-string came off, his pants came down, and he showed her just how blessed he was. Having a big dick was something he was very proud of.

The Magnum condom snug around his thickness and length, Devon wanted to fuck her doggy-style. Primed behind her, with her legs spread and pussy throbbing, he gripped her big booty and thrust himself inside.

She groaned from the impact. He was bigger than average, but she was a professional at taking any size dick.

It was definitely where he wanted to be. In some pussy. He wasn't ashamed to pay for sex. It was worth it.

He grunted, and she cried out. He wanted his money's worth and subsequently came like thunder after being inside her pussy for fifteen minutes.

Afterward, that bitch didn't walk right. It was money well spent.

***

Kip arrived in Harlem with Papa John riding shotgun. He was a bit disappointed that Big Sean was still alive, but there was going to be a next time. He stopped in front of a brownstone on 158th Street and let Papa John out of the vehicle. Papa John had plans on spending the night at the house of one of his baby mamas, who'd been calling him repeatedly that night, wanting a booty call with her daughter's father.

Papa John was eager to see her, knowing Lana was a freak and gave the best head. "One, my nigga," he said. "And ease up. Get laid tonight. I know I will." He laughed.

Kip sat indifferently in the seat, not really listening to his friend. His attention was elsewhere.

Papa John shrugged and turned, and made his way up the stairs and into the brownstone where Lana already had her door open, waiting for him to come in.

Kip drove off and went home. The night was still young, and he was far from tired. Kid was fast asleep. The apartment was too quiet.

He lit a Black & Mild and sat on the couch. After a few puffs, he picked up his cell phone and made a call.

"Hello," Eshon answered her phone.

"Hey, what you doing?"

She was excited to hear from him. "I'm just lying in bed watching TV. Why?"

"So you're not busy?"

"No!" she quickly answered.

"I want you to come over."

"Now?"

"Yeah, now."

"Okay, give me fifteen minutes."

"A'ight." He hung up. Eshon was the perfect woman to make him feel good tonight. She always knew what he liked.

He continued smoking his small cigar and sat slouched on the couch, his gun on the table in front of him. He was in a minor zone.

Twelve minutes later, he heard knocking at the door. He stood up and walked toward the door. He looked through the peephole to see if it was her, and it was. She was three minutes early. He took a deep breath and opened the door.

Eshon immediately smiled at him.

He looked her up and down. She came dressed like it was date night, wearing a trench coat, heels, and lingerie underneath. Her long, silky black hair was flowing superbly. Kip couldn't take his eyes off her. He had to admit to himself that Eshon was a beautiful woman.

"You like what you see?"

"You look good," he said.

"And you look great."

Kip stepped to the side and allowed her into the apartment. Her walk was always fierce, and she was working her shoes in the short distance from the hallway to the living room. Kip caught himself staring at her ass—apple bottom at its finest. The sex between them used to be mind-blowing. Why did they break up? She could be a little crazy and overzealous. He became aroused.

"I missed you," she said.

"I missed you too."

He moved closer to her, and they locked eyes. Kip could feel the heat and the passion bubbling inside of him.

She sighed heavily. Her apprehension disappeared when Kip wrapped his strong arms around her and started to kiss her.

While kissing slow and deep, he moved his arms down her curvy physique and grabbed her ass and squeezed. He started peeling her coat away. He was getting her naked in the middle of the living room.

"What about your brother?"

"He's sleeping."

They landed on the couch, with Eshon on her back, her legs upright in the air as Kip pulled off her panties. The only clothing left was her bra. Her flesh was perfection. She had a shaved pussy, no tattoos, no scars or blemishes. Her body would undeniably hypnotize any man.

Kip touched her skin tenderly and then kissed her stomach. His lips tickled her. She giggled. He removed his jeans and boxers, and his erection shot up vertically like a missile ready to launch. He placed himself between her parting legs.

She asked him, "You got any condoms?"

He paused. "Huh?" *Damn! Why she ask that?*

Eshon felt ambivalent about having sex with him unprotected. She loved him and wanted to have his baby, but who else was he fucking? She didn't know. She took STDs and HIV seriously. She didn't want that type of shit in her life.

Kip looked at her. They'd used condoms before, and sometimes they didn't. In fact, given the way they used to fuck raw and the many times he came inside of her, he was surprised that she had never gotten pregnant by him.

"I'm just asking."

"Yeah." He got up and went to his bedroom.

He came back with a Rough Rider condom. He tore the pack open and rolled the latex onto his erect dick. He then repositioned himself between her legs and thrust into her excitedly.

Eshon breathed out, feeling his dick pulsating inside her. She gripped the back of his neck tightly and pulled him closer to her naked body. She straddled him with her long, defined legs, while he was pressed down against her. His mouth latched onto hers, and they kissed wildly.

While making love on the couch, a single tear seeped from Eshon's eye and trickled down the side of her face. After his nut, where would she be? Was this a mistake? Should she have made a statement by putting her pussy on strike? She felt she had let him back into her too easily. But, damn it, the dick was so good inside of her.

Kip thrust in and out, feeling her warm, tight pink lips wrapped around his dick. He thrust hard and deep inside her, holding her sexy frame lovingly and ready to explode.

Eshon closed her eyes and moaned, "Ooh, fuck me!"

After an hour of fucking, their bodies twisting and turning from position to position, from the living room couch, and into his bedroom, Eshon came in breathless anticipation, not once, but twice. Kip's body shook with an ejaculation that rushed through his whole body, his dick twitching as the last of his semen spurted into the condom while still inside her paradise. He ended up lying down fully atop Eshon.

The two lay nestled on his bed. Eshon rested her head against his chest, and she closed her eyes in his comforting arms. Once again, she exhaled, knowing this was where she wanted to be for the rest of her life.

TWELVE

Eshon woke up to Kip nudging her side roughly. She felt him tugging at her like there was an emergency going on. She opened her eyes to find Kip fully dressed. She lay still and naked underneath his sheets, still rejoicing from the night before.

"Eshon, you gotta get up and get dressed," he said. "C'mon, you gotta go."

The high afternoon sun seeped through the bedroom window. The time on the digital clock read 1:15. She didn't know she'd slept that long. But some good dick could put her into a long coma.

Kip forcefully pulled the bedroom sheets off her body and tossed them to the floor.

"Kip, what the fuck is your problem?" she hollered.

"Right now, you're a problem. You need to leave."

"What?"

"I got something to take care of today," he said.

"And? Why can't I just stay here and wait for you to come back?"

"You can't. It was fun, but you know, we still ain't together."

Eshon frowned. She knew it, she fuckin' knew it. He had gotten the pussy, busted a good nut, and now he was kicking her out. Eshon leaped from the bed. "You're a fuckin' asshole, Kip! Fuck you, fo' real!"

They argued while she quickly collected her things and got dressed. Kip looked unconcerned about her feelings.

"I'm always good to you, Kip. Always! Why can't you be the same toward me and my feelings?" she screamed.

"Yo, Eshon, fall back on the drama."

"Fall back? Nigga, is you fuckin' serious? You telling me to fall back on my fuckin' feelings? You dumb fuck!"

"Look, we had fun last night. I just got shit to handle today."

Eshon wanted to slap him so hard, it would make him cross-eyed. "FUCK YOU! I can't fuck with you, Kip. You're always hurting me when I do nothing but love you all the time."

Their argument echoed through the walls. Dressed and visibly upset, she took off out of his bedroom and right into Kid, who was in the hallway coming from his bedroom. She stormed right by him and out of the apartment, slamming the door so hard, it almost knocked the pictures off the wall.

Kip walked out of his bedroom and into Kid.

"What you do to her?"

Kip glared at his brother and screamed, "Mind ya fuckin' business!"

Kid glowered. "You know, you can be an asshole sometimes, Kip. Eshon is good peoples, and the way you dog her sometimes, it's disgusting."

"What, you Captain Save-a-Ho now?"

"No, but I do know a good thing when I see one, and you just too stupid or too blind to fuckin' see it."

Kid angrily wheeled by his brother, hoping to run over his toes, and went back into his bedroom, slamming the door behind him.

Kip stood in the hallway, looking unmoved by anything Eshon or Kid had to say. He went into the living room and soon heard several hard knocks at the door. He was familiar with the hard knocking. His heart skipped a beat as he slowly walked toward the apartment door and looked through the peephole. He saw his nightmare come true—the police were at his door.

"Muthafucka!" he cursed silently.

They continued to knock.

Kid, alerted to the knocking, and came wheeling into the living room, looking worried and asking Kip, "What's going on?"

Knowing they weren't going to go away, Kip opened the door and was greeted by two plainclothes detectives.

"Kip, it's good to see you again," the black male detective said. He was dressed in a black suit, white tie, and black fedora, his holstered Glock showing. He had a sharp chin with a dark goatee and small, shifty eyes.

Kip had crossed paths with Detective Albright several times. His partner was Detective Yang. He was dressed in a suit and tie too, with spiky jet-black hair. He was shorter in stature, clean-shaven, and was a veteran detective at the 32nd Precinct on West 135th Street.

Kip asked harshly, "What y'all want?"

"We just want to have a few words with you, Kip," Detective Yang said.

Kip wasn't intimidated by their presence. He was a hardcore thug that didn't shiver or become panicky when approached by cops. "Y'all got a warrant? Am I under arrest?"

Detective Albright said coolly, "No, not right now. But you know me, Kip. We can do this the easy way or the hard way; it's your choice."

Kip grimaced at them both. He relented and left with them, telling his brother, "I'll be right back. Don't even worry, Kid."

Kid sat there in his wheelchair looking despondent. He prayed that it wasn't anything serious. But knowing Kip, it was definitely something serious. Was it about the shooting in the park? Kid had so many worries flooding through his mind, he felt like he was about to have a panic attack.

THIRTEEN

Jessica removed herself from the bathtub and toweled off. She contemplated if she should call Maserati Meek. She was nervous, not knowing how he would react if or when she called? Was it just a stunt? Was he serious about linking up with her? She wouldn't know unless she called.

She placed the towel around her body and knotted it. She stared at her reflection in the foggy mirror. She heaved a sigh, hearing her family outside the bathroom door. It was her, her mother, brother, her two aunts, and her grandmother in one cramped two-bedroom apartment and one bathroom. It was too much going on, and she had no privacy.

"I need to get the fuck outta here," she said to herself. "This place is driving me *loco*."

Her brother knocked on the door. He needed to use the bathroom.

Jessica swung open the door with an attitude and scowled at him.

He pushed by her. "You ain't the only one living here," he said.

At least in L.A., they'd had a three-bedroom house. In Harlem, it felt like the walls were closing in around her.

Jessica went into the bedroom she shared with her aunts and mother and got dressed. Her outfit was always put together correctly. She couldn't slack in that department. Her looks and her crew were all she had right now.

She left the apartment with her cell phone. She went into the stairway to make the phone call that would probably change her life for the better.

She sat on the concrete steps and slowly dialed the number given to her. Anticipation swelled inside of her as the phone rang several times before someone finally answered.

"Hello," a male voice answered.

She smiled and asked, "Is this Maserati Meek?"

"Nah, not him, sweetheart," the voice said.

Jessica felt like a balloon deflating.

"Who looking for him?" the man asked.

"This is Jessica, from the club. This number was given to me by one of his men, and he's expecting my call."

There was silence on the other end of the phone. She didn't know what was going on, or what game was being played, but she didn't like it at all.

The voice then said, "You'll get a callback."

The phone suddenly went silent, leaving Jessica clueless. It looked like her hopes of snatching a baller like Maserati Meek went down the drain. She lingered in the stairway, looking like someone had stolen her puppy.

"Really," she muttered. "These the games muthafuckin' *hombres* are still playing today?"

Jessica needed a timeout; she needed a strong drink or maybe some good weed to erase her mind of what had just happened.

Just as she was about to give up hope, her cell phone rang. It was a private number. Something told her to answer. She pushed the accept button on her phone, answering the incoming call, saying, "Who this?"

"You called looking for me, right?" someone said.

"Maserati Meek?" she inquired skeptically.

"This is him, eh. That night I saw you in that sexy dress, you blew me away. You're gorgeous, I say."

His charm caused Jessica to smile broadly. "Thank you."

"Where you from?" he asked her. "Brooklyn? Queens?"

"L.A."

"L.A., crazy town. I like it, though. But, listen, I'm not the one for small talk, eh. Are you busy?"

"Excuse me?"

"Tomorrow, what plans do you have?"

"None."

"Then give me your address, and I shall come get you."

Was she hearing him right—come get her? "You want to pick me up, homes?"

"Homes. How cute," he said, admiring her slang. "Yes. Do you have a problem with that?"

"I don't, fo' real," she answered quickly. "I'm in the projects though, in Harlem."

"You think I'm afraid of the projects? You do know my reputation?"

"I do."

"Okay, so let's not make this difficult."

Jessica gave him her address. He promised to pick up her by noon. He wanted her to be ready and for her to wear something nice and sexy. Their conversation ended leaving Jessica blown away.

Wow! she thought. *Am I really in that easy?* If so, then look out, world. She was about to latch onto him and get the advantage she needed in life.

***

The following afternoon, Jessica stepped out of her building looking fabulous in a pair of tight jeans that accentuated her figure, a blazer with a corset, and heels. Her silky, long hair was flowing down to her shoulders, as she carried her Louis Vuitton tote bag. It was a beautiful warm and sunny day. It was the perfect day to get with a baller like Maserati Meek.

She walked onto the pavement and toward the street.

The fellows were gawking her way, looking thirsty. "Damn, Jessica! When you gonna let me get that?" one thug joked.

Jessica threw him the screw face and then flipped her hair from his direction. Her attitude was stink and fierce toward these broke, whack niggas in the projects. She knew she was the shit and everyone wanted a piece of her booty, but only a handful got to fuck her.

She waited on the corner of 133rd Street and Old Broadway, the back of the projects, away from the busy streets of Amsterdam Avenue. She didn't want everyone in her business. She was hoping Maserati Meek would be on time. She didn't want to wait long and end up looking stupid. She'd texted him her location.

He replied: TWENTY MINUTES.

She sighed, hoping it would all be worth it. It was quiet where she waited. She glanced at her watch every three minutes and tried not to become impatient.

It was a quarter to one when Jessica saw a pearl-colored convertible Maserati GranCabrio Sport. Meek was behind the wheel looking super handsome and super rich. Jessica was in awe.

He pulled up to where she was standing and smiled at her. "Good afternoon, Jessica." Maserati Meek couldn't take his eyes off her. She looked stunning and breathtaking with her long legs, long hair, pretty eyes, and vixen figure. Her heels strutted against the ghetto pavement, and she slid into the passenger seat of the car.

Jessica grinned like a lottery winner.

Finally, they were face to face, and Jessica could feel her pussy throbbing already. She loved his hair; it was long and silky like hers, and he wore it in a bun on top of his head. Sexy!

She gave him a kiss on the lips like they were a couple. "Hey." She smiled.

"You ready?"

"Yes. Where we going?"

"Vegas!"

"Whoa! What? Excuse me, homes, did you say Vegas?"

"Yes, I'm taking you to Vegas, eh."

"I didn't pack. I have nothing to wear."

"You'll be okay, eh. I'm going to take you shopping out there."

It was all happening too fast. He was definitively eccentric. But what did she have to lose? She did want to escape and she had never been to Las Vegas, though she'd once lived in L.A.

"A'ight, homes, Vegas it is then. Let's go," she said.

Maserati Meek grinned and nodded. "You're fearless. It turns me on." He put the car in drive and headed for John F. Kennedy Airport in Queens.

Jessica was ready to enjoy herself, and in doing so, she planned on laying it down on Maserati Meek something special. She was ready to show him how special she really was. She sat back in the convertible Maserati. She could definitely get used to this.

FOURTEEN

Kip sat in the windowless interrogation room unworried, though he was a bit perturbed that cops brought him in for questioning on some crime. Whatever it was, he was innocent. He had nothing to say to the police. He wasn't a snitch and he wasn't a punk bitch. It was a routine he was used to. It wasn't his first dance with detectives, and it damn sure wasn't going to be his last. He lived that life and he was about that life, and that life came with run-ins with the law.

He sat in the metal chair at the long metal table. He had been waiting for over two hours in the room. Kip knew how cops worked. It was a game they liked to play. They would keep you in a room for a long time, watching you to see how you hold up under the stress of the unknown criminal charges.

The door to the interrogation room opened, and Detective Albright walked in, followed by Detective Yang.

Kip glared at them, remaining silent.

Both men took a seat opposite him. Albright removed his fedora and placed it on the table. The standoff was about to begin.

"What y'all muthafuckas want?"

"We know you heard about the shooting in the park a few days ago," Albright said. "Three dead."

"I wasn't there. I ain't got shit to do with that," Kip said.

"C'mon, Kip, your brother was there playing in a tournament, and we know he got into an argument with a man named Mark Sparks. Now this same man ends up dead."

"My brother ain't got shit to do wit' no murder, and I don't know any Mark Sparks."

"So we gonna play this game, Kip?" Detective Yang chided.

"Call me Parker Brothers."

Albright banged his fist on the metal table. "You think this is funny?"

"I think y'all got the wrong man up in this bitch," Kip replied.

Detective Albright sighed, keeping his cool. He leaned closer to the table, placing his elbows against the metal, and locked eyes with Kip. He was a seasoned interrogator. He read body language and looked for changes in speech and eye contact. Every fiber in his body told him that Kip was a guilty man. He was tired, though. Tired of men like Kip constantly getting away with crimes because witnesses refused to come forward and testify and because of lack of evidence.

"We know you were there, Kip," Albright said.

"And if I was, I was there to watch my brother play chess, and then I got distracted by some pussy. Didn't see shit go down," he announced coolly.

Yang said, "What about your friends, Papa John and Devon?"

"What about them?"

"You think they're that loyal? If we get them in here on an unrelated charge, have them looking at twenty-five years to life, you think they're gonna be so loyal?" Yang asked roughly. "I've seen men like y'all break before, and I'll see it again."

Kip chuckled. "Whatever. Y'all niggas got a charge on us, then fuckin' charge us. If not, I'm a free man, right? And if not, then I want my fuckin' lawyer. I'm tired of talkin' to y'all. Bring me down here on some bullshit!"

Albright and Yang were at their wits' end.

Detective Albright, fed up with the thug's cockiness, wanted to wrap his hands around Kip's neck and choke him. "You know about a shooting two weeks ago near Club Revolt?"

"What? I thought we were done with this shit. I want my lawyer."

"Oh, we're done, and you can have your lawyer. I'm just talking, that's all. But, anyway, I have to ask—Where were you on the night Jason Miller was robbed and shot?"

"I was home, fucking this bitch; she had some good pussy too."

"And I suppose you have a bitch already to verify your alibi, huh?"

Kip nodded. "Of course. She ain't gonna forget this dick."

Albright added, "Well, there's surveillance in the area."

"And I'm supposed to be worried about being someplace that I wasn't? You're reaching, detective, and that's some petty shit, even for you, nigga!"

Detective Albright stared Kip down from head to toe, but there was no panic or no change in his body language. Kip continued to be an arrogant, cocky son of a bitch, acting like a man with nothing to hide.

"Once again, is there a charge, detectives?"

Yang said, "No, asshole, there's no charge."

"Okay then. Then I guess that means I'm fuckin' free to go, right?"

"Get the fuck out this room!" Albright said, clearly frustrated.

Kip sprung up from his chair and smirked. The men sat at the table looking defeated by the interrogation.

Before Kip left the room, he spun around with an afterthought for them. "I guess we'll talk soon, huh?"

Detective Albright shot up out of his seat and charged toward Kip. He got into Kip's face and exclaimed, "Oh, we gonna talk real soon, you ignorant nigga, believe that! And when we do, I'm gonna lock you so far inside the jail, you gonna forget what daylight even looks like."

Kip had nothing else to say. Seeing the cop riled up was entertaining enough. He chuckled and made his exit, leaving the cop fuming.

***

An hour later Kip arrived back at the apartment to find Kid still there.

Seeing his brother walk through the doors again, Kid exhaled. "Kip, you're home!" he exclaimed animatedly.

"Of course, I'm home. I told you I was coming right back."

Kid was elated. The spat they'd had that morning had been completely forgotten or forgiven. Kid thought he had lost his brother to incarceration, but good fortune brought him back home once again.

"We need to leave, go for a drive or something," Kip suggested.

"Leave, and go where?"

"Upstate to see Nana."

Hearing that woman's name had created a foul look on Kid's face. "What? Are you serious?"

"Yeah, Kid, I am. It's about time you go and see her and stop being so fuckin' stubborn. She raised you and took care of us when she didn't have to."

Kid sighed.

"Look, do it for me, just this once. She asked about you, so be the bigger person and come say hi."

Kid relented. He knew it would mean a lot to his brother. But for him, it was going to be an agonizing trip. He'd always believed that Nana was a materialistic, conniving bitch who only used people to get what she wanted or needed in life. She had everybody fooled, but not him.

FIFTEEN

Jessica couldn't believe that she was in Las Vegas. Maserati Meek had flown them first class on an American Airlines flight, and so far, everything was going well. Flying first class was the best—more leg room with fully reclined seats, privacy, wine, and gourmet meals. She was becoming spoiled already.

She stepped off the plane, still elated. She was over the moon being in Vegas with a baller and shot-caller like Maserati Meek. Just like that, she had gotten her wish.

Jessica strutted through the airport terminal with Maserati Meek and was ready to leap out the doors and into the desert sun and crash into nothing but luxury and opulence. She wondered what he had planned. Where were they going to stay? Already, there were signs of wealth and escapism, people everywhere looking eager to go gambling, catch a Vegas show, or sin somehow and somewhere, leaving whatever troubles behind. Vegas could easily change a person from a mild-mannered nobody to feeling like a rock star.

McCarran Airport had palm trees in the terminal. Palm trees? The feeling of nostalgia for her hometown was overwhelming.

Maserati Meek was dressed in white shorts, a white button-up shirt, and white loafers, looking more like a vacationer than a drug kingpin. His diamond Rolex gleamed around his wrist. His Middle Eastern accent and appearance turned heads.

Jessica couldn't wait to get their day started.

Walking through the terminal, Maserati Meek pulled out his cell phone and made a call. He seemed easygoing at the moment, contradicting the eccentric and unpredictable behavior he was known for. He was nice and sweet.

Their conversation on the plane was stimulating. He was educated, funny, and thoughtful. He spoke about growing up in Egypt, living briefly in England, then Brussels before settling in the States. There was a lot more to him than met the eye. Jessica was stirred up with intrigue and thrill.

He kept promising to give her the world, only if she remained loyal to him, kept their affair private, and stimulated him in the bedroom. He didn't want a boring woman, and she didn't want a broke and boring man. It seemed like a match made in heaven.

They stepped outside, and immediately the dry desert heat hit her like a ton of bricks. Being from L.A., she was used to it, but Nevada had a different type of atmosphere. It wasn't humid heat, but it was still hot.

"How soon?" Jessica heard Maserati Meek say to someone over the phone. "Okay. Good."

He hung up and smiled at his newfound jump-off. "I know I'm going to enjoy you this weekend," he said.

They exited the terminal walking casually, and unlike the other suckers waiting in long lines for cabs into the city, Maserati Meek already had something special planned. The moment they were outside, a four-door black Bentley Mulsanne pulled up. The driver stepped out and opened the back passenger door for them. Maserati Meek helped Jessica into the car, and she slid into pure lavishness—leather recliner seats in the back, flat-screen TVs, an 8-inch touch-screen computerized control system, and pricey champagne.

"Wow!"

Maserati Meek sat near her and smiled. "You like?"

"I love it," she uttered wholeheartedly.

"Now, let's take you shopping."

The driver slowly pulled away from the airport terminal and joined the clutter of cars, mostly taxi cabs leaving from the terminal and heading toward the nearest freeway.

Jessica sat back and gazed out the tinted windows. *This is what a princess must feel like*, she thought. She was in a grand chariot and on her way to enjoy her kingdom with her prince.

The first stop was Crystals at CityCenter, and then the Forum Shops at Caesars, the Grand Canal Shoppes between the Venetian and the Palazzo, and last, but not least, the Miracle Mile Shops near Planet Hollywood.

Jessica racked up expensive clothes, lingerie, shoes, purses, bathing suits, and jewelry. Maserati Meek spent roughly forty grand on her shopping spree with his Amex Black Card, and it wasn't a dent to him. Forty grand was like forty pennies.

Next, they pulled up into the entrance area of the MGM Grand, the third-largest hotel in the world. The driver opened their door, and they both climbed out of the Bentley and stepped foot onto superiority.

Once again, Jessica was awe-struck. Although she was getting money with Kip and rubbed elbows with ball players and drug dealers, her background was gangs, murder, and poverty. She had been suddenly thrust into a world that only the fortunate were meant to experience.

She had over a dozen shopping bags for the bellhops to carry into their suite. She walked into the hotel, eyeing everything. The place was huge, and luxury couldn't even describe its atmospheric lobby.

Jessica strutted through the opulent lobby, her high heels click-clacking against the extensive marble flooring. Flanked by Maserati Meek, the bellhops were behind them carrying their items to the elevator and into their room.

Maserati Meek placed his keycard into the lock. The small light went from red to green, and he pushed open the door.

Jessica entered the luxurious 950-square-foot corner suite with a magnificent sweeping view of the Vegas strip and other tourist attractions. It had sleek furnishing in the extended living room, an oversized marble bar, a Roman spa tub, and a dining area for four. "Ohmygod!" she exclaimed, absolutely floored.

Meek smiled. He tipped each bellhop a fifty and sent them away.

Jessica explored the room. The place was flawless. The room was fitted with electronic sheer blinds, as well blackout ones, keeping out the bright lights of Vegas along with the bright sun for better sleeping. The plush accommodations and amenities were everything she could ask for.

Before they did anything, Jessica felt she owed him. Now it was her turn to make him happy. She looked his way and smiled. She undressed right there in the living room, took off everything but her high heels, and approached Meek, biting her lip and touching herself.

"C'mere, homes. *Te quiero.*"

Her ghettoness and the Spanish turned him on completely. Meek stood there, ready to be victimized by her.

She dropped to her knees in front of him and started to undo the buttons and zipper on his white shorts. She reached into his shorts and pulled out his manhood. Surprisingly, it was bigger than she thought it was going to be, but not huge. It was pinkish but solid. Her manicured hand slowly jerked him off, and then she wrapped her lips around his dick and shifted back and forth, wetting and pleasing his erection with her full lips, cupping and massaging his balls. Her mouth was like a vacuum.

Maserati Meek pulled her off his dick and lifted her to her feet.

Jessica wiped her mouth and looked surprised that he didn't let her finish. Usually, when she gave a man a blowjob, he was overwhelmed with stimulation and ready to come.

"Let's continue this in the bedroom," he suggested.

She was down for whatever.

They entered the bedroom where Maserati Meek took Jessica and placed her on her back, on the comforter of the bed. He removed his shirt and shorts and positioned himself between her legs, making himself comfortable. His thing was eating pussy. It gave him great pleasure to pleasure women.

He found her sweet spot and saw how wet she was for him. He fingered her for a moment and then licked his fingers, tasting her sweet, sticky juices. He spread her legs farther apart to view all of her. She was amazing below—completely shaven clean, her lips pink, smooth, and glistening with moisture.

"You are beautiful," he murmured.

Jessica's chest heaved up and down when he parted her lips again, revealing her pink center, and fingered her momentarily.

He placed his lips to her core and tasted her sweetness. He dug his tongue into her middle like a drill and sucked her juices. He nibbled at her clit.

"Oh god! Ooooh shit!" she groaned, squirming.

"Keep still," he told her. He encircled his arms around her thighs to make sure she couldn't get away from him.

Her body went into overdrive with pleasure as he licked and sucked on her more and more. He was going to make her come. His shit was raw and unadulterated. He was a freak.

He wanted to eat her pussy out in different positions.

Jessica went from lying on her back with her legs spread to being placed on all fours with Meek attacking her goodies from the back. She then straddled his face. His tongue was rigid inside of her, and before she knew it, she was coming on his face, exploding, and trembling uncontrollably from an intense orgasm.

"What the fuck!" she uttered, feeling spent, her head spinning. She had no complaints; no complaints at all.

Maserati Meek looked like a man who just constructed the world's tallest building. "Get dressed. Let's go have some fun, eh."

Any more fun and she might just have a heart attack from happiness. She got dressed in one of the many outfits he had bought her, a Victoria Beckham dress, printed with a kaleidoscope of color.

They went to the casino, where Meek gave Jessica ten thousand dollars to gamble with. And she had good luck. She won at blackjack and doubled his ten thousand to twenty thousand.

Day one with him and she was in love. The only thing Meek asked for was her loyalty. But could she be loyal to him? She was heartless and had seen many murders in her young life, and been through countless of experiences from L.A. to Harlem, and didn't know a thing about loyalty. She was only loyal to herself.

SIXTEEN

Kid had a thousand questions to ask Kip. Why had they come for him? What were the charges, if any? How did he get out? Would they come for him again?

Kip didn't want his brother to worry about the police and his lifestyle because he had everything under control. He told Kid to relax and chill.

Kid was too revved up to relax. It had been an exciting morning, and he had a lot going through his mind. *Why did I relent?* he thought. He had better things to do with his time than visiting someone he despised.

Kid was riding comfortably in Kip's minivan, which was tricked-out to fit him and his wheelchair. Kip hadn't held anything back with the expenses to his ride, making it wheelchair-accessible for his brother. It was fully loaded with TVs and leather interior.

They were an hour from Nana's place in Poughkeepsie, New York. Kid was still uneasy about seeing Nana. Why? Why?

It was early evening when Kip helped Kid from the minivan and wheeled him toward the over-the-top retirement community Nana was stashed in.

Kid looked at the white, two-story building with the towering pillars and shook his head in disgust. He knew it was expensive. Nana had Kip eating out of the palm of her hands.

They entered the building, Kip signed in, and they headed toward the elevators.

Before knocking on her door, Kip looked at his brother and asked, "You gonna be cool? You gonna behave yourself while you here?"

"What am I? Five years old?"

"Nana don't need the extra stress from you, Kid."

"Then why bring me in the first place? You already know how I feel about her, Kip."

Kip sighed. "Just be nice to her, Kid. Just this once."

"I'll try, but I'm not making any promises."

Kip knocked on Nana's door.

"Who?" Nana asked from the other side of the door.

Kip hollered, "Hey, Nana, you got visitors."

She didn't hesitate to open her door. Seeing Kid there too, she was shocked. She smiled. "Oh, my. Both my boys came to see me today."

She hugged Kip. When she went to hug Kid, he was aloof with a weak greeting. "Come in! Come in!" she said.

Nana was dressed in a blue muumuu, house slippers, and her hair was in curlers. She closed the door and grabbed a walking cane from out the corner.

Kip was surprised. Last time he'd seen her, she was walking fine. "Nana, what happened? Why the cane?"

"Oh, I'm an old woman getting older, Kip," she said. "Lately, my knee's been bothering me, and it's my back."

"Nana, sit and relax. We here now."

"You two boys are looking so handsome. I'm so proud to call y'all my sons."

Kid rolled his eyes and sighed under his breath.

Kip shot a displeased look at him.

Kid fell back on his rudeness. It was torture for him.

Nana ignored him and went on being the kind, old, sickly lady.

They talked while Kid stared out the room window. He heard Nana complain about her medication, how it had gone up. Kip was listening to her, but Kid was completely sicker than her inside and out. He felt his stomach churning from hearing her bullshit. She walked with a cane that Kid felt she did not need. He wanted to push her out the fucking window.

Nana said, "I'll tell you, Kip, the way things are today, this system is going to send an old lady like me to an early grave."

"Nana, I told you to stop talkin' like that. You gonna be fine."

"With what their charging for my medication, they want the elderly to become sick and move on."

"How much is your medication? What do you need?" Kip asked.

"Kip, you've already done too much for me," she said.

Kid muttered under his breath, "Damn right, he has."

They both heard him.

Kip shot his brother a screw face.

Nana sighed. She sat her old, aching bones in a chair near Kip, looked at him with simplicity and said, "If I'm not mistaken, at least nine hundred dollars."

"For what?" Kid said, taken aback by the price. "What medication you're taking that cost nine hundred dollars?"

Kip hollered, "Kid, chill. What's wrong wit' you?"

"*She's* what's wrong with me, Kip! That woman ain't sick! She's obviously faking it."

"And you know this how, huh? You a damn doctor, Kid? You're smart, but you ain't a doctor. And I don't like how you're coming at Nana."

Nana sat there silently. She always thought that she had been good and fair toward both brothers, but Kid's animosity came toward her like a ninety-mile-per-hour pitch from the mound aimed for her head.

The brothers argued for a short moment.

Kid said, "You know what? I'll be downstairs in the lobby. Y'all two have fun." He stormed toward the door, wheeling himself quickly into the hallway and to the elevator. He didn't want anyone's help or sympathy. He couldn't tolerate her fraud and his brother's foolishness.

"I'm sorry, Nana. He's just going through some things, that's all."

"It's okay, Kip. Your brother is just upset and angry. He's in that chair . . . maybe he feels vulnerable and needs someone to hate."

Kip didn't respond. He just wished that the two favorite people he loved would just get along.

Before leaving, he gave his Nana twenty-five hundred dollars for her expenses and some spending money.

Nana looked reluctant to take it, but Kip wouldn't take no for an answer. She beamed inside. The cash was more than plenty for her to have a good time with. Tonight, she would hit the casino and play her slot machines and the blackjack tables then maybe attend the local bar for a drink. Nana was living the good life, and she had Kip to thank for it.

***

The brothers were silent on their way back from Poughkeepsie. Kid was upset with Kip because he felt Nana was playing his brother for a fool. Why couldn't Kip see that she was a fake? Now suddenly she had all these medical problems and injuries. And the cane was the icing on the cake. He didn't plan on seeing that old bitch again.

Kid sat in his seat and stared aimlessly out the window. Traffic on the highway was flowing, which was a good thing. He wanted to hurry up and get home. He needed some sleep. It had been a long and trying day.

Kip drove and listened to the disc jockey. He would rather listen to the radio than beef with his brother. He soon heard that there was updated news on Jason Miller's condition. He turned up the volume slightly.

The news announcer went on to say that the assault on Miller had cost him his career. The two gunshots to his ankles shattered bones and tore tissue. His rehabilitation would be extensive and expensive, and several doctors all came with the same bleak news—he would never be able to play basketball at a professional level again.

"Animals, whoever did this to Jason Miller!" the disc jockey exclaimed. "Whoever is responsible for shooting this man and taking away his livelihood should be locked up for life! Jason Miller was a good man and a great basketball player. The NBA will miss him. I knew he would have brought the Nets a championship."

Kip smirked at the man's comment. Jason Miller wasn't a good man. He was a jerk and a bully, and Kip was the bigger bully. Kip had no remorse for what he did, and like he'd told Jason before the shooting, he could kill him and still keep him alive. Without basketball, Jason Miller was nothing.

Hearing enough of the radio, Kip turned it off. The media and the sports world were going crazy over the athlete's tragedy as the manhunt for the assailant continued. The police still had nothing. Their case was at a standstill. Kip felt he'd gotten away with it. *What will the Brooklyn hoops star do now?* he wondered.

Kid muttered, "I have therapy tomorrow."

Kip had forgotten about his brother's physical therapy. It had been years and still no positive results. "How's that going for you?" Kip asked.

"I'm still in this chair, right—that's how it's going for me. Why do you keep paying for something that's never going to happen? Huh? I'm never going to walk again, Kip. I accepted it, but you can't."

"We never give up."

"I'm fine, Kip! I am, and I don't need your charity all the time."

"Yeah, you say that now, but tomorrow you'll be whining about something you need."

Kid sighed in heavy frustration. He just wanted to get home and slam the bedroom door in his brother's face. Nana had gotten to him. She had made him so upset, he was taking his anger out on his brother.

Kip glanced at his brother through the rearview mirror and shook his head. Arrogant and stubborn, he was, but that was Kid. There was a lot going on with Kid, and Kip knew it. Whenever he decided he wanted to talk about it, Kip would be there. Until then, he allowed his brother to have his foul mood and express his anger since Kip had other critical issues to deal with.

Kip's cell phone started to ring. He glanced at the caller ID and saw that it was Papa John. He ignored the call, thinking it wasn't anything important, but more calls started to blow up his phone. Other people were hitting him up, including Eshon.

He then received a 911 and a 411 text from Devon and Papa John. Something was definitely up. Whatever it was, it couldn't be said on the phone. Kip needed to get home fast.

"What's going on, Kip? Why is your phone ringing so much?"

"It's nothing," Kip answered, but his mind was racing. Did it have something to do with the detectives he'd encountered early this afternoon?

"Don't lie to me, Kip. What's going on?"

He barked, "It's nothing, Kid. Not your concern."

Kid frowned and folded his arms across his chest. He hated not knowing what was happening. It had to be something major. He didn't want to be treated like a child or some handicap, although he was in a wheelchair. He wanted the same respect as everyone else.

But Kip shut down, ignoring his brother's questions, and sped down I-87 toward the city.

Back in Harlem and back on the block, Kip helped Kid out of the van using the access ramp, and when he volunteered to escort him to the apartment, Kid fussed and bickered at him.

"I don't fuckin' need your help, Kip. I'm good! Go handle your business." Kid wheeled himself toward the building lobby, leaving Kip standing there.

Kip simply said, "Fuck him!" He turned to see Devon's black Expedition pulling up on the block.

Both men climbed out and approached him.

Kip was ready for whatever they had to tell him. "What's up? Why y'all niggas blowing up my phone?"

Papa John told him, "Yo, them niggas from the park the other day, them Brooklyn niggas that was beefing wit' ya brother, including Uncle Junior, them niggas got bodied last night."

"What? Fo' real?" Kip was stunned by the news.

"Yeah, all three gunned down," Devon said to him, excited about the murder.

Kip wasn't going to lose any sleep over it, but he asked, "Who did it?"

"We don't know," Papa John said.

Kip felt it was payback, karma biting them back for messing with a cripple. But he was also aware that the blowback might come back on them. Uncle Junior was fresh home from prison and a major somebody in Brooklyn.

Devon said, "It's all over the news. Whoever bodied them niggas almost tore them muthafuckas in half wit' machine gun fire right outside Marcy Projects. Some Scarface type of shit."

"Damn!" Kip felt strongly that a war was coming their way. Of course, Brooklyn would feel that Harlem had something to do with it.

Mark Spark's death was on Devon, and Kip had his friend's back completely, but the other gangland-style murders on their own turf? Someone crazy had done it.

Kip was ready for whatever came his way. Trouble wasn't anything new to him. He lived his life a quarter mile at a time, meaning he took life's situation as they came, and he planned on living his life to the fullest.

SEVENTEEN

Yo, we slippin', my niggas. This muthafucka been alive for too long. Two weeks already and he still breathing," Devon griped. "How we lookin'? We lookin' like we can't hunt a nigga down and take care of him when this is what we do, steal and kill." He sat in the backseat of Kip's minivan smoking a blunt. He was anxious to put down the murder game and get paid. He needed the money. The cash from their last score had already been spent mostly on hookers, weed, things for his truck, and guns.

Kip said, "Yo, Devon, chill, a'ight! I got this."

"I'm sayin', Kip, the longer it takes lookin' for this muthafucka, the more incompetent we lookin' to Maserati Meek."

"You think I don't know that, nigga!" Kip replied in frustration.

"It feels like Big Sean knows we lookin' for him," Papa John chimed. "We been lookin' everywhere for this nigga, and he ain't been at the spots he usually be at."

"I know," said Kip.

"Now what?" Devon asked.

"We keep lookin', that's now what. What, y'all niggas think because two weeks went by this nigga still can't get got? Every contract ain't gonna be swift like that, y'all niggas know. Fuck. Get y'all minds right, niggas, and stay focused on what we getting paid to do. Y'all niggas sounding like y'all becoming discouraged by the time."

Devon and Papa John didn't argue with Kip, knowing he was right. It was just taking them longer than usual. Big Sean was out there somewhere, most likely still in New York, and they didn't know whether he had been tipped off about the contract on his life.

"So, that thing wit' the police, they sweatin' you hard about that park shooting?" Papa John asked, changing the subject.

"They ain't got shit on us, and they know it. Them muthafuckas just fishing, that's all, and they came at me because they know I'm the biggest fish in the pond."

"Fuck it, I'll kill a cop. I don't give a fuck. All them niggas need to die anyway," Devon said seriously.

"Yeah, we know you would, wit' ya crazy ass," Papa John replied.

"Still, we need to be extra, extra careful, still do what we do, and watch our backs doing it," Kip said.

Devon and Papa John nodded.

Devon passed the blunt to Papa John as they sat parked on a Queens block, not too far from his cousin's place. It was dark, it was late, and they were moving around inconspicuously.

"Devon, you need to stay in Queens and keep cool. Harlem ain't the place for you to come back right now. Not until shit gets breezy and blows away like the wind."

"I miss the block, my niggas, and the hood, yo. Queens is dead."

"And the cops are still pressing niggas out there. I can't afford to have you locked up right now," Kip said.

Silence struck Devon as he looked out the window and took a pull from the blunt that was passed back to him. Kip had always been the smart one and the cautious one. Devon knew he had fucked up by shooting that boy in the head in the park with so many people around, and though no one was talking yet, it still wasn't wise for him to be in Harlem. Kip always advised well. It was one of the reasons they hadn't been incarcerated yet.

Committing a crime was like artwork. You had to pay attention to the details—you had to take your time. The pistol was your brush, and the street was your canvas.

With cash getting low, each man was desperate for another robbery to commit. And Big Sean was out there somewhere. Kip knew it. He felt the nigga was close but just fortunate not to cross paths with them so far.

The men continued smoking and talking before parting ways that night. Devon went back to his cousin's place, and Kip dropped Papa John off at a different baby mama's place in Washington Heights.

Kip didn't drive straight home. He drove to Riverside Park, where he liked to go to think and be alone. He parked his vehicle and stepped out into the warm spring night and into the park. With it being so late, the park was quiet and still. From where he stood, Kip had a beautiful view of the GW Bridge crossing over the Hudson River and into New Jersey. The Hudson River was God-made and wide and stretched for miles. With a full moon above, the lights that illuminated from the bridge to the shores of New Jersey were hypnotic.

Kip lit a Black & Mild and smoked. He had a lot to think about. He eyed a few boats floating on the Hudson and wondered what problems them people had. They lived on a boat and maybe sailed the world. They could just float away and be someplace else the next day.

With a handicapped brother, not knowing his parents, and living in the ghetto, Kip had to become a man overnight. If not, the wolves of the ghetto would have devoured him and his little brother.

Kip took a few more pulls from his burning Black and flung the rest into the river. He sighed. Time was winding down and Big Sean needed to die. He was determined to find him. He had scouts looking everywhere, calling in and informing him on locations. Big Sean wasn't a hard man to miss. He looked like he weighed a ton. The spread of money to different people Kip trusted brought back some information, but nothing concrete.

As he stood in the park staring at the picturesque scenery under a clear night, his cell phone rang, breaking his thought. "Who this?" he asked sharply.

"You lookin' for Big Sean, right?" the caller said.

He caught Kip's attention immediately. "Depends. Who the one calling me?"

"Look, I know he likes to gamble. He be at this gambling spot in the Bronx, a warehouse in Hunts Point."

"The address?"

"I'll text it to you," the caller said.

"And what you lookin' for? How much?"

"Nah, no payment. I just want the same thing you want—that nigga dead. He killed my cousin a month ago, and I would do it myself, but I'm no killer like y'all niggas anyway."

The caller hung up.

The call had Kip on edge somewhat. Who was he? How did he know about Kip being a killer? Could it be a setup? Most importantly, how did the nigga get his number, never mind it was a burner phone he was using? Kip wasn't stupid enough to give people his real cell phone number. He had to think. It seemed like solid information. He and his peoples would check it out tomorrow. If it was legit, then he would be grateful.

He stood in the park for another fifteen minutes and then left. He needed to sleep and he needed to check on his brother. Tonight, he would recharge and then be ready to go hunt and earn his payday.

***

Kip sat riding shotgun in Devon's Expedition and smoked his Black. They crossed over the Willis Avenue Bridge into the South Bronx and made their way toward Hunt's Point. It was after midnight. The men were dressed in black, and eager to get the job over with.

Papa John handed Kip a .9mm. He quickly inspected it, removing the clip. It was fully loaded—new, no bodies, no heat. Perfect.

Papa John handed Devon a similar .9mm, the same origin, and he held on to the .45. He then handed them two silencers to suppress the gunfire if needed.

They were mentally ready and equipped. This was a job for them. You just did it and got paid.

The mood in the truck was chill. No stress. If they stressed and became nervous then that meant making mistakes, and they couldn't afford to make any mistakes. So they smoked and thought about what they needed to do.

"How far?" Kip asked Devon.

"GPS says three more miles away," Devon replied.

Kip nodded. It was about to be game time soon, and the men already had their game faces on.

They neared the location in Hunts Point and soon arrived at the after-hours gambling spot— a decayed-looking brick warehouse on Oak Point Avenue. Several cars were parked around the location. The area was industrial and commercial and was a ho stroll, where a few pimps stood on certain blocks and watched their hoes flag down cars and work tricks.

The men sat parked across the street from the place, watching the front area. Few people came and went. The place was definitely low-key. They had no idea if Big Sean was inside.

"How we gonna do this?" Devon asked.

Kip said, "Simple. I'll go in, scope it out, look for this nigga, and if I see him, I'll text y'all niggas. I'm gonna lure him outside, and we hit that nigga then."

It was a straightforward plan, but they could be walking into a setup. Kip was determined to fulfill the murder contract and end this hunt. He climbed out of the truck, leaving his gun behind. He knew there was a chance he would be searched at the door. He casually crossed the street and walked toward the front entrance, ascending the small concrete steps leading to a black door. There were no bouncers outside, but he was sure they were inside.

Kip knocked, and soon the black door swung open. He was led inside. Two men flanked him. They asked, "Who you?"

"I'm here to win some money," he replied composedly.

"How you hear about this spot?" one of the bouncers asked him.

"Nigga, who ain't heard about this spot?" Kip then reached into his pocket and pulled out a wad of cash to impress them and to show that he was serious.

The men looked more relaxed, seeing his wad, and eased up on their quick grilling. They searched him for any weapons and allowed him access to the place.

Kip walked through the foyer and into the spacious black room filled with gamblers and dealers. The underground casino looked like it was generating tons of money for the owner or owners with blackjack, dice games, roulette tables, and several slot machines. Men in black, presumably bouncers, were situated everywhere looking for cheaters or troublemakers.

The first thing Kip looked for was surveillance, and fortunately for him, there wasn't any. The last thing he needed was his face captured on video cameras while looking to murder someone. He walked around the room shrewdly, searching for Big Sean, and soon found him gambling at the roulette table.

Kip remained expressionless. He quickly texted his crew: HE'S HERE, 20 MINS, BRINGING HIM OUT, PARK AROUND THE CORNER. Kip blended into the crowd easily. He sat at the blackjack tables and placed two hundred dollars in front of him, faking interest in the game. He received two hundred dollars in chips from the dealer.

From his location, he had a clear sight of Big Sean's every movement.

The cards were dealt. Kip landed a king of spades and then a five of hearts, totaling fifteen. "Hit me," he told the dealer, knocking his knuckles on the table.

The dealer removed a card from the deck and placed it upwards near his other cards and he was out, losing with king of hearts. He lost fifty dollars.

Kip bet another fifty, and the cards were dealt again. He received a ten of diamonds and the next card was a ten of hearts, totaling twenty. "Staying," he told the dealer.

The dealer dealt himself a nineteen, and Kip won fifty dollars.

Kip continued to gamble while watching Big Sean play roulette. Not caring if he won or lost, his eyes were on a different prize.

Ten minutes went by, and he mostly won, but he still sat watching Big Sean.

Taking his small winnings, Kip removed himself from the table and went toward his target. Deliberately, he made himself known to Big Sean. He was surprised to see Kip there. They started to chat like old friends.

Kip said to him, "Yo, we did another score the other night, came off nice on some jewelry, and got some shit outside in the car. You wanna take a look?"

"Oh word, you ain't hit up Meek yet?" Big Sean asked.

"Not yet, but I got you, my nigga. You can have first dibs on the stuff."

Kip noticed that he was wearing the watch Meek had given him. It was a bright piece of jewelry with diamonds that stood out. Big Sean flossed it around proudly.

Hearing that he had first dibs on stolen jewelry before Meek could take a look at it, Big Sean was enthused. "I'm down, let's go take a look."

Kip smiled. "Follow me then."

He and Big Sean moved toward the exit. They walked out of the building and onto the quiet street, nothing coming or going for blocks.

DIRTY WORK - PART ONE

"Follow me."

Big Sean walked behind Kip. They went up the street and turned the corner, and were on a barren street, no cars, except for Devon's parked Expedition, closed buildings, and darkness.

"Yo, I need a chain," Big Sean said. "A diamond Jesus face. You got one of those?"

"We got a lot of shit. When you see what we got, you gonna love it." Big Sean smiled.

As they approached the truck, Devon and Papa John climbed out. They opened the back gate and lifted the door. There was nothing back there. It was empty. The back was lined with a plastic tarp.

Big Sean looked at Kip with confusion. "What is this?" he asked.

"Yo, my bad, my nigga," Kip said. "We still got you."

"What?"

Kip extended his hand for a handshake from him. Big Sean reached out to his hand, and there was a firm handshake between them. With his free hand, Kip put the gun to Big Sean's chest and pulled the trigger.

Bak! Bak!

Big Sean's eyes widened from shock, his body went limp, and then his large frame dropped to the ground right before Kip's feet.

They picked his big ass up and placed him into the back of the SUV. Before they closed the back gate, they removed his watch and rummaged through his pockets. The man had eight grand on him. It would be divided between them. They drove off and dumped his body into a nearby alley.

Big Sean may have been a killer and one of Meek's lieutenants, but he definitely wasn't the sharpest knife in the drawer. In fact, he may have been the dullest.

They were satisfied. It took long enough, but the murder contract had been fulfilled. Now it was time to go and collect the rest of their money from Maserati Meek.

EIGHTEEN

Kip knocked on his brother's door and then pushed it open. He didn't wait for an answer. Kid was already dressed and in his wheelchair. Though it was a gloomy day, looking like rain sooner than later, Kid was ready to go down to the park and play some chess. He looked up at his brother and groaned, still feeling some type of way about the other day.

"What you want, Kip?" he asked with a slight attitude.

"Look, little brother, I know you're still upset wit' me, but I need for you to stay away from the park for a few weeks."

"What? Why?" Kid hollered, taken aback by what he just heard.

"There's some shit that went down, and things are 'bout to heat up, and I don't need you in the line of fire."

"Then what I'm supposed to do?"

"I don't know, but that park, it's not safe right now."

Kid glared at his brother and spat, "It's because of some shit you did, right?"

"Look, I'm not tryin' to argue wit' you. I'm just tryin' to keep you safe."

"I already don't do much around here, Kip. Now you're trying to keep me on house arrest and stop me from doing what I love."

Kip sighed. He moved closer to his brother.

Kid wheeled himself farther away, moving toward the window. He didn't want to be close to Kip. What he wanted to do was jump up from his chair and punch him in the face. Chess was his hobby and his livelihood too. It was his girlfriend, the woman he fell in love with. Now Kip was breaking them apart.

"Look, how about you play here?" Kip suggested.

"What?"

"I mean, call up some peoples you trust and play in the living room."

"It won't be the same."

"Look, nigga, I'm tryin' to work wit' you here, a'ight! Fuck, Kid, compromise wit' me," Kip hollered.

Kid frowned. He wondered when Kip ever compromised. "Okay, I'll play here. You happy?"

"Nah, but I feel better."

"Can you leave, please? I just want to be alone," Kid said sadly.

Kip shook his head and left the room, closing the door behind him. He knew it was hard for his brother to leave the park alone, but it had to be done. Everything was changing, and there were people out there that would use Kid to get at him, and he wasn't about to let that happen.

He left the apartment with his gun in his waistband. He had some business to take care of with Maserati Meek.

✳✳✳

Kip drove alone this time to meet with Maserati Meek. He was on the Long Island Expressway doing sixty. It was late morning, and the sky looked like it was about to burst open with rain. It was a cooler day with the fall-like weather. He wore a hoodie and his beige Timberlands. Droplets of rain began to spray against his windshield. He turned on the wipers and continued east on the highway.

Kip listened to the radio while on the way to Meek's stash house. The media were still talking about the Jason Miller incident, the robbery, the

ERICA HILTON

shooting. Who were the culprits? What were the NYPD doing to find them? The morning disc jockey did a segment on the protection of athletes when they were in the clubs, at their houses, or with their families. How safe was it for them? The woman read statistics on how many athletes were robbed each year, and it was a staggering number.

Once again, Kip didn't want to hear it. He turned off the radio. He had other things to focus on. Jason Miller, the police, the radio, they were the least of his problems.

A half-hour after noon, Kip arrived at another of Maserati Meek's hideouts. He climbed out of his minivan and felt uneasy for some reason. His .9mm was tucked snugly in his waistband. He didn't want to leave it behind, but to meet with Meek, he would have to. His security wasn't going to allow it. He removed the gun and placed it underneath his seat. He took a deep breath and approached the house. Like always, there were exotic cars parked out front. This time there was an Aston Martin and a yellow Lamborghini, along with two black Maseratis.

Kip wanted to collect the money he was owed and be out. He climbed the stairway and knocked on the door. It soon opened. He was met by two of Meek's men. They searched him thoroughly, and he proceeded inside the home.

Maserati Meek was in the living room sipping hot tea, dressed in a white robe and slippers, looking relaxed today. When he saw Kip, he smiled. "My nigga," he greeted in his strong Middle Eastern accent. "I've heard the good news. Eh, my problem, it isn't my problem anymore, eh, my friend."

He was lively, dancing around in his robe and slippers, while Kip stood in the living room stoically.

Meek gestured to the chair. "Have a seat, and let's talk."

A few of his men joined them in the living room. They stood around looking cold and calculating.

129

Kip was feeling really uneasy. "I just came to collect my money," he said respectfully.

"Yes, yes, your money, eh. You did right by me," Maserati Meek said. "Excuse my jolliness. I recently came back from Vegas and had a wonderful time. I had some of the best pussy in my life. This woman, she is phenomenal, I must say, eh."

Kip didn't care for the particulars about his trip. The only thing he cared about was his fifty thousand dollars.

"Are you single, my friend?" Maserati Meek asked Kip.

"That ain't your business."

"I know. Why did I even ask?"

To Kip, it felt like Maserati Meek was stalling in paying him for some reason. He started to feel a lot edgy. He scanned the room and saw more of Meek's goons around than he'd anticipated, different faces, different lieutenants. If it went down, could he fight his way out? Most likely, he wouldn't stand a chance. And Meek wasn't a dude to be trusted. He was known to be paranoid and crazy.

Kip now felt that coming alone was definitely a mistake. "Meek, I just want my money and to leave. We did a job for you, so pay me," he said more sternly.

"Yes, yes," he said. He snapped his fingers toward one of his goons. "Go get this man his money."

The man nodded and left the room.

Kip's uneasiness jumped from a five to a twenty on the Richter scale. If it came down to it, fight or flight, what were his odds? It wasn't looking good at all. The man who had left, would he come back with his money or murder?

As Kip waited, Meek's cell phone rang, and he picked up.

Kip just stood there coolly. *Never let them see you sweat,* he always told himself. He took a deep breath and waited. It was all he could do.

Maserati Meek was engrossed with the caller on the other end. He paced around in the next room.

Kip could barely hear what was being said. Did it concern him? At that moment, he wished he could read lips.

Maserati Meek then hung up and came back into the room he stood in. He looked at Kip. His expression seemed to change. He no longer looked upbeat, but more serious. Who did he talk to? "It seems that I may have another job for you, my friend," he said to Kip.

"What kind of job?"

"One that will pay really well, eh. But I'll fill you in with the details soon." Meek looked into the next room and nodded slightly to someone.

Soon, the same man that had left the room reentered with a small backpack. He tossed it to Kip, who crouched and quickly picked up the bag. He unzipped it and saw fifty thousand dollars in ten-thousand-dollar stacks inside. Cool, but could he sigh with relief? Not yet. He was still in the house.

Meek said, "You can leave."

Now suddenly he was rushing Kip out of his house. Something was definitely up. Kip left the house and finally felt relieved when he was inside his minivan with his money. He removed the gun from underneath the seat. He started the ignition and lingered behind the wheel for a moment, wondering what the fuck had just happened back there.

As he sat, he noticed a car approaching. Kip gripped his gun, which was already cocked, and kept his attention fixed on the vehicle. It was Jay P arriving. He remained cautious as he eyed Jay P climbing out of his dark green Yukon. He looked worried about something.

Kip rolled down his window, and Jay P came to the van. At the window, the two men dapped each other up.

Jay P was about to tell Kip about Big Sean's murder, a devastating blow to him. But something quickly caught his attention. He noticed the diamond watch around Kip's wrist, It was the same watch Big Sean had on—the one Kip stole, sold to Meek, and Meek gave to Big Sean. How did Kip suddenly get possession of it again? There was only one way he saw how—He'd murdered Big Sean himself and took back the watch. Jay P knew the hit had to come down from Maserati Meek himself. But why? Suddenly, his mood changed. Kip suddenly went from acquaintance to public enemy number one.

"I'm out," Jay P said without emotion. He stepped away from Kip's minivan and got back into his SUV.

Kip made his exit right after. And like Phil Collins once sang, there was definitely "something in the air tonight."

***

Maserati Meek stood in the living room brooding, his lieutenants confused. What happened? They thought they were there to murder Kip today. It was supposed to be swift, a fast bullet to the back of his head, but they didn't question Meek's change of plans.

Maserati Meek wanted Kip dead because Kip had renegotiated the price for the hit on Big Sean. Meek had a set price, and he felt that Kip had gotten too greedy charging him fifty thousand when he'd just paid the nigga two hundred grand for the jewelry. And, no one talked back to Meek. No one. Once Meek said something, it was set in stone. In Egypt, the alpha is the man with the biggest guns and the largest gang.

Maserati Meek looked at his men and said, "He's still valuable for the moment. I still need him."

Maserati Meek was just on the phone with Panamanian Pete. Panamanian Pete's name was major and had been ringing out for years through the Carolinas, Georgia, and Alabama. He ran those states with drugs, nightclubs, and goons. Panamanian Pete wanted to purchase a large shipment of kilos and guns from Meek, but Meek was paranoid. Why the sudden phone call? Meek felt it was a setup. He was aware that those alphabet boys wanted to arrest him and put him inside a cage for the rest of his life. He couldn't risk someone in his organization getting jammed up. Every move he made had to be a wise, cautious one. He figured Panamanian Pete was either working for the Feds or planning to rob him. He needed Kip to take the hit if there was one planned. The young thug all of a sudden had a purpose.

Kip's greed had rubbed him the wrong way. Kip didn't know it, but they had a plastic tarp covering the floor in the next room, the room where he was supposed to be led to and violently murdered. Then they were going to roll his body up and dispose of it like it was trash.

NINETEEN

Ooooh shit! Oh, baby, right there. Right fuckin' there, homes, right there. ¡*Mierda!* ¡*Mierda!*" Jessica cried out in heated passion. She closed her eyes, bit down on her bottom lip, and squirmed around on the bed.

Maserati Meek went to work on her. He held her legs vertically in the air, his hold around her secure, his tongue inside her sweet core as he tasted every inch of her nice and slow.

Her pussy flowing like a river, Jessica announced, "I'm gonna come!" She couldn't take it anymore. Her entire body felt lit up so bright that she was oozing natural power. Her legs quivered intensely. She wanted to drop them around Meek's shoulders, rest them against the bed, but he continued to keep them vertical.

Her clit was trembling with intense sensation as his tongue darted in and out, and he wasn't shy of tasting her anally. Meek pushed Jessica's legs back more and continued to feast on her wetness. He lapped gently, making her howl.

"Come in my mouth." He licked her clit tenderly, and he softly sucked her pussy lips as he slid his fingers in and out of her.

Maserati Meek was putting Jessica in that mental room of pure, unadulterated gratification. The more he licked and fingered her, the more she squirmed, crushed her teeth against her bottom lip, and the more her juices flowed.

Quickly, he pulled Jessica on top of him, and she started to ride his tongue to near orgasm.

Maserati Meek felt the warmth of her thighs against his face. Her breathing became labored. Whipping Jessica up into an orgasm required work, and it was work that Meek loved putting in.

"I'm gonna come!" she screamed out.

Moments later, her body reacted to the licking and the sucking, and she burst open like a piñata at a Mexican birthday party, her juices all over his face.

She rolled off his face and collapsed on her back, her chest heaving up and down.

Meek pulled himself up from his back and stood erect in the room. "I need to take a shower," he said.

Jessica smiled at him.

"You care to join me?" he asked.

"Give me a minute."

He walked into the bathroom adjacent to the bedroom. He didn't have the perfect ass, and he was a bit hairy in some places, but his money and power made up for any physical flaws. The dick was good, but the way he ate pussy was explosive.

Jessica heard the shower turn on. She rolled around in his bed feeling like a spoiled child. Her body felt healed, and her pussy still quivered from the tongue action. The expensive silk sheets made it feel like she was lying on clouds. His bed was so soft.

Maserati Meek was spoiling Jessica rotten with gifts. Overnight, she was swamped with Gucci, Prada, Chanel, Versace, Christian Louboutin, Armani, and so much more. She had jewelry and shoes. And he was filling her pockets with cash. It was a dream come true.

Even with her new clothing and her new man, she was still living in a cramped apartment in the projects with her family. She was spending more and more time with Meek; her new life with him was pulling her farther away from her friends. There was also another problem she had to deal with—he still had that bitch Nia in his life. She didn't want to look jealous, but she was. She didn't want to share him anymore.

Jessica rose up and peeled herself off the comfortable king-size bed. She walked to the wall-to-ceiling windows in the bedroom and gazed out at a vibrant, well-lit New York City. She was twenty floors up in his penthouse suite, surrounded by opulence in the romantic bedroom with an ultra-luxury king bed, large TV, and a cozy sitting area. The bathroom had a Kohler-jetted tub, a furniture sink vanity, and plush soft towels.

She pressed her tits against the glass and laughed. God, she was having the time of her life. She felt like a kid. She wanted to stay naked and free. Free from poverty and free from her crowding family. This was the place to be free. Her view of the city from so high was exhilarating. It felt like she was flying.

She thought about her options with Kip and his crew. She loved getting money with them; it kept her updated with fashion and things, but she and her friends had to take risks. Sometimes she felt like a prostitute, and Kip and his peoples were her pimps.

But with Maserati Meek, she pleased him and he pleased her, and they were falling in love. He gave her everything she needed without risk, and without any drama surrounding it.

She turned and made her way into the bathroom to join Maserati Meek in the shower. She stepped into the tiled shower with the warm water cascading down on her, and they wrapped their arms around each other and kissed passionately.

Touching Jessica again made Meek completely aroused and hard. The two couldn't get enough of each other. It was hot and steamy passion sex continuously when they connected. It was just them—sucking, licking, and fucking their brains out with no thought of the outside world. They sexually contorted their bodies underneath the steamy, cascading water and their tongues and mouths wrestled fervently.

Jessica then lowered herself down to her knees and took his erection completely into her mouth and thrust her action forward, her full lips wrapped around his hard, pale flesh like a blanket. She felt he had made her come; now she wanted to make him come.

Meek cooed and groaned. He closed his eyes and enjoyed the pleasure.

Later in the night, the two lay nestled against each other on the bed. He didn't want to let her go. She didn't want to wake up from this dream. Everything about it felt so wonderful. From there, the pillow talk started.

"You're wonderful and beautiful, you are, eh."

She definitely had him sprung.

And although Maserati Meek required complete secrecy from her regarding their sexual interactions, now that he seemed pussy-whipped, he started to run his mouth to friends and people. He put Jessica on a pedestal and made it clear to everyone that they were fucking. His eccentric behavior couldn't allow him any confidentiality.

He looked her in her eyes and asked, "You ever killed anyone?"

What kind of question was that to ask, especially after their intense lovemaking? But Jessica wasn't appalled by the question; she remained chill. Death wasn't anything new to her.

Meek continued with, "How do you feel about death, eh? I mean, does it turn you on like it does me?"

"Hey, homes, I've seen my fair share of it over the years. The world I come from, it's an everyday thing, ya feel me?"

"Oh, I do. Besides you, power and murder turn me on, stirs me up. Just the other day, I let a man live when I was so erect to have him killed."

She was listening. The things men said after sex, or when they were in love with someone. "Who was it?" she asked.

"Oh, this young thug named Kip."

Jessica's facial expression didn't change at all when she heard the name. She acted like she'd heard the name for the first time. She simply asked, "Why did you want him dead?"

"His greed, but I let him live because he's still needed for now. But his death is inevitable. Maybe I might bathe in his blood, eh."

It was a sickening thought, but Jessica didn't take any offense to it. She continued to lie next to him indifferently. He talked about murder like it was changing a TV channel.

Although Jessica had known Kip for years, and he was the love of her best friend Eshon's life, she didn't plan on warning him about the threat. The moment she'd connected with Maserati Meek, she'd already made her choice about where her loyalty lay.

Kip and his brother were nothing to her. It was good while it lasted with him and his crew, but now that she'd found the next best thing, she wasn't about to ruin it, even if it meant Kip's demise.

TWENTY

It was the middle of May, and except for a few rainy days, the weather was consistently warm. Spring was in full-blown effect, with the trees full and green, their leaves dancing in the wind. The grass was soft and plush, and the sky a blanket of blue. It was the perfect day, and with Memorial Day approaching, there was barbecue in the air, especially in the Manhattanville projects.

Kip was cooking a few burgers outside of the project building he resided in. It was a small gathering with music playing from two speakers and several folks scattered around, talking, eating, and enjoying a beautiful day. Kip looked in high spirits as he stood by the small black grill flipping burgers and turning hot dogs. The thug and murderer he was didn't show today. Instead, he treated his friends to food and music, like he was a pillar of the community.

For several weeks now, he had been low key. Though money was running low, his intuition told him to take a chill pill and relax. The neighborhood still had cops patrolling, and detectives Albright and Yang were still lurking around and still investigating the park shooting. New York homicide was relentless in solving the murders of three people.

The Nets didn't make the playoffs, and a lot of basketball fans believed it was because of the absence of their star shooting guard. Had he not been shot, and had his career not come to a sudden end, the Brooklyn Nets would have been playing for a championship. There was absolute outrage.

Folks were ready to take out their pitchforks and torches and hunt the monster themselves. The fans and the media wanted justice.

With Kip barbecuing, the ladies came out in droves to get some free food and some time with him. He was the center of attention. He looked extremely handsome with his fresh cut, long black cargo shorts, matching black Nikes, and wife-beater, his gold chain swinging.

Kid was lingering near the spontaneous cookout with a burger in his hand and a smile on his face. It was moments like these that he cherished—his brother doing something positive in his life. Though it seemed minor, to him, it was memorable. Kid was ready to get back to the park and continue his reign as the best chess player in the city, if not the state.

He'd done what Kip had advised, inviting a few people over to play in the apartment and staying away from St. Nicholas Park for a beat, but it just wasn't the same. He missed the feel of the park, the concrete tables, the people around watching, and the competition.

It was a glorious afternoon, with the residents enjoying the food, the kids, the music, and Mother Nature. Kid was showing off in his wheelchair, doing wheelies and spin moves. It was impressive. Kid was laughing and playing around.

Kip smiled at his brother. This was life. No drama. Just spending time with friends and family.

Eshon and Brandy soon made their way to the makeshift barbecue. Eshon was extra excited. Seeing Kip cooking and enjoying himself was a turn-on for her. All had been forgiven from when he'd kicked her out so suddenly the next morning after sex. In fact, she was with him a week ago. They had intense sex, raw this time, and in the heat of the moment, she allowed him to come inside her. When he exploded into her, and she shuddered from her own orgasm, a million thoughts raced through her head. What if this was it? What if she was pregnant this time? Could she ever stop giving in to his needs, though she had her own needs?

Eshon continued to take chance after chance with Kip, not knowing where her fate might turn up with him. Surprisingly, after they fucked, she spent the night at his place again, and in the morning he didn't rouse her to wake up or rush to kick her out. She had woken up to find him gone. He let her sleep in his bed. She was taken aback. What did it mean? Was Kip coming around finally? Was he about to give their relationship a second chance? She was nervous and excited at the same time.

Eshon and Brandy walked closer to the activity. She saw the sharks swimming around Kip. His being single was the smell of blood in the water to a shark, and the thirsty bitches came swimming toward him to fasten their sharp teeth around some new meat.

Brandy noticed her friend's facial expression. She quickly said, "Just chill, Eshon. It's a nice day, niggas is barbecuing, and we look good. Make that nigga sweat you for once."

It was sound advice, but would she listen? Only time would tell.

Eshon had come out her apartment looking on point. If Kip wasn't looking her way, there were plenty of niggas around gawking at her and hungry for her attention. The ladies went toward the men and women. Eshon immediately approached Kip and threw her arms around him for a loving hug. He hugged her back, and she said to him, "I missed you."

He simply smiled.

She didn't attempt to kiss him in public this time. She had learned her lesson. She didn't want to look desperate around some thirsty bitches. Besides, Kip couldn't get enough of what she had between her legs. Good pussy always brought a nigga back.

"You hungry?" he asked her.

"Of course."

Kip placed a few more meat patties on the grill, and Brandy struck up a conversation with one of his friends.

Kid came rolling over, noticing one girl was missing in action. He looked at Eshon and asked, "Where's Jessica? I haven't seen her around lately."

"Yeah. Where is she? She's been MIA for a moment now," Kip said.

Eshon shrugged. "I don't know. She ain't been chillin' with us like that lately. I think she met some nigga and been fuckin' with him."

Kid looked saddened by the news. Jessica was his crush. The girl he wanted to marry. He always tried to amuse her and be kind to her with gifts, but most times she didn't even acknowledge him.

The rest of the afternoon was spent joking around, drinking, and smoking blunts, along with dancing, more eating, dominoes, and spades. Eshon and Brandy were partners against Kip and Devon.

As evening fell, the party moved into the building lobby, where a group of men started a dice game near the stairway entrance. There was still music playing, and Eshon and Brandy continued to stick around.

The one man absent from the festivities was Papa John. He hadn't been seen all day. Kip had called his cell phone a few times, but it went to his voicemail. Kip wasn't worried about his dude. Papa John knew how to handle himself. Kip figured he was laid up with one of his baby mamas or some new chick he'd met, and was somewhere in the city putting his dick to good use.

Kip smoked his Black & Mild, loitering near the front entrance of the lobby. Though everything appeared fine on the outside, he felt some trepidation. His cut of the fifty grand was almost gone, and they hadn't done a job or murder contract in several weeks. They needed to get back out there and make some real cash. But he wanted to wait until some of the heat died down around them.

Devon was feeling the effects too. While others were busy with gambling, the ladies or music in the lobby, he stepped to Kip and said, "Yo, let me holla at you for a sec, my nigga."

The two men walked out of the lobby and into the street. Devon lit up a Newport. His skin looked ashy, and his clothes were dingy like always. He wore a faded dark hoodie on a beautiful warm day and old Timberland boots that had seen better days. He was sockless with smelly feet and sweaty armpits. And concealed in his waistband was a .9mm. Devon the Devil, as they called him, was ready to raise hell again.

"It's been a minute, nigga. When we gonna get live again?"

"Soon, Devon. Not until things cool down."

"If shit get any cooler, I'm gonna have frostbite. Ya feel me? Shit, my pockets is low, Kip. I need to eat again."

"And we will, *D*. I'm 'bout to look into something."

"Like what?"

"Something. You know how this goes—We don't rush into anything if it doesn't feel right. We stay cool and alert, and most important, we stay patient. We get antsy, we get stupid and sloppy, then we get caught or worse. And you already know what that worse is."

"Yo, we already know where there's enough money and shit around to set us up for a lifetime, my nigga. We just need the balls to go take that shit, yo." Devon clapped his hands together gleefully to make his point.

Kip already knew who he was implying. He was absolutely against it. Maserati Meek was too powerful for them to try and rob. He had an army behind him with guns that the streets had never seen before. And he was smart, crazy, and eccentric. Trying to rob him was like trying to rob Fort Knox; it was damn near impossible.

"It ain't happening, *D*," Kip said.

Devon frowned. He wanted to make it happen, with or without Kip.

"That's suicide, nigga. We don't shit where we eat. We stay smart wit' our shit."

Kip knew that Devon was right about one thing—they needed to get back to work. His bills were starting to come in, and the rent needed to be paid, his and Nana's.

Devon took one last pull from the cigarette in his mouth and flicked it away. He was displeased with the conversation, but Kip was the boss and knew best. Devon pivoted from his friend and walked off, refusing to rejoin the party happening inside the lobby.

Kip kept his eyes on Devon until he could no longer see him. Lately, he had been worried about his friend. Though Kip wanted Devon to stay in Queens longer with his cousin, Devon couldn't take the quietness and the boredom of the borough any longer. He had packed his things and returned to Harlem against Kip's wishes.

Kip stepped into the lobby. The music was loud, louder than before. The dice game near the stairway was in full effect, and the ladies were flirting with the men, drinking alcohol from red cups, and everyone was having a good time all around. Kip looked around for Eshon and spotted her talking with Brandy.

He went toward them, looked at Eshon, and said, "Can I talk to you for a minute?"

She grinned. Of course, he could. She nodded. She stepped away from Brandy and followed Kip down the hallway, where they could chat in private. Any time alone with Kip was a good time for her.

"What's up? What you wanted to talk about?" she asked, feeling slightly giddy from the alcohol she'd consumed.

"We need to get back to work," he said.

"Huh?" Now she was confused. She thought he meant he wanted to talk about them—their relationship. Last week was fun. She wanted to repeat it with him.

"Look, money is gettin' tight, and we need another score," he said.

"Oh," she murmured dejectedly.

"Find your girl, Jessica, and y'all start keepin' ya eyes and ears open for drug dealers. Find out where they keep their stash houses, get close to a nigga. You know the routine, Eshon."

"I do," she said.

"I wanna get us paid again."

"I'm on it, Kip."

"Good."

He was ready to leave, but Eshon stopped him. "You wanna go up to your place and chill? I mean, fuck? I missed you."

No other man would pass up the chance to lie down with Eshon and spread her legs, but Kip had other things on his mind.

"Next time," he said aloofly and walked away.

Eshon stood there feeling disappointed. She really wanted some dick tonight, but Kip put her and her needs second. It was a crushing feeling. She no longer wanted to stay at the party, so she left suddenly with Brandy following behind her.

"Eshon, you okay?" Brandy asked.

"Yeah, I'm fine. I just needed some air."

Brandy knew it was much more than her needing some air. She knew Kip had said something that had unsettled Eshon.

TWENTY-ONE

Eshon heard the rumors, but she didn't want to believe it, nor did Brandy. The two girls sat in Brandy's bedroom on a warm Sunday smoking a blunt. The tension and drama between them and Jessica had come unexpectedly. They'd heard that Jessica had been talking shit about them. Jessica had become vulgar and disrespectful to her friends out of the blue. What could've sparked it? She had separated herself from them and the projects and started acting shadier and shadier. Eshon felt it was because of the stranger she had been seeing for the past month. Neither Eshon nor Brandy knew who Jessica was seeing. Was he getting inside her head? Was he brainwashing her with nonsense, trying to turn Jessica against her friends and family? The one thing both girls did know—Jessica had changed and become a major bitch, and not just with her friends, but her family too.

"She said what?" Brandy hollered through the cell phone, standing suddenly from her bed. "Who that bitch think she is?"

Eshon sat in the background watching Brandy become upset. It was a mutual friend of theirs on the other end, feeding them with the latest Jessica nonsense. Judging from Brandy's reaction, it was something big.

"Yo, that bitch 'bout to get sent packing back to L.A. Who the fuck she think she is?" Brandy griped loud and clear.

Eshon was itching to know what had happened or what was said. Lately, Jessica had been strutting around the neighborhood like her shit didn't stink. She was wearing the best clothing, showing off the priciest shoes and pocketbooks, and acting brand-brand new. She moved like she was the one calling the shots. It meant that whoever she was dealing with was a boss nigga and a man with wealth and status. He'd amplified the arrogance and conceit in Jessica.

Brandy hung up.

Eshon asked, "What happened?"

"Yo, we need to fuck that bitch up," Brandy growled with contempt for their former friend.

"What the fuck she said?"

"She called you and me Kip's whores, screaming to niggas about how he pimping us for bread crumbs."

"What?" Eshon shrieked.

"She talkin' shit, Eshon—out there telling people how she made us look good. If it wasn't for her, we would still be some bum bitches."

Eshon was now on her feet with her fists tightened. Jessica had gone too far. All they had done was be friends with her, and now she was trying to ruin their names by spreading lies about them. But why, though? Eshon couldn't understand it.

Eshon had heard enough. She wanted answers, and then she wanted to beat Jessica's ass.

Brandy exclaimed, "I knew that bitch was fake."

Eshon marched out of Brandy's bedroom and stormed to the front door with Brandy right behind her. Jessica needed to be taught a lesson. So what she was from L.A. and her family was connected with some gang? This was Harlem, and bitches got stomped out like roaches in this city.

Eshon and Brandy stormed into the building, took the elevator to the eighth floor, and walked to Jessica's apartment door. There was no hesitation or fear of confrontation with her. Eshon balled her fist, raised her arm, and banged intensely on apartment 8E.

"Who is it?" a lady asked from the other side.

"Is Jessica home?" Eshon asked.

They heard the Spanish lady scream out, "Jessica, *alguien está a la puerta para ti!*"

They didn't know what the bitch said. But they were waiting eagerly in the hallway to confront her. Soon, the apartment door opened, and Jessica came into their view, dressed like she either was going out or had just come in.

"What y'all want?" Jessica asked them with an attitude.

"Why I keep hearing that you talkin' shit about us? Huh, bitch?" Eshon shouted. "What's up with that?"

"Look, bitch, don't be fuckin' comin' to my door wit' all that drama. I don't know what you heard, but you fuckin' heard wrong, *puta!*"

"Nah, you the one lying, bitch! What? You got some rich dick in your life and now you wanna act like we're beneath you, bitch?" Brandy chimed angrily. "Don't get it twisted and get fucked up, bitch!"

"Fuck you, Brandy! You always been jealous of a pretty bitch like me! Don't hate on me, homes, cuz your ass got flaws."

"You fake-ass bitch! Keep our names out your fuckin' mouth!" Brandy warned her.

"What, bitch? Don't tell me what to do. I'm not worried 'bout y'all at all."

"Look, you need to shut the fuck up and chill, bitch," Eshon hollered, raising two fingers into Jessica's face.

The war of words between Jessica and Eshon and Brandy was on. They started to scream and curse at each other in the hallway. The commotion was loud. Eshon was up in Jessica's face in a threatening manner, but Jessica wasn't backing down.

The argument escalated until Jessica swung at Eshon, striking her in the face. Eshon didn't go down, but she ferociously struck back with several punches and hair pulling, backing Jessica into a corner, and dazing her with several right hooks.

Brandy immediately jumped in, and a full-scale fight ensued. Though she was a tough girl from L.A.'s mean streets, she was no match for Eshon and Brandy.

"Fuck you, bitch!" Eshon screamed out.

The heated commotion in the hallway attracted Jessica's family. Soon after, all of her family came pouring out of the apartment. Seeing Jessica assaulted by her two close friends, they immediately intervened. There was no way they were going to allow one of their own to get jumped in front of their own home.

The mother and aunt went for Eshon, who suddenly had her long hair being ripped from her head as punches were thrown at her face and body. The cousins and brothers attacked Brandy with force. They threw her against the wall and then kicked her down to the floor, and stomped on her angrily. Jessica's family was hardcore bangers, and once they got started, it was hard for them to stop.

Though they were swiftly outnumbered, it didn't mean Eshon and Brandy were about to give up and be beaten to death. It was pound for pound, screaming, hair pulling, and punches thrown wildly.

Eshon held her own, taking out the mother with a punch and then wrestling with the aunt near the stairway. They were like two wolves sinking sharp teeth into each other. Everyone's hair was in disarray, their clothing ripped and torn.

Neighbors came into the hallway to break up the fighting. It was hard to keep everyone apart. A tenant had already dialed 911. The cops were coming. Nobody wanted to stick around for questioning or a possible arrest.

Eshon and Brandy quickly snatched their belongings from off the floor and hurried away from the scene, cursing out Jessica and her family.

Eshon shouted furiously, "You gonna get yours, bitch, all y'all. Best believe that shit."

Eshon and Brandy made their exit from the eighth floor via stairway. Both girls looked like they had been in a slugfest.

Jessica's expensive outfit had been ruined, and her hair was sweated out. She had a bloody lip and a blackened eye. Eshon had put a hurting on her, but she still stood tall and proud. She was upset, though. It was embarrassing to her family and her neighbors. The first thing she wanted to do was call Maserati Meek and tell him about the incident. Eshon and Brandy had no idea who they were now fucking with. Her man had serious juice, and Jessica felt that if she wanted to, she could have them bitches killed before the next day came.

✳✳✳

The hard and loud knocking at his front door caused Kip to jump up and reach for his pistol, which he kept close. It even caused Kid to wheel himself from out his bedroom. Kid looked nervously at Kip, while Kip remained straight-faced. Was it the police again? He cautiously made his way to the door and glanced through the peephole. It was Eshon. He sighed with relief, seeing a friendly face, and opened the door for her.

Once face to face with her, he said, "Damn, bitch! Why you knocking on my door like you the police?"

Eshon pushed past him and stormed into the apartment. She was upset. She was emotional. She was in tears.

Kip noticed her disheveled appearance. "What the fuck happened to you?"

"I need a fuckin gun, Kip," she said, distress in her voice.

"Eshon, you okay? What happened?" Kid asked with much concern.

"I'm gonna kill that fuckin' bitch, I swear."

Kip asked, "Kill who? Who you beefin' wit'?"

"Jessica! I'm gonna shoot her and her whole fuckin' family."

Kid looked at Kip, and Kip looked at his brother.

"Yo, Eshon, just chill and calm down," Kip said.

Eshon screamed out, "Nah, fuck calming down. That bitch wanna be a goon and talk shit and think she can't get got. Fuck that bitch! That bitch about to get got!"

"Eshon, relax and talk to me. What happened between y'all?"

Kid moved closer to her. Hearing Jessica's name made him nervous. He didn't want anything bad to happen to her.

Kid asked her, "What happened to Jessica?"

"Yo, don't ask me about that bitch! Fuck her! I'm gonna kill that nasty fuckin' bitch."

"Baby, just calm down and talk to me," Kip said evenly.

Eshon took a deep breath and looked into his eyes. Only Kip could relax her. She took a seat on his couch and started to open up about the incident with Jessica, and then informing the brothers how she'd met a new man. Since she'd met him, she had changed into a bitch.

This was intriguing information for Kip but painful news for Kid. She was the love of his life.

"Hold up, what nigga she dealing wit'?" Kip asked.

"I don't know. We never saw or met him. But I know he got money because he got Jessica stuntin' in nice clothes, jewelry, money, and shoes."

"Wait, wait. Jessica got herself some baller nigga like that, and she ain't put me on to him to have him robbed? What the fuck, Eshon!" Kip frowned. "Yo, who is this nigga?"

"I don't know, Kip. We never met him before. She's keeping him a secret for some reason."

"Why the fuck she keepin' this nigga a secret?"

Eshon didn't have an answer for him. She continued talking; telling them more about the fight and what was said. Eshon wanted to lean on his shoulder and be hugged and consoled. But Kip soon became bored with her story and upset with Jessica for holding out on him. He planned on talking to her. He needed the money.

"I need a gun, Kip . . . please," Eshon begged.

Kip sucked his teeth. There was no way he was about to give her a gun to shoot Jessica. It wasn't happening. "Yo, y'all just need to kiss and make up. Y'all friends."

"What?"

"Eshon, you ain't gonna kill her. You ain't no killer. You're just highly upset right now, emotional and shit. And Jessica's still cool peoples. It's just jealousy shit between y'all, and I bet y'all gonna be friends again before the summer starts," he said with confidence. "I'm not giving you no gun."

Eshon didn't like what she was hearing. He was supposed to have her back. Why was he defending Jessica after everything she had told him? She became even angrier. Everything out of Kip's mouth was wrong and more hurtful.

"You know what, Kip? Fuck you too!" She spun around and stormed out of his apartment, tears trickling down her face.

Kip shrugged his shoulders and closed his door, muttering, "Fuckin' dramatic bitches."

TWENTY-TWO

Kip sat in his Nissan Quest smoking a Black & Mild. He was parked on West 133rd Street, across the street from the Manhattanville projects. It was a busy night in the ghetto. He watched the residents move easily on the block, enjoying their spring. He had to think and get his mind right, though. With a civil war between Jessica, Eshon, and Brandy, his dynamic trio was put on hold.

He kept his gun close, his eyes open, and his head swiveling. He was always on alert—no matter where—either sitting in his hood or on foreign territory. A man had to keep his focus and he had to keep his momentum. Trouble had no boundaries.

Kip took another pull from the small cigar, listening to the radio, having his moment of solitude on the Harlem block. Get niggas and get money was on his mind. He was itching for another taste of cash flow.

Reclined and unwound for the moment, he soon noticed Papa John coming up the block. His friend looked troubled about something. He approached the minivan and climbed into the passenger seat.

"What's good, nigga?" Kip greeted him with dap.

Papa John looked like he had something on his mind. He wasn't his good-humored and perverted self like usual.

Kip noticed a few cuts and bruises on his hands. "What happened?"

"I'm good, nigga," Papa John replied gruffly.

"Nigga, whatever it is, don't come at me wit' it. I'm your boy, nigga. Talk to me. You got beef wit' someone?"

"Nah, it ain't like that."

"Then what's goin' on? You ain't come to the barbecue I threw. We had plenty of bitches there. Your flavor, nigga."

"Yo, when we gonna do another lick? I need the cash, for real."

"I'm workin' on somethin'," Kip responded.

"Workin' on what?"

"Yo, what's goin' on wit' you, Papa John? Huh? 'Cuz right now, you comin' at me a little suspect," Kip asked with a minor frown.

"I just got a lot of heavy shit on my mind. Family shit."

"Family?"

"My kids," he said.

Kip passed the Black & Mild to Papa John, and he took a pull. He said, "Nigga, you ain't got nothin' stronger than this shit? No fuckin' weed?"

"Y'all niggas the potheads."

Papa John took a few drags. He needed to hold back his tears. He wasn't the one to cry in front of anyone, especially his homeboys. So he kept his emotions strongly contained. He was a womanizer—an asshole, a freak, and a violent man, but when it came to his children, he was a father and he liked the job. He had six kids, and all four of his boys were named John Jr.

Unbeknownst to his crew, one of his sons had recently been diagnosed with autism. He had gotten the disturbing call last week from his baby mama, Lana, who had called him howling about the diagnosis. She cried out to Papa John, saying she had to raise a retarded baby and called Papa John's seed inferior.

The remark infuriated him. He rushed to her house and stormed inside, and they'd gotten into a heated argument, which led to Papa John attacking her and beating her down. It was his son, and he wasn't retarded, and his sperm wasn't inferior. He then took his son, John Jr., and left. The next day he took him to see a top physician who had confirmed the diagnosis. His son would need to see a specialist and receive therapy if he was going to live a somewhat normal life. But therapy for autism was expensive, between three to eight thousand dollars, and the therapy wasn't fully covered by Lana's medical insurance. But whatever his son needed, he was willing to pay for it in cash.

It was getting late. Papa John had to leave and check on his son. He had his five-year-old autistic son, John Jr. staying with his other baby mama, Tina, who had his three-year-old son, John Jr. Tina didn't have a problem with it. She loved Papa John deeply, despite his womanizing ways.

"Yo, I'm out, I gotta check on my son," he said to Kip.

Kip nodded. They gave each other dap, and Papa John climbed out of the van. Papa John walked toward the avenue while Kip remained seated and smoking. His people were starving for some cash, and he needed to provide another score for them. It felt like they were drowning in problems all of a sudden.

Kip took one last pull from the Black, flicked it out the window, and shouted, "Fuck this!" He started his vehicle and drove off. His plans tonight were to go to the bar, get a drink, and chill. Maybe he could find an easy nigga to rob at the bar, or not. But he needed to do something.

He then thought about Devon's plan, robbing Maserati Meek. Nothing was ever impossible, but damn, it was still suicide. But if push came to shove, and they became desperate, then would it be a bad plan for them to execute? They needed to eat by any means necessary.

TWENTY-THREE

After checking on his son, Papa John was satisfied he was safe at Tina's place. He then went to his father's place in Whitestone, Queens, a quiet upper middle-class neighborhood.

The cab came to a rolling stop in front of a three-bedroom, two-story home on Third Avenue. Papa John paid the driver and climbed out. He looked around far and wide at the manicured lawns, picket and bricked fences, detailed shrubberies, orderly driveways, and nicely paved streets surrounding him. It was the opposite of Harlem—quietness and affluent folks with expensive hobbies and 401(k)s. His father was living great. And he didn't really care for the man. Papa John felt his old man was a traitor working for the NYPD.

He approached the home. He noticed one car parked in the driveway, a white Lexus. The last time he checked, his pops was driving a Mercedes-Benz. He ascended the brick stairs and rang the bell. He hated reaching out, but he needed a place to stay temporarily. Lana had called the cops on him after he had beaten her up bad, and he feared there might be a warrant out for his arrest.

He rang the doorbell several times and waited. He glanced around. He soon found himself in Devon's situation, most likely on the run for doing something stupid. But that was his son, his seed, and his baby mama had no right calling his son retarded and stupid. Papa John had immediately snapped and went ham on the bitch. He knew John Jr. was in good hands with Tina. She had her ways, but she was a great mother, and Papa John trusted her with his other son. Anyway, he felt that John Jr. and John Jr. were brothers and needed to know each other.

"Who is it?" he heard a female voice say.

"It's Papa"—He quickly had to correct himself—"It's John. Where my pops at?"

The door soon opened, and his father's young and beautiful twenty-two-year-old girlfriend stood in front of him.

"He's at work," she said.

Papa John had seen her only a handful of times, but he had to admit, his pops had great taste. Dina was a beautiful, curvy woman. He looked her up and down, admiring her wear, a printed romper, her long legs glimmering, her pedicure showing her small feet and pretty toes.

"You here by yourself, huh?"

"What you want, John?"

"I need to talk to him."

"Well, he's at work. He won't be home until after nine tonight."

"So what you saying? I can't come inside my own father's house?"

"We didn't know you were coming to visit."

"I came to have a talk wit' my pops, and last time I checked, I was still his son."

She sighed. "You wanna come inside and wait?"

"Yeah, I would appreciate that."

Dina stepped aside, annoyed, and Papa John marched inside. His father had fine taste in women, cars, and homes, plus furniture. The décor was high-end and contemporary. The TV was so big in the living room, it looked like a Mack truck could literally come through it. The leather furniture was comfortable, the artwork tasteful, and the stereo system was the best. He had parquet flooring with a stylish rug tying together the place.

"You thirsty?" she asked.

"Yeah, I'll take Pepsi."

She strutted into the kitchen, and he took a seat in the living room. He couldn't keep his eyes off Dina. If his pops hadn't snatched her up first, then he would have. She came back into the living room with his cold Pepsi. She sat.

Papa John smiled, and he couldn't stop being himself, not even around Dina. He rudely asked, "You pregnant yet?"

"Excuse me? What?"

He laughed. "I mean, with a woman like you, is my pops tryin' to make me any little brothers or sisters yet?"

She scowled. "You're disrespectful, John!"

"I'm just making conversation, that's all."

"By asking me that shit?"

"My bad. I apologize."

Dina shook her head in disgust at him and sucked her teeth. "If you're going to be rude, you can leave."

"Nah, I'm not tryin' to be rude or disrespectful. Sometimes I can be a little blunt wit' mines."

"A little?"

He chuckled. "So I see my pops bought you a Lexus. Nice. He gotta be in love with you."

"We're getting married. You didn't notice?" She held up her left hand, showing off the diamond engagement ring.

"Oh shit, I didn't even peep that. Damn, my pops banking like that? How much that ring cost?"

"I don't know, but it's expensive."

"Your pussy must be"—He simply chuckled. "You're a lucky woman, and he's a very lucky man. Congratulations."

She cut her eyes at him. "Thank you."

Papa John took a sip from the Pepsi then suddenly wondered why he'd asked for a soda. "Yo, y'all ain't got nothing stronger, no liquor, in here?"

"I thought you wanted a Pepsi."

"I need a real drink . . . some weed too. You smoke?"

She grinned. "Occasionally."

"Well, I occasionally got a twenty sack on me," he said, pulling out the small Ziploc bag containing some potent kush. "I just need me a Dutch Master."

Dina tried to be conservative, but her age was breaking through, slowly but surely. Her fiancé didn't smoke, but he did drink. Dina didn't mind getting high with Papa John. He seemed like fun.

*

Several hours later, Papa John had his father's fiancée high like a kite and a bit tipsy, and it didn't take long for him to pin her against the bedroom wall with her legs straddling him as he slammed his goliath-size dick deep into her. She panted and chanted, feeling the dick cemented into her, her pussy dripping like a leaky faucet. Papa John was a beast on her, fucking her raw with her tits pressed against his bare chest.

She clawed at his skin, definitely feeling the difference between father and son. "Fuck me!" she cried out.

It was wrong, fucking his father's girl, but Papa John had no morals. He needed to get his mind off his son, and his other troubles. And for the moment, Dina was his healing. They were in a frenzy, fucking hard.

She could feel herself about to come. "Oh shit! Damn it, fuck me!" Dina hollered. "You black, big-dick, thug muthafucka!"

Suddenly, the faint sound of a car door slamming caught their attention. Darryl was home early.

Dina slammed her hands against his chest and pushed him out the pussy. She stood to her feet and hurried to the nearest window. She saw his black Mercedes-Benz parked in the driveway, and he was approaching the house.

"Shit! Your father's home early!" she said in a panic. She hastily put on her panties and clothing.

Papa John threw on his jeans and shirt, splashed some cold water on his face, and rushed downstairs. He slammed himself on the living room couch just in time before his father walked inside.

Startled by his son's presence, Papa John's father asked, "John, what the hell you doing here? Where's Dina?"

"She's upstairs."

"And you're here, in my house, because?" his father asked suspiciously.

"Pops, I'm your son. I can't come by and say hey?"

"You never come by."

Darryl moved toward his son. Exposed fully on his hip was his holstered Glock and gold badge. Darryl was an intimidating figure, standing six one, robust with a dark goatee and strong features.

"I need to talk to you, Pop."

"Yeah, we need to talk all right," Darryl responded sternly.

Before anything else was said between them, Dina came down the stairs looking fully refreshed in a pink sweat suit and trying to look innocent. She smiled at her fiancé, threw her arms around him and gave him a kiss. "How was your day?" she asked him.

Darryl kept his eyes on his son, ignoring her question momentarily. It felt like a critical moment between them. "Fine," he answered dryly.

"Baby, you hungry? You want me to make you something?"

"No, I need to talk to my son about something," he said seriously. "Give us some privacy."

Dina nodded and left the room. When she was gone, Darryl quickly stepped to his son, grabbed him by his shirt, and threw him against the wall in the living room. The impact of it rattled a few pictures.

"What the fuck, Pops!" Papa John hollered, in shock. He could feel his father's entire strength on him. The man was forty-nine years old and still had The Hulk inside of him. He had aged, but he was still quick and fierce.

Darryl hollered, "I'm about to fuckin' retire soon, and I have lots of connections in the force—Harlem, Brooklyn, Queens—so why do I gotta hear about my son's name coming up in several investigations? One is even a fuckin' murder!"

"I don't know what you talkin' about, Pops," Papa John quickly denied.

"What are you doing out there? Are you a fuckin' criminal, John? Huh? Tell me this some bullshit I'm hearing about you."

"It is! I have a legit job."

"Where? Doing what?"

Papa John needed to think fast. "At McDonald's."

"McDonald's," Darryl repeated, looking dubiously at his son. He thought his son lived off women. "You know I'm a detective, boy. If you're lying to me, my son or not, I'll lock you up so fast, your head will spin."

Both men locked eyes with each other. Papa John didn't flinch. He was sticking to his story.

His father released his stronghold and backed away a little.

"I'm good, Pops, believe. I'm no criminal."

"Why are you here?"

Papa John had to swallow his pride and ask for his help. It had been two years since he'd moved out of his father's house and been on his own. He took a deep breath, continued looking at his father, and said, "I just need a place to stay for a short moment."

"Why?"

"I got a lot going on."

"A lot going on like what, John? You're gonna have to fuckin' elaborate a lot more for me to even consider opening my home to you."

Papa John sighed and finally relented to his pain, saying to his father, "One of my sons was diagnosed with autism." There, he'd finally told his father.

Hearing about his grandson's diagnosis changed Darryl's demeanor. Though he rarely saw any of his grandchildren, it didn't mean he loved them less. Darryl said, "If you need to talk, I'm standing right here."

Papa John put on a show for his father—emotions, tears, and pain. It was the first time anyone ever saw him cry.

Darryl showed empathy and invited his son into his home.

Papa John felt confident that his criminal life wasn't going to catch up to him. Though his father was a seasoned detective, he felt he was the wiser. Besides, he'd just fucked his father's bitch in their bedroom and seemed to have gotten away with it.

For a long time, Papa John had been getting away with murder, and with a place to lay his head, at the home of an NYPD officer no less, he felt almost invincible.

TWENTY-FOUR

Nana, AKA Rhonda, took a pull from her Newport 100, moving on the dance floor like she was in her early twenties. With a cigarette in one hand and a cup of corn whiskey in the other, she moved to Al Green's "Let's Stay Together" cheerfully. It was one of her favorite songs. She twirled and glided with her old-school generation of friends, and they sang along to the song that had Blue's lounge full of life with fun, laughter, drinking, and dancing.

Nana looked good in a red-and-black sexy dress, her hair flowing and jewelry showing. She threw back the corn whiskey like it was water and continued to smoke while dancing the night away. She was definitely the center of attention and a regular at the lounge. They knew her name, her drink, and her choice of men.

Soon, Nana started to dance intimately close to a younger fellow stylishly dressed in a black suit and a garish red tie, with a dark, trimmed beard and bald head. His eyes were dark, his smile mischievous, and his demeanor shady. He was handsome to the aging woman. They wrapped their arms around each other and started to bump and grind on the dance floor, thrusting and protruding their bodies in some dirty dancing. She was familiar with the man, who wasn't shy feeling on her booty and kissing the side of her neck. They laughed and played together like school kids. He whirled her around a few times on the floor and then spun her around like she was thirty-something. Nana was having the time of her life with him.

When the song ended, Nana looked winded. She joked, "Ooh, chile, you about to give this old lady a heart attack with all that jiving against me."

He laughed. "Old lady where? There ain't no finer, younger, prettier thing in this place than you."

She blushed. His compliments were inflating her ego. She smiled widely.

His hands groped her body publicly, no shame in his game. "C'mere and let me give my woman a kiss," he said.

Nana shoved her tongue down his throat and French-kissed him like there was no tomorrow. When it came to showing each other public affection, neither one of them was shy at doing it.

Finally pulling his lips apart from hers, he smacked her on the ass and said, "Hey, go get me a drink. I'm thirsty again."

She nodded. Nana went to the bar, opened her purse, and pulled out a few hundred-dollar bills, money given to her by Kip. She wasn't cheap in splurging on herself, her young stud, Curtis, and her friends. She ordered two more corn whiskeys. She joined her man again by an open table, and they drank and talked.

Nana was head over heels in love with Curtis, who she'd met eight months ago at the casino. He was an intriguing guy, tall and handsome. He'd initiated the conversation, she liked his personality, and as a lonely old woman, she soon became swept up in his charm and the sex. Whatever Curtis needed, she easily provided.

Nana was feeling hot and bothered. She wanted some dick. She was all over Curtis at the table. She fondled his crotch and put her tongue into his ear. "You ready to go, baby? And have mama tuck you in snugly tonight?" she asked him.

"Yeah, in a beat, honey. I just wanna finish this drink." Curtis downed his liquor.

Nana continued touching him. Her promiscuous movements clearly indicated her needs. Curtis looked at her and smiled. "Hey, sexy, before we leave, let me rap to you about something."

"What is it?"

"I hate to ask, but I'm short on my rent this month."

"How much do you need now?"

"Four hundred."

Nana went into her purse and pulled out her wad of cash. She then peeled off five hundred dollars and handed it over to Curtis, who took the money from her in a heartbeat with the brightest smile.

"You're the best, gorgeous. I love you."

"I love you too," she declared.

She gave him the extra hundred because she could. To Nana, forty-five-year-old Curtis was her breathe-again man. But, in reality, he was a fraud and a con, a two-bit hustler and loser who had never worked a real job in his life. He knew he'd hit pay dirt with Rhonda.

Since the day they'd met, she had been tricking on him with money and gifts. Nana, or Rhonda to him, had become his sugar mamma. And he treated her wrinkled pussy like it was gold to him. Definitely an act, but a believable act to her. He was also growing weary fucking the old bitch and wanted one last payday from her before he left her completely and headed to Baltimore with his younger, sexier chick.

Two hours after midnight, the two left the lounge together. She climbed into his old '67 Chevy Impala and went to a cheap motel for a night of lovemaking. An hour later, Curtis was fucking her from the back, a position he frequently performed on her, so there wouldn't be any eye contact as he was inside of her. Nana loved it, being on all fours and taking a big dick hard like stone from a man twenty-something years younger, thrusting in and out of her.

Usually, he would eat her pussy, but tonight's treat had been absent.

She wasn't complaining though. He fucked her vigorously, and they went from doggy-style to her on top, riding his dick like a surfer on a wave.

Soon, he made her pussy come like a dam had burst open, and Nana was having almost the perfect orgasm. She shuddered immensely on top of him, her manicured nails digging into his chest as she felt such a needed release.

He smacked her firm ass and then pushed her off the dick. He needed a cigarette.

Nana lay next to him, completely satisfied. Her smile could light a dark room. She exhaled.

Curtis took a puff from his cigarette and shared it with her. The two lay on the bed feeling a post-coital moment. Subsequently, the pillow talk began, with Curtis saying, "Time is winding down with this business I want to invest in."

"And how much you need again?" she asked.

"A hundred thousand dollars."

Curtis was pressuring her to help him invest into buying a nightclub with a friend. A man named G-G was selling his nightclub for two hundred thousand dollars. The place already had a name and reputation, and G-G simply wanted to retire a well-off man. They needed some startup money; he would put in a hundred thousand, and so would his friend.

But Nana didn't have it. And now, all her lies were catching up to her. In the beginning, she had told Curtis that she was a wealthy woman that had sold her successful business for millions over a decade ago, and she was living off the interest. He had been pretty much begging for the money for over a month now.

"I need to talk to my accountant," she said.

"Rhonda, you told me the same thing last week. I really need this money, or else, this opportunity of a lifetime will slip from my hands, and G-G gonna sell the club to someone else."

Rhonda didn't know what to tell him. She felt stupid lying to him. Now the frustration was building up, and she didn't want to lose him over a lie. "I'll get you the money," she said.

"When?" he asked harshly.

"I just need some time, baby. That's all."

"I don't have time. It's been over a month now, and I still have nothing from you but promises and procrastination." Frustrated, Curtis removed himself from the bed and reached for his clothing. He hurriedly got dressed.

"Baby, don't leave me, please," she begged. Nana jumped from the bed, desperate for him to stay.

Curtis ignored her, throwing on his shoes and grabbing his cell phone.

"How will I get home?" she asked.

"Call a cab." With that being said, Curtis stormed out of the motel room and slammed the door behind him.

Nana stood there naked, looking downhearted from his abrupt departure. Tears started to well in her eyes. She didn't want to disappoint him and felt she had to get him that money somehow. The only way she saw it happening was through Kip. She would have to tell him one of the biggest lies ever for him to come up with a hundred thousand dollars to help her boyfriend. And she planned on getting it done very soon.

TWENTY-FIVE

Kip stood on the rooftop of his building, underneath a sky full of stars, on a warm spring night with his Timberlands crunching against the gravel beneath his feet. He smoked his Black & Mild as he gazed at an illuminated Harlem and the George Washington Bridge in the distance. It was a beautiful night with a faint wind brushing against his face. He seemed to be in a trance, enjoying his smoke and solitude once again.

He took another drag and spun his head, alert to his surroundings. Even on the roof of his tall building, he was on guard and armed with a .38 special. He stepped closer to the ledge and gazed over. It was a long drop to the ground.

Just then, his cell phone rang. Kip removed the phone from his hip and looked at the caller ID. It was Maserati Meek. Kip felt a tinge of apprehension. His last meeting with Meek didn't feel right, and he didn't trust him. But business was still business, and Kip needed some work. He answered his call, "What's up?"

"We need to talk," Meek said.

"When and where?"

"Same place, tomorrow afternoon."

"Okay," Kip replied, keeping things simple.

The call ended.

Kip wasn't going to make the same mistake as the last time. This time he wasn't going alone to meet with Maserati Meek.

***

Kip stopped his Nissan Quest in front of Maserati Meek's lavish place in Long Island, and he, Papa John, and Devon climbed out of the van. There was a fourth man with them too, a hood acquaintance named Maniac, who remained in the van holding onto an Uzi submachine gun. He was extra backup just in case shit happened.

Kip wasn't taking any chances this time around. He was more on point and ready for anything. He said, "Maniac, if we ain't out here in fifteen minutes or less, you already know what to do."

Maniac nodded. He held the Uzi like it was his own child. When it came to crazy, he was up there with Devon. Just didn't give a fuck.

Kip told them to be on high alert. The three men walked toward the door, and until they rang the bell, Devon was still in Kip's ear about robbing Maserati Meek. But, once again, Kip was against the idea.

Maserati Meek's goon answered the bell. He stared at Kip and his cronies and allowed them inside. But before they could take a step farther into the house, he had to perform the routine body search to make sure they weren't carrying any concealed weapons.

"You know, this is becoming a real bore between us," Kip said.

"Doing my job, nigga!" the man said roughly.

"Yeah, a'ight," Kip said.

Cleared of being a danger to his boss, they proceeded inside the place.

Immediately Maserati Meek met them. He smiled and said, "I see you brought your bodyguards with you, eh. Let's have some fun then."

Kip didn't find him funny. The three men stood there expressionless, making sure things weren't about to get real funny.

"We here; let's talk," Kip said, wanting to get down to business and make his exit without incident.

"Yes, let's talk, my friend. But only you and I . . . alone," Maserati Meek instructed.

Kip turned to look at his friends and gave them a nod of assurance. They nodded back. Kip left the room with Meek, leaving his two goons to play with the other men in the room. Kip followed Maserati Meek outside onto the patio. His backyard was quiet and concealed, with trees decorating much of the place.

Meek said, "I have another job for you."

Kip nodded. He thought it was another murder contract.

"I need for you and your crew to make a drop for me."

Kip was somewhat taken aback by the job. A drop? They weren't UPS. It was the first time Meek had asked them to deliver something. Usually, it was murder, or Kip was selling him stolen goods. Kip was skeptical about the job. "You want us to deliver what?" he asked Meek.

Maserati Meek exhaled and then answered, "I need for you to drop off fifty kilos and two dozen guns to a certain location and also to collect my money—eight hundred thousand dollars."

"Why us?" Kip asked, trying to make sure it wasn't a setup.

"Because I do not trust many of my men to execute this drop, eh. I feel that some may have been, what's the word, compromised," he said. "And some are just idiots."

It still didn't add up for Kip, who continued to feign interest in the job. He locked eyes with Meek, looking for a flaw in his story. Why would Meek suddenly trust him with such a large quantity of drugs, money, and guns? Who was to say they weren't going to rip him off?

"And you trust us with this much amount of shit?"

"You, my friend, are loyal, and you know respect. And you know my power and my vengeance. If you were to rob from me, eh, you do understand there is nowhere you can run or hide where I would not find you, your friends, and your family. And, besides, you're not a stupid man, Kip. I do respect your intelligence."

It still didn't feel right to Kip, but he decided to accept the job. "When and where?"

"There's a man named Lance, and you are to meet him at a specific place near the Brooklyn Bridge at a certain time. He will be expecting you in three days, eh."

"And our cut for this transaction?"

"Five percent."

Five percent wasn't going to do for Kip. "Make it ten percent."

Maserati Meek kept his cool and continued to grin, even though once again, Kip defied him by renegotiating a price that was already concrete in his mind. Although bargaining was a huge part of his native culture, where most were offended or lost respect for you if you did not negotiate terms, Maserati liked the Western way of thinking. When you're a drug boss, what you say is law.

"Ten percent then," he said to Kip, fuming on the inside.

Maserati Meek knew, just like a child, Kip would continue the disrespect. He wanted to chop off his head right there but kept his cool.

Maserati Meek gave him details on how the drop should be implemented. The drugs and guns would be cleverly stashed inside of a gray Nissan Altima. Kip and his crew would pick up the car from an auto body shop in Harlem. Papa John and Devon would drive the Nissan, while Kip would drive the Expedition. They would head to the location near the Brooklyn Bridge to meet with Lance. At the drop, Papa John and Devon would exit the gray Nissan and get into a black Toyota Camry, where the payment of $800,000 would be concealed inside the car. No one would leave the destination until both crews checked that all the merchandise was accounted for. Kip and his crew would drive the black car with the cash to Meek's place on Long Island, and hand it over, minus their ten percent. The whole thing sounded and looked to be easy-peasy.

Skeptical still, Kip shook hands with Maserati Meek, promising him results, and the men left the house. Maniac seemed almost disappointed that he didn't have to use his Uzi, but he was happy to see his friends come back out alive.

They sped away, and a few miles away from the house, Kip went over the job with them.

"Yo, we need to take all that shit, nigga." Devon blew out a long whistle. "Eight hundred G's is a lot of cheddar." With that much cash, drugs, and guns, he felt they could equal Meek's power and become kingpins themselves. He was truly excited.

Papa John was in too. The cash could definitely help with payment for his son's treatment and therapy. That much cash on hand was life-changing.

The men did the math. Ten percent of $800,000 was a paltry eighty grand. Divided among the three of them, it was close to twenty-seven thousand dollars apiece. It wasn't much, and Kip's crew was becoming hungrier for much more.

Kip felt the job was odd and could be a setup. There were so many what-ifs—what if the car was wired with GPS and tracking, or Maserati Meek was tailing them? And what if there was no transaction, but they were simply on their way to their deaths, where they were to be killed once arriving at the location? Kip had to think so many moves ahead, and sometimes it was exhausting. What to do?

TWENTY-SIX

Kid sat by his bedroom window and gazed at Jessica strutting through the projects looking like a beauty queen in her colored skinny jeans, a white tee, and a pair of peep-toe heels. Kid's eyes were hooked on her the entire time until he observed her climbing into the front seat of a lavish, black Mercedes-Benz. He felt depressed. Jessica was a beautiful woman, and he wanted her absolutely, but she wasn't into guys like him—crippled, powerless, and young.

Kid wanted a change in his life. For once, he wanted to look and feel powerful and independent like his brother. He wanted the respect like everyone else, and though he was a chess prodigy and got his respect playing the game, he was tired of being looked at as Kip's little brother and being treated like he couldn't handle himself. The girls liked him. They thought he was cute and adorable, but as a boyfriend, they didn't give him the time of day. No one looked past the chair. Sometimes he felt alone and unwanted. He wanted to leap from his chair and show the world a different him. He was smart, and he could be patient, but where was his future?

He continued to sit by the window, feeling the afternoon sun splash against his face. The warmth of the day was inviting. He was itching to go down to the park and play a game of chess. It was what kept his mind free from troubles and worries. The game was his escape. He mobilized his chess pieces so well because he himself was immobile, so he gave his king, queen, pawns, knights, and rooks legs to travel freely and conquer. Though he felt powerless, his chess pieces gave him power.

While sitting and contemplating, his cell phone rang. Kid wheeled himself toward it and answered. He didn't recognize the number.

"Hello," he said.

"Good afternoon, Kid. It's your Nana."

He frowned. Why was she calling him? He didn't even think she had his number. "What you want?" he asked harshly.

"I don't mean to disturb you, but I'm calling looking for Kip. For some reason, he's not answering his cell phone, and I'm concerned."

"Maybe he finally came to his senses."

Nana sighed. "Why such hatred for me, Kid? I did nothing but love and take care of you and your brother the best I could."

"Because I know what you are. I see you, and you may have Kip fooled with that old sick-granny routine, but you don't have me fooled."

"But I am sick, Kid."

"I call bullshit!"

"Kid, please. This is important. I need to contact your brother. I need to tell him something that he needs to know. I'm a dying woman, Kid."

Kid felt nothing for the old lady. If she were to drop dead that day, he wouldn't feel any contrition. He knew the bitch's crocodile tears were only about money. He didn't believe she was sick at all, and if he could prove it, he would. But for now, he could only trash her and lash out with words.

He hung up. He didn't plan on passing any messages to his brother about that woman. She'd never called, and they'd never spoke.

Feeling alone and gloomy on a sunny day, Kid needed to get out. He was tired of the apartment and tired of looking out the window and seeing the woman he loved love somebody else. Though Jessica and Eshon had beef, he was still with team Jessica. She could do no wrong in his eyes; it all had to be a misunderstanding.

Later in the day, Kid went down to St. Nicholas Park, played a few games of chess, and won over three hundred dollars. He spent four hours in the park and then arrived home as the sun was setting over the horizon.

An hour after he came home, Kip walked through the door. Kid could see he was in a sour mood.

"What's wrong?" Kid asked him.

Kip didn't have any words to say.

The look on Kip's face already told Kid that he must have spoken to Nana, and she had gotten to him already. Kid felt there wasn't anything he could do about it. Kip was silent and acted like he wasn't even there.

Kid rolled himself into the bedroom and closed the door. *That manipulative bitch,* he thought. She was always messing with his brother's psyche and creating stories to make him feel sorry for her.

***

The next day, Kip was in his minivan, speeding on the interstate, on his way to see Nana. By early afternoon he was knocking on her door and dying to speak to her.

Nana answered the door in her teal housecoat, fuzzy slippers, and curlers, clutching her walking cane.

Kip gave her a hug and took a seat inside the room. "Nana, tell me what you said yesterday isn't true. You ain't got cancer, right?"

Nana, looking bleak and sickly, took a seat opposite him. She had told him that she had been diagnosed with stage 3 breast cancer that could have already invaded nearby lymph nodes and muscles. And though the cancer was advanced, a number of effective treatment options were still available.

Kip didn't want to believe she was dying from breast cancer, but she had the proof, the letter and her diagnosis from her doctors. He looked downhearted. Nana was the only woman in his life that he loved and cared for so much.

"What are the doctors saying? You can fight this, right? It's treatable?"

Nana released a deep, sorrowful sigh. "I don't know, Kip. The insurance company is refusing to pay for my chemo and the experimental drug treatment."

Kip was floored. "What the fuck you talking 'bout, Nana? Why? You sick, they should be helping to take care of you."

"Calm down, Kip."

"Nah." He jumped up, agitated and upset. "These muthafuckas shouldn't be playing games wit' your life like this, Nana."

"They're saying that there's some discrepancy with my insurance company and"—Nana looked like she was about to break down in tears—"And I might have to pay out my own pockets. It's an expensive treatment, Kip, but I don't want you to worry about it."

"What you mean, don't worry about it? I'm fuckin' worried, Nana. You need help. You need this treatment done. This chemo, if it's gonna help, then we're gonna get it for you."

"I'm an old woman, Kip. I'm dying anyway, with or without it."

"Nana, you need to stop talkin' like that. You gonna be fine. I promise you that. I'm gonna get you the money," he assured her.

"Kip, between treatment and medication, things can get really expensive. We're talking about a minimum of five chemo treatments, costing no less than twenty grand."

"Don't worry 'bout the money. I'm gonna handle this for you, Nana. You just relax and let me deal wit' the finances." Kip was confident but worried at the same time.

Kip believed her health was failing, and he didn't want to lose her. And if he had to kill a few niggas to pay for her chemo treatments, then there wouldn't be an ounce of hesitation on his part.

Before his departure, he hugged his Nana tightly, and as he did so, a few tears trickled from his eyes. He quickly wiped them away, took a deep breath, and left distraught from the news. She meant the world to him, and he was ready to do what needed to be done. It was going to be his longest trip back home.

***

It had been a rough day for the brothers, and it became an even rougher day when the two argued over Nana's cancer. Kip had come home and told Kid about Nana's breast cancer, the chemo treatments, the payments, and her medication.

Kid felt that they should get a second opinion.

"Why would Nana lie about having cancer?"

"You can't be so fuckin' stupid and naïve, Kip!" Kid had screamed out. "She's a lying and conniving fuckin' bitch, Kip! Get a second opinion!"

"You always tryin' to put Nana down, after everything she did for us. No!"

The two brothers got into an intense shouting match. Then Kip became so angry at his brother, he punched him in the face, pulled him out of his wheelchair, and tossed him to the floor. He then pushed his wheelchair across the room, way out of Kid's reach.

Towering over his crippled little brother with anger, he screamed, "You stay there, muthafucka, until you come to your senses!" Kip stormed out of the apartment, leaving his brother sprawled out and glued to the floor.

Kid was shocked by the action. Nana was coming between them. He detested her more and more. He had to crawl to his chair. It took a long, embarrassing while. When he finally got settled back into his chair and propped up, the tears came streaming from his eyes. He couldn't believe that his brother would do him like that—straight attack him like a stranger, and take Nana's word over his.

TWENTY-SEVEN

I t was the morning of the drop, and the day reflected Kip's mood—cloudy and bleak, and a bit chilly. Kip was in a very dark place. He didn't know what the outcome would be this evening, but he said to himself, *Fuck it.* He called his crew. They needed to meet and talk before they did the drop in Brooklyn.

Two hours later, Devon and Papa John were on the building's rooftop having a critical meeting with Kip, smoking his usual Black as he stood on the roof with a cold, scheming gaze.

"What's up? Why we here on the roof in this wind?" Devon asked.

Kip looked at both his friends, two men he considered his brothers. They had been through thick and thin, and they were still standing when the worst of the worst had tried to put them down.

Kip took one final drag from the Black and flicked it off the building. He then said coldly, "We gonna rob these niggas. Y'all good wit' that?"

Devon smiled like it was Christmas Day. "Fuck, yeah, I'm good wit' that shit, nigga! It's about time you came to the realization." Devon slapped him a hard five.

Kip looked at Papa John. "And what about you?"

Papa John looked his friend in the eyes. "We like the Three Musketeers, right? One for all, and all for one."

"One for all and one for what?" Devon replied with a puzzled look. "Yo, fuck them corny niggas! Nigga, we like those niggas in that movie

Goodfellas, feel me? Now those niggas got shit poppin'!"

Kip loved his crew. He even managed to laugh at their antics.

Devon and Papa John were down for different reasons. It was a risky lick, but they were confident it could be done.

Kip had to break down the plan to them. He explained that they would go there, kill whoever, take the $800,000 and give Maserati Meek back his kilos and guns, with a lie, saying that the guys they were to meet never came with the money and had planned on robbing them. Kip figured they could actually be walking into a setup and a death trap, and his mentality was, "it's either them or us."

Devon felt they should keep the drugs and guns too. "Fuck Maserati Meek! That nigga can bleed too."

Kip was against it. Maserati Meek was a harder target and was always protected. Kip knew that would bring too much heat on them. The plan was set—Kill these fools, take the money, and implement the lie.

TWENTY-EIGHT

It was leading to the moment of reality for them, the biggest payday they would ever see if everything went as planned, or their demise if things went bad. Either way, all three men were determined and not backing out of it. They were winging it, not having time to scout the location, know the players they were going to jack, or how many there would be. They had to play things by ear, rely on their instincts, and have each other's backs at any cost.

Kip didn't know if there would be an army of men at the meeting. How would they pull it off? There was some trepidation lurking inside of him, but he was confident they could make it happen.

Devon's Expedition came to a stop in front of the greasy-looking auto body shop on Broadway. Kip, Papa John, and Devon climbed out and entered the establishment. The inside was busy with mechanics working on cars, despite the late hour.

Kip said to one of the mechanics, "We lookin' for Nino."

A greasy mechanic pointed to the makeshift office near the back of the shop.

Kip went alone. He knocked on the old wood door.

Nino, a heavyset man with nappy hair, dressed in greasy overalls, came to the door. He quickly sized Kip up. "You Meek's people, right?"

Kip nodded.

Nino already knew they were coming. He had photos of all three men, courtesy of Meek. "Follow me," he said to Kip.

They came to a gray 2012 Nissan Altima that looked brand spanking new and unassuming.

Nino tossed him the car keys. "You're the driver?"

Kip shook his head no and then called over Papa John and Devon.

Nino gawked at them, already feeling that they were bad news.

Kip handed the keys to Devon.

"Everything's ready, placed where it should be." Nino removed a few Polaroid pictures from the pockets of his overalls—they were of the car, dismantled—and then he showed them several more pictures of where the kilos and guns were concealed inside the car.

Kip was shocked. How could an average-looking car hold so much shit? It looked like it had never been taken apart.

"We okay, right?" Nino asked.

Kip nodded. "Yeah, we good."

Devon got behind the wheel, and Papa John rode shotgun. Nino seemed almost relieved to have the car leave his shop.

Kip got into the Expedition, and their scheme was now in motion.

The location on Water Street was an abandoned, graffiti-scrawled factory on a cobblestone street and just a stone's throw away from the Brooklyn Bridge. It was late, and the area was sparse of traffic and people. It was perfect for a setup—no operating businesses, no residents, no people—just silence and buildings for several blocks, and an up-close and personal view of the Brooklyn Bridge.

Devon pulled up to the entrance of the place and honked the horn quickly, signifying their arrival. Right away the rolling metal gate lifted, giving the men right of entry into the place. The Expedition followed behind the Nissan into a vast area of concrete, pillars, and emptiness.

Parked in the empty building were two cars, a black BMW 750 and the black Toyota. Four men armed with machine guns stood by the vehicles.

Kip stared at them; it already had gotten complicated. He was still adamant about going through with their plan.

Everyone climbed out of the cars. Meeting with armed strangers when tons of cash and drugs were involved was always a risky business.

Kip held a straight-faced glare and approached Lance, the man in charge. Lance was average height, and he was a dangerous-looking man with a protruding chin and cold eyes. He was dressed in a white tank top with gangland tattoos up and down his arms. He flashed a gold grill and exposed a pistol in his waistband.

"So, you the man, huh?" he said to Kip.

"Yeah, and I just want to get this over wit'."

"It's just the three of y'all?" Lance asked.

"Why the questions?"

"Just making conversation, yo. Relax," Lance said in a greasy way.

There was a quick size-up from both sides, and then Kip started to politick with Lance. Kip already saw the man's arrogance, his overconfident body language suggesting that since his goons had the machine guns and there were four of them, they obviously had the upper hand. Kip was quickly feeling things out. He couldn't wait too long to make his move. If it was a setup, then they had to do their part fast.

Lance looked around, and then he nodded to one of his henchmen. The machine gun-toting goon stepped away from the group and proceeded toward the Expedition and the gray Altima.

"What's going on?" Kip asked.

"Just checking things out," Lance said. "Relax. Why you so paranoid?"

If Lance told him to relax one more time, Kip was going to chop his head off. Things were going from uneasy to extremely tense in a heartbeat. Something was wrong.

Kip threw a subtle head nod Devon's and Papa John's way. They watched the goon approach the SUV and the Nissan. He carried his machine gun in a hostile manner. He moved closer to the vehicles in silence.

Kip, Papa John, and Devon were strategically placed, so they wouldn't be hit with friendly fire. And as the man walked closer to Devon's SUV, it happened suddenly—a burst of machine gun fire erupted deafeningly, and the goon was hit violently with a barrage of bullets. Maniac, who was hiding in the back of the truck, gripped the smoking Uzi and tore into the man with vengeance.

"What the fuck!" Lance screamed.

Before Lance and his men could react, Kip and his men were already on them. Kip swiftly put a Glock to Lance's head and fired—*Boom!*—blowing his brains out. Stupid muthafucka should have had his weapon in hand and ready, instead of in his waistband.

The other two goons desperately lifted their weapons, but Papa John and Devon lit into them with automatic weapons, striking them with head and chest shots. They collapsed on their back, dead.

The bloodshed happened in a matter of seconds. Kip and his men breathed out with some relief. They were still alive. They looked at each other intently. Everyone was okay, no holes in them, no blood.

"That's what the fuck I'm talkin' about, my niggas!" Devon hollered.

They looked around. The bodies were slumped on the cold concrete floor, a testament to their ruthlessness.

Maniac grinned. Finally, he had gotten to use the Uzi. The smell of blood and death was an exhilarating feeling for him. He was psychotic. He was the perfect piece in Kip's plan.

"Papa John, check the car and see if the money's there," Kip said, doubtful that there was any cash.

Papa John went to the black Toyota, where there was supposed to be $800,000 inside. He lifted the trunk and saw two large duffel bags.

He unzipped one, and bingo! Cold, hard cash. "Yo, we rich, bitch!" he shouted elatedly.

Everyone smiled. It was a great feeling.

Kip loved it when a plan came together perfectly. It definitely had to be a setup—an ambush from Maserati Meek. Kip still couldn't wrap his head around it. Why would Meek trust them with that much cash, guns, and drugs? He thought there wouldn't be any money, but there was plenty of it. "Yo, grab that shit and let's be out," he instructed.

Papa John removed the cash from the trunk and hurried toward the SUV. Kip and his men carefully removed the dead men's jewelry, cash, and cell phones, wearing latex gloves to make sure not to leave behind any fingerprints. They then dumped the bodies into the black Toyota.

Devon climbed back into the gray Altima, the others piled into the Expedition, and they left the crime scene. Their hearts were still beating intensely. The easy part was done. Now they had to face Maserati Meek and tell him what happened.

Kip turned off the men's phones and tossed them over the bridge, and into the water.

"Y'all niggas be on point," Kip said to his men on their way to Maserati Meek's place.

They all nodded. They had to make everything look as real as possible.

Kip was upset. He wanted to confront Meek and beat him down, but that wasn't possible. Not now anyway.

The SUV came to a screeching stop in front of Meek's place next to Devon in the Altima, and all four men climbed out the vehicles heatedly.

Kip pounded his fist on the front door. He had his gun visible, and so did the others. His heart was still pumping a million times a second, and when the front door opened, and Meek's goon loomed, Kip and his men charged into the place, and pointing their weapons at Maserati Meek's men, who in return, lifted their weapons and aimed back.

It became a Mexican standoff quickly.

"What in the hell, Kip! Are you out of your mind, my friend?!" Maserati Meek shouted.

"You tell me, nigga," Kip hollered. "You set us up!"

"What? I set you up?"

"Yes. That drop wasn't a fuckin' drop, it was a fuckin' ambush!"

Maserati Meek smiled ironically.

Kip shouted, "You think this shit fuckin' funny?"

"So it was a setup, eh," Maserati Meek said.

"You admitting it, huh? I should blow your fuckin' head off," Kip threatened.

The cocking back of machine guns and pistols were heard. Meek's men were ready for bloodshed, as were Kip's.

"Relax, relax. I didn't know," Maserati Meek said, casually.

Kip was tired of hearing the word *relax*. He wanted to shoot Meek just because of that word. "Don't fuckin' tell me to relax!" he shouted.

"You got balls, Kip, eh. I give you that," Maserati Meek said. "But I didn't set you up. I did not know. The deal was supposed to be legit. It seems we've both been double-crossed. And a question for you: What happened to the men?"

"They're fuckin' dead!"

"Impressive!" Meek said.

Maserati Meek believed his story. He believed all along that Panamanian Pete was up to something. As a drug connect, Maserati Meek carefully looked for new accounts, but he vetted, and if he liked what he saw, then he came to you for business, or he was introduced to someone in a nightclub. Pete calling him out of the blue spooked him, so he used Kip and his crew to do the dirty work.

"Everyone, put your guns down. And, Kip, let's you and I talk, eh. You've done me a great favor, my friend," Meek said.

Maserati Meek was happy to have his merchandise back. The two men talked privately without guns being pointed at each other. Meek still wanted Kip dead, but for now, he would keep him alive. Kip proved that he was a survivor and still reliable.

When the bullshit was explained, and Kip was somewhat satisfied with the explanation, Meek said to him, "I have another job for you."

"What job?" Kip asked.

"I want you to kill Panamanian Pete."

It was a job Kip wasn't too sure of. Besides, unbeknownst to Meek, they were eight hundred grand richer. "I'll have to get back to you on that."

Meek didn't like waiting for an answer. He wanted to know now. Kip was always pushing his limits.

✳✳✳

Panamanian Pete was a tall black male with a powerful build. His fairly cut body filled out the three-piece suit he wore as he sat at the table playing high-stakes poker with a few acquaintances with over a million dollars on the table. Their location was classified, but in the back of a barbershop, a front for drug running. Protected by armed security in every direction, the men talked and laughed.

Pete looked cool and affable at the table, with his gold Rolex peeking from underneath his white cuffed shirt, but he was known to be a brutish muthafucka with notable power. He was arrogant and moved with confidence wherever he went, owning people like he owned buildings.

Soon, a man entered the backroom. He was stopped suddenly by security. He asked to speak to Pete. He came with urgent news.

Pete nodded to the security, allowing the man closer access to him. The man approached urgently Pete's way. He lowered himself to Panamanian Pete and whispered into his ear. Pete's demeanor didn't change at all when he heard about the slaughter of his men in Brooklyn, though among the men killed was his cousin Lance, not to mention the missing $800,000. Pete simply nodded, understanding the verity of the situation. The man was dismissed, and Pete continued playing cards. Inside, he was filled with rage, sorrow, and yearning for vengeance. He sat stoic though.

Maserati Meek had struck first, and now it was war.

TWENTY-NINE

The men divided the cash, each of them receiving a healthy cut. It was enough money to aid some serious issues each man was having in their life. Devon stopped his Expedition in front of the projects. The hour was really late, with dawn soon coming. The block was calm, people were asleep, and the projects were still.

Papa John yawned loudly.

Kip climbed out of the SUV and gave his goons dap. "Tomorrow afternoon," he told them.

They nodded. Devon drove off, leaving Kip alone on the sidewalk, his gun tucked snugly in his waistband.

Kip started to walk toward the building lobby. He was the only soul outside at three in the morning. He could hear his own breathing. As he got closer to the lobby, an eerie feeling came over him. He turned around, only to see Jay P in all black, gunning for him with a .45.

"You bitch-ass nigga!" Jay P shouted.

Boom! Boom! Boom! Boom!

Kip scurried for safety while trying to pull his own gun from his waistband to return fire. Bullets ricocheted everywhere. He made a dash for his building.

Jay P was reckless with it. He fired more wild shots, shattering glass.

Kip felt a sudden sting on his arm. "Ouch!" he shouted. He stumbled.

He was able to return fire, but Jay P was already gone. He had been grazed in the arm, but it hurt like a muthafucka.

***

Kip was able to get himself patched up at Harlem Hospital on Lenox Avenue. While being treated, he received an unwelcome visit from detectives Albright and Yang. They had heard about the shooting and came to chat with him.

Kip scowled at their presence, having nothing to say to them. They tried to grill him on the shooting, wanting him to give a name, but he remained tight-lipped. Tired of the harassment, he let the detectives know how he felt about them. Once again, they had nothing and were forced to leave.

Devon and Papa John were already aware of the shooting, and they rushed to the hospital. Kip told them to wait outside. He didn't want their faces seen inside the hospital.

Finally released from the hospital in the early hours of the morning, Kip climbed into the back seat of the Expedition, and they rushed home. Kip was extremely worried about his brother. He needed to move Kid. Their apartment was no longer safe. They discussed what happened, and each man thought the failed hit had come on Maserati Meek's orders. Meek didn't believe a word they'd said, and probably figured out they had stolen the money.

All three men went up to Kip's apartment with their guns drawn and ready for anything. Kip cautiously put his keys into the lock and pushed the door open, expecting a gunfight, but there was nothing. The place was still and quiet. He rushed toward Kid's bedroom with his gun still in hand and pushed open the door, only to find his brother still sleeping.

"Kid, wake up! Wake up!" Kip said, rousing his brother from his sound sleep.

Kid finally woke up, looking disoriented for a moment. The sun was still new in the sky and percolating through his bedroom window. He lifted his upper half from the bed, propped up on his hands, and quickly took in that something was wrong when he saw Devon and Papa John and the bandage around Kip's left arm.

"Oh shit! What happened to you?" he asked fearfully.

"I got shot."

"Shot?!"

"I ain't got time to explain what happened. We need to go," Kip said sternly.

"What? Go where?"

"I ain't got time to explain shit to you, Kid. Just pack some things into a small bag and let's go."

Kid looked agitated and almost reluctant. He knew Kip wasn't taking no for an answer. He packed a few things, including his chess set and his game systems, into an overnight bag. They were going to stay at an Extended Stay America hotel in Mount Vernon for a few weeks. The hotel had kitchenettes and was quite a distance from Harlem. Kip felt his brother would be safer there, and Kid didn't object.

The men left the apartment. No one knew how long they would be gone. With war escalating, everyone's lives were about to get a lot more dramatic and dangerous.

At the Extended Stay hotel, Kip helped his brother get unpacked, and then he dropped the duffel bag filled with cash onto the bed. He unzipped it, showing his brother what was inside.

Kid was in awe. Kid knew one thing for sure: However Kip attained that large amount of cash, it was done illegally, and most likely, someone had ended up dead.

"Kid, if anything happens to me, I need you to take care of this," Kip said. "Keep this safe."

Kid said, "Don't talk like that, Kip. Whatever happened, whatever you did, we gonna get through this. We always do."

Kip wasn't so sure. A lot of shit had gone down, and there was a lot of heat on the streets. A war had started, and many men were going to die.

Kip zipped up the duffel bag and shoved it under the bed. He tucked his pistol into his waistband and prepared to leave. With Kid hidden safely in a hotel in Mount Vernon, he felt okay. He stared at his little brother before he walked out and smiled.

"Just be careful out there, Kip. Please."

"I will."

All was forgiven between the brothers. The fight they'd had was long behind them. Kid couldn't lose him; Kip was the only family he had.

Kid sat in his wheelchair and just stared at the door, wondering if his brother would walk through it again.

***

Kip made the trip upstate to see his Nana once more. It was early morning when he knocked on her door, and she answered in her usual attire. She had a chronic cough and looked fatigued. Kip hated to see his Nana in such poor condition. But he had something that was going to cheer her up.

He closed her door and walked toward her bed with an overnight bag in hand. He dropped the bag on her bed. He hugged and kissed his Nana on her cheeks. "I got something for you, Nana. You gonna be okay." He unzipped the overnight bag and showed her the cash inside—one hundred thousand dollars for her treatment and medication.

Nana was flabbergasted by the amount of money on her bed. She had never seen so much cash before. Her eyes lit up brightly like Times Square at night.

"Holy shit!"

"I told you, Nana, don't worry 'bout anything. I was gonna get you that money."

She wondered how he got it. Did someone die for this amount of money? She picked up a ten-thousand-dollar stack and gazed at it like it was exotic. "Kip . . . how?"

"Nana, don't worry about how I got it. I just got it for you to get better and live."

Kip was in a rush and couldn't stay long. He hugged and kissed his Nana again and left her small apartment.

Nana started removing the stacks of cash and placing it on her bed. She counted it; it was all there—$100,000. Kip never failed to impress her. She then picked up her phone and called Curtis. When he answered, she boasted, "Guess what, baby? I got you your money."

"I knew you wouldn't let me down, Rhonda. I'll come get you in about an hour. We'll go out to eat and celebrate." He hung up.

THIRTY

Eshon sat in the comfort of her bathtub, soaking in the warm waters with soft bubbles. She was hassle-free and calm for the moment. She had scented candles burning and a glass of white wine close by, enjoying the perfect scenery she created for herself. She felt enchanted tonight, feeling great to be in her own world.

She sang along in perfect harmony to one of her favorite tracks, "Part II (On the Run)" by Beyoncé and Jay Z.

She was always thinking about Kip. Every love song, every breakup song, or just another sad love song, for her, was about Kip. Every word sung was about him and their relationship, their love life forever on repeat on the radio.

Eshon shed a few tears just thinking about the ups and downs with Kip, wondering if he would ever love her like she loved him. There was no hesitation when it came to loving him, and she let it clearly be known how strongly she felt about him. She wanted marriage and kids with Kip, and whether it was a life of crime with him or a life of stability with a family and a nine-to-five, she would be there.

Eshon lingered in the tub for about an hour, drowning in love and heartbreak simultaneously. She finished her wine and wiped away a few more tears. She stood up from the tub, stepped out, and toweled off while looking at her image in the bathroom mirror. What she saw was extraordinary, and she hated to be conceited. What was there not to like about her curvy figure, perky tits, round chestnut-colored eyes, full lips, and soft skin? She could easily become a singer or a model, or maybe both. Eshon knew she was a great catch, and while every nigga in Harlem was chasing and yearning for her, she didn't give them the time of day, because she believed wholeheartedly in what she had with Kip. Some might say she was delusional.

She tied the towel around her body and knotted it. Stepping out the bathroom and into her bedroom, she noticed she had several missed calls and a few voice messages, including texts. Immediately, she knew something was up. Brandy had called her four times, and a few other home girls had reached out. There was a text from Brandy, saying: URGENT, CALL ME BACK.

Eshon wasted no time calling her back. Brandy's phone rang twice before she answered, saying to Eshon, "You ain't heard?"

"Heard what?" Eshon asked, trepidation slowly building inside of her.

"Kip got shot last night."

Eshon immediately went blank. She thought she'd heard her friend wrong. It had to be a joke, but Brandy wouldn't joke like that.

"What?" She was scared to ask if he was alive or not. Her heart fluttered with fear, not wanting to hear the worst, but she needed to know. "Brandy, is he dead?" she asked, her voice quivering with apprehension.

"He went to Harlem Hospital, but they say he's okay."

Eshon felt like she herself had just escaped death row. "What happened?" she asked.

"He got shot in the arm. I thought you knew."

"I didn't. Is he still in the hospital?" Eshon didn't know it, but her body was already dressing, and she was ready to rush to his aid.

"I don't know, but it was over some beef wit' some nigga."

Eshon was fully dressed; she had set a record for dressing. She then flew out the door like a flash of lightning and hurried to Kip's apartment. Once there, she knocked several times, but there was no answer. She knocked again. Again, no answer. She sighed and took a seat on the ground. She was worried about Kip. Was he still in the hospital? She doubted it. He had gotten shot in the arm; it couldn't be that serious. She knew Kip had to be out there looking for revenge on the man who'd shot him. It was in his character.

***

Devon smoked a blunt while sitting shotgun in his own vehicle. Papa John drove, and Kip sat in the backseat clutching a black 12-gauge pump shotgun, itching to use the fully loaded weapon against Jay P. Kip was looking for him, and anyone working or associated with him was a dead man too. He wanted to blow Jay P's head off, and Maserati Meek's too. No more Mr. Nice Guy.

They drove to Long Island and went to both of Maserati Meek's stash houses, but both houses had been abandoned.

"Muthafuckas is running from us because they know we comin' fo' that ass," Devon exclaimed.

Kip had no words. They all believed Meek had left the houses, and probably left town, because of the failed hit on Kip, who was grateful that Jay P had poor aim. And Maserati Meek's cell phone was off.

But they had no idea that Meek was in hiding, and in Mafia terms, "going to the mattresses" because of the sudden conflict with Panamanian Pete. Maserati Meek was at war with a man just as powerful, resourceful, and deadly as himself. And Pete didn't take kindly to losing his cousin and $800,000 in cash.

***

Panamanian Pete thought it was a petty robbery, and that his cousin's murder was uncalled for. Why would Maserati Meek do something so stupid? Why would he risk both organizations going to war over $800,000, when they both had more money than they could count? What was Meek's goal? Panamanian Pete planned on asking Meek that before he beheaded him for violating him, his family, and his organization in the worst way.

✳✳✳

The entire night, Kip and his crew drove around the city, going from borough to borough, looking for Jay P, going to locations he was known to frequent, but there was no sign of him or of anyone connected to him.

The next day it was the same thing, hunting urgently for Jay P or anyone close to him. Four days passed, and Jay P was nowhere to be seen. He seemed to have vanished into thin air.

THIRTY-ONE

Jay P slept like a baby next to his naked whore. After some intense sex, he was spent. It was the middle of the night, and he didn't hear a sound where he laid his head. After shooting Kip in the arm, missing his target completely and fucking things up, he had to leave town immediately. He didn't trust anyone, and he knew there would be a price on his head. He went north, to Connecticut, where he stayed in a cheap rental in West Haven. He kept things low-key, paid for everything in cash, and left his entire identity back in New York. In West Haven, he was Mitchell from Albany. He had gotten a fake ID, always carried around his Ruger .9mm, and did his best to stay out of trouble. His only weakness was pussy. He'd spent a week in West Haven and frequented a strip club in New Haven called The Bottom, where he met Star, and she became his freak of the week.

Something suddenly woke Jay P out of his peaceful sleep. The room was dark and quiet. His stripper, Star, was wrapped around him intimately, still asleep. Jay P felt like some kind of entity was in the room with him. He pulled himself from the woman's naked body and looked around the darkness, feeling a bit of paranoia overcoming him. His Ruger .9mm was on the nightstand, but still a tad out of his reach.

He sat there on the bed, one leg propped on the mattress, the other on the floor. Then something caught his eye in the shadows of the room—a man. Jay P knew it wasn't a friend. He lunged for his pistol, but a bullet quickly tore through his leg. It came from a .9mm with a suppressor at the end of it.

Jay P dropped to the floor, bleeding and immobile.

The man dressed in black stepped closer to his victim.

Jay P stared up at him in awe and whispered, "I know you."

The man in black aimed his gun at Jay P's head.

Jay P pleaded for his life. "Please . . . don't do this."

The man fired three times at Jay P's head and completely disfigured his cranium with large holes. Jay P's body slumped in a pool of crimson.

Star, awakened by the commotion, was wide-eyed with terror and about to scream.

The man trained his gun on her. "You scream, you die."

"I don't wanna die," she murmured, panic in her voice.

He glared at Star. He was only there for Jay P, not her, but she had seen his face. He locked eyes with the naked woman and said, "I'm sorry."

"No!"

Pwoot! Pwoot!

He put one in her head and chest, and she lay there dead. He couldn't take any chances.

***

Two days later, Jay P's naked, bullet-riddled body was found in a park in Queens with half his head blown off. Someone had taken a razor and carved the word *war* into Jay P's chest. A man walking his dog came across the gruesome sight in the early morning and immediately called 911.

The news quickly spread through the Tri-State. It was believed that Jay P was killed by one of Panamanian Pete's men in retaliation for the death of his cousin and his missing $800,000.

***

Kip held Eshon in his arms as they lay in his bed, naked and chilling comfortably after two hours of passionate sex. She wanted to be held by him forever. Seeing Kip alive and in good health, she was able to breathe again. But for how long would she breathe freely until something else came up? But Eshon didn't want to think about that. She wanted to enjoy Kip, his body, his kisses, his everything. It had been a breathtaking evening for her. For them. She and Kip went at it like they would never see each other again. She kissed every part of him, and she felt him so strongly when he came, it almost felt like her soul had lifted from her body for a second.

She toyed with his chest and rubbed her leg against his fine physique. She kissed his lips softly, looked into his eyes and uttered the words, "I love you."

He looked at her, exhaled, and said, "I love you too."

Eshon almost jumped up with joy. Her pussy throbbed. She truly didn't expect that from him. Was Kip finally seeing the light with her? Was he changing? This had to be the best day of her life.

"I don't want to lose you, Kip," she said, as they stared into each other's eyes.

"Where I'm gonna go?"

"This life you live, Kip, do you ever think—"

"Eshon, don't even think like that. You know this is me, what I do, and you've been riding wit' me for the longest. So don't act like you brand new to this shit."

"I know, but—"

"But what? What you think this is? *The Cosby Show*? You Claire and I'm Cliff? You know what my reality is, and how I survive out here."

"But you got shot."

"And I got stabbed, arrested, and shot before. I'm a thug, Eshon, and if you want a normal fuckin' life, then you meet a normal fuckin' man. I'm not that."

And just like that, his saying "I love you too" to her went to shit in a heartbeat.

Just then, Kip's cell phone rang. He reached over to answer it. It was Papa John calling him. "Yo," he answered.

"I got news for you, nigga," Papa John said, sounding a little upbeat.

"What is it?"

"They found Jay P."

Kip lit up from the news. "Where he at?"

"He dead in Queens," Papa John said.

"What?"

"They found his body fucked up—three shots to his head and the word *war* carved into his chest."

"Shit."

"Yeah, so he ain't a threat anymore."

Kip felt somewhat ambivalent by the news. The nigga was dead, but he'd wanted to light him up himself with the shotgun and crack his fuckin' head open. Was Meek cleaning house? Or was it some other gangsters at play? Either way, they could cross one more enemy off the list. What were the odds?

Kip removed himself from the bed.

"You leaving?" Eshon asked him.

"I got shit to do," he said, being short with her.

Eshon got an attack of separation anxiety, fearing that, once he was gone, he would never come back.

Kip left the hotel room, and all Eshon could do was wait and hope he would be fine.

***

Two men, both armed with automatics holstered underneath their denim vests, exited a brownstone in East New York, Brooklyn carrying a black bag on a warm, cloudless night in Brooklyn. The brownstone was one of Maserati Meek's stash houses for drugs and cash; it was where he supplied the area with coke and dope, and the cash collected from the streets went there to be picked up by one of his collectors.

The block was active with Bloods, but the location was a sanctuary for his goods coming and going. Everyone knew not to try anything with the house. The wrong look that way or a slow walk in front of the building could mean death. Residents minded their business and looked the other way when obvious drug activity was taking place.

It was a scary place for the innocent, but even a scarier place for any man looking to make a quick come-up. The place was fortified with steel doors and surveillance cameras everywhere, along with lookouts on the block, not to mention the killers inside.

The two men, Cold and Harold, approached a silver Lexus, where the driver waited for them to come out. His head swiveled as he did his best to observe his surroundings, looking cautiously for any potential threats. A hundred thousand dollars was being collected from the place. Business was good, and heroin sales were up. Way up.

Both men stepped foot on the sidewalk, and from both directions, everything was clear. There were a few Bloods lingering at the corner of the block, flaunting their red bandanas.

While the men were walking toward the vehicle, an adolescent boy appeared on the block riding a bicycle. The two men glanced his way and thought nothing of him. He neared the silver Lexus, and as he passed nearby, he tossed a small object into the car and sped off.

Caught off guard, the driver searched for the item desperately, only to find that it was a grenade without the pin. Wide-eyed at the sight of it, he uttered, "Oh shit!" and frantically tried to flee the car, but it was too late.

DIRTY WORK - PART ONE

BOOOM!

The explosion shook the car violently, blowing out the windows and twisting the car metal. The driver was instantly killed, his body contorted inside the warped wreck.

The explosion, heard for blocks, threw Cold and Harold backward and off their feet. As they quickly collected themselves, rising to their feet and removing their weapons, a shadowy figure emerged from the side of the brownstone and opened fire on them with a submachine gun, killing them instantly.

The killer quickly picked up the dropped bag of cash and jumped into a stopping black BMW. The BMW took off, leaving Maserati Meek's three men completely destroyed. It was payback from Panamanian Pete.

THIRTY-TWO

Loon, a trusted lieutenant in Meek's organization, cruised through the streets of Hempstead, Long Island with an arsenal of weapons inside the trunk of his Accord. On high alert, he kept his .380 close, along with an MP5K. Things were tense since Panamanian Pete had struck back with vengeance.

***

The other day, Brooklyn detectives had found a charred body in the trunk of a car. It was one of Meek's men—captured, tortured, shot, and then burned alive inside the car. Meek and his organization started to feel the effects. It seemed like Panamanian Pete and his goons were everywhere, trying to hit Meek where it hurt—his pockets.

In two weeks, Meek had lost over a million dollars in cash and product, five of his men were dead, and one of his places was destroyed. The five boroughs had become too dangerous, so Maserati Meek and his men went into hiding at a secured warehouse in Long Island. Meek surrounded himself with men and guns and ran his business from there, sending messengers to talk for him and do his dirty work. He didn't trust cell phones. He didn't like talking on them, especially when it came to murders and drugs. If it wasn't a face-to-face, where he was secure and could look a man in the eyes, then he wasn't with it.

Meek knew that information was power, and he was willing to go to any limits to pay for any information regarding Panamanian Pete, his family, and his men. He had duffel bags filled with cash, and he had put the word out.

Soon enough, information about Panamanian Pete and his peoples started to pour in. Meek found out that Panamanian Pete's older brother Mike was staying at an unassuming apartment near the bus station on Main Street in Hempstead with his wife and kids. Mike wasn't a criminal like his kingpin brother, but had worked in transit for ten years and was a law-abiding citizen. Meek didn't care; he put out the hit and sent his killers to retaliate for the brother's sins.

***

The day was clear and sunny when Loon came to a stop in front of the five-story brick building. He had an address, a picture, and a motive. His lips pulled on a Newport, and then it went flying out the window. Evening time was approaching, meaning people would soon be on their way home from work, creating rush-hour traffic. Loon sat coolly across the street from the building. He just had to wait, be patient, and then create hell when it was time.

***

Two hours later, a white Civic parked on the street, near the building, and a man in his early forties climbed out with his two children, ages five and ten. Loon watched the man in his work uniform grab a few things from the backseat of his car and proceed toward his residence.

It was time for Loon to make his move. He donned a black ski mask and picked up the MP5K, cocked it back, and got out the car with urgency. He kept his eyes stuck on his target and hurried his way. He lifted the submachine gun in the victim's direction, and when Mike finally noticed the threat looming his way, he stood wide-eyed and almost frozen with fear. He was holding his little girl's hand when the gunman opened fire on him.

Over a dozen rounds instantly slammed into the man's chest and torso, his grip around his daughter's hand released instantly, as he was violently gunned down. His body was lifted from the pavement and then crashed right back against it.

When the gunfire finally ceased, the kids were heard screaming from the top of their lungs. Their father was dead, his blood spilling all over the sidewalk, his torso deformed with bullets.

Loon quickly retreated, his mission accomplished.

***

Detectives Albright and Yang stepped into the room with the witness. She sat silent and afraid. They had finally tracked down the woman from Club Revolt, the one who was with Jason Miller the night of the shooting. She had dyed her hair from brunette to blonde and gone to Boston after the incident, afraid for her life. Albright and Yang were relentless in finding the shooter and bringing him or them to justice. The security footage from the club had finally been released, no thanks to the owner's reluctance and his lawyers putting up a wall behind him. But Albright got his warrant for the security footage at Club Revolt and went through it meticulously, looking at every minute of it. He found out that Kip was in the club that night. Albright and Yang knew they needed more evidence on Kip. His attendance at the nightclub would simply be considered circumstantial evidence during litigation. They needed more, such as a witness to place Kip as the shooter.

Both detectives sat across from Kimberly Bush. She was beautiful, with nice curves, and a nervous smile.

Albright placed a cup of coffee in front of her and said, "You'll be okay."

"I don't know anything, detectives," she said.

"We just want to talk, that's all," he replied calmly, not wanting to spook her or push her too far.

Yang chimed, "We just want to know what happened that night."

"I had a good time, and then I left," she said.

Albright said, "But you see, security footage shows you leaving the club with Jason Miller the same night, and moments later, he's robbed and shot. We simply want to put the man behind this behind bars for a very long time. And we need your help. We just want you to look at some pictures and point out the man who attacked and robbed y'all."

Several sheets of men's mug shots were placed in front of Kimberly. She still looked reluctant, but that night had haunted her for weeks, and many nights she couldn't sleep.

Although Albright and Yang weren't the primary investigators on the Miller shooting, they took the initiative to investigate it on their own. Albright had been after Kip for a long time now. He knew if he got something on Kip, the dominoes would start to fall.

Kimberly stared at the mug shots. She went through quite a few photos until she saw the shooter—Kip. His mug shot was scary, his eyes intense. She stared at the picture, her heart beating fast. Exhaling with uneasiness, she pointed to his photo and uttered the words both men had been waiting to hear for a long time.

"That's him!" she said.

"Number seven?" Yang asked her.

She nodded.

Both men smiled.

"We need you to circle and initial the picture," Albright said.

She took his pen, circled the photo, and initialed her name next to it.

Detectives Albright and Yang felt that they finally had their man.

**

After the death of his older brother Mike, Panamanian Pete went no holds barred on Maserati Meek's drug organization. Two of Meek's soldiers were decapitated, their heads left on display on the street.

Then a week after that, they hunted down Nia, his main girl, and tortured her. They recorded the entire incident and sent it to Meek. She had suffered for hours. They beat her tirelessly, shot her in the head, and left her body in the city dump for Sanitation to find.

Nia's murder hit Maserati Meek hard. Everyone close to him was being hunted down, but fortunately, his family wasn't in the States but in Egypt.

Maserati Meek needed reinforcement, and though he hated to ask, he needed Kip's help. He needed the extra manpower, and the man's adept skills to hunt and kill a man.

THIRTY-THREE

Kip thought, *the audacity of Maserati Meek, reaching out to me to help fight his war.* The man had put out a hit on him, a failed hit, and now he was asking for his help. Did he think they were fools?

Kip, Papa John, and Devon were outraged, and they were ready to part ways with him for good. Devon had been itching to kill him anyway.

One of Meek's men had reached out to Kip and gave him an address for the meeting. Meek wanted to have a direct talk with Kip, to work something out with him and his crew. Kip agreed to the meeting, but he was coming for warfare.

The following day, an hour before they were to meet with Maserati Meek, all four men, including Maniac, put on Kevlar vests then loaded bullets into several machine guns and automatic pistols. They were ready for war. This was it, feeling like the final battle.

Kip had been through hell before, but going against Meek was a troubling thing, knowing the man was going to have a wall of men protecting him.

Devon drove his Expedition, Kip rode in the front, and his other two cronies were in the back. The ride to Long Island was silent. Each man entertained their own thoughts as they cruised on the Cross Island Parkway. It was a new address, and there was no time to scout the location. Like the meeting at the abandoned factory near the Brooklyn Bridge, they had to wing it. They'd come this far and weren't backing down.

With the sun completely set, Devon navigated his SUV toward the meeting place in Baldwin Harbor. Quiet and out the way from homes and businesses, and the freeway, he parked on a barren street near an empty park.

Maserati Meek was already present, sitting in the backseat of his SUV, waiting patiently for Kip to arrive. He came with five men, each one heavily armed with machine guns and bad attitudes. Both vehicles sat parked opposite each other, but in a straight line parallel to the park.

Devon killed the headlights. "How we gonna do this?"

Kip sighed. He was never someone to back down from a fight, even if he was outnumbered, or if the person was bigger, or maybe stronger. There had been minor moments of peace in his life, but the majority of his twenty-two years on earth had been a battle with the streets, life, and himself. He thought about his brother, Nana, and even Eshon. He would always do for those he loved, even if it meant risking his own life.

He clutched the submachine gun and stared intently at the black Escalade Maserati Meek sat in. How could they do this and not lose their lives? Kip had a plan. His cronies depended on him, so he couldn't let them down, no matter how bleak the situation looked.

"Y'all niggas ready?" he asked them.

They all were, especially Devon, looking like a pit bull ready to be unleashed.

Kip swore he heard him snarl. "Just be cool, Devon."

"I'm cool. I'm good," Devon replied, his voice brimming with excitement.

"Just follow my lead, and let's be smart wit' this nigga," Kip said. "He ain't no off-brand nigga, remember that."

The doors opened, and all four men climbed out of the SUV wearing war paint, their expressions manifesting their hate and distrust.

Maserati Meek exited the Escalade and smiled at Kip and his crew.

"My niggas, eh! Why the guns? Why the hostility toward an old friend, Kip? I come in peace."

Kip didn't find him funny. Gun-toting henchmen flanked Meek. Kip took one step toward Meek, and then unexpectedly, chaos happened.

Devon couldn't control himself. The sight of Maserati Meek ignited him with rage. He raised his Heckler and let loose on his foes, and a hail of bullets went flying the enemies' way.

Meek's men returned gunfire, and everyone scattered, shooting at each other. Meek took safety behind the SUV, while his men went to battle with Kip and his crew.

Rat-a-tat-tat-tat-tat-tat!

Bratatat! Bratatat! Bratatat! Bratatat! Bratatat!

The block sounded like Syria as the night was lit up with intense gunfire from machine guns.

Two of Meek's men went down from body shots.

Devon was the devil that night, possessed like a hellspawn, with a murderous rage that fueled a complete bloodshed. "Fuck y'all muthafuckas! Fuck y'all!" he screamed madly.

Bullets slammed into the vehicles and ricocheted off the concrete, and somehow, Maniac and Devon were crazy enough to drive Maserati Meek and his men back. Impervious to death, they moved like they were made of Teflon from head to toe.

Rat-a-tat-tat-tat-tat-tat!

Meek rushed into his Escalade and managed to speed away from the craziness. He had come to talk, but Kip and his crew had other plans.

Devon continued to release hellfire at them but then fumed that Meek had gotten away. "Fuck!"

Papa John cried out, "Oh shit! Kip!"

Devon spun towards his friend's howling. What he saw nearly took the life out of him. Kip was down, shot in the neck and bleeding profusely.

Devon and Maniac rushed to Kip's aid. His eyes were still open, but he couldn't move. He was choking on his own blood.

"C'mon, my nigga, don't die on us! C'mon, nigga, not like this ... not like this!" Devon cried out.

"Kip, you good, nigga. We gotta go!" Papa John shouted, tears welling from his eyes. He tried to lift his friend, but Kip was in grave shape.

It couldn't be. They stood crouched around him, panicking as their friend's life faded. Almost immediately, he was dead.

"We gotta go!" Maniac hollered.

Devon and Papa John couldn't leave him. They didn't want to leave him. It had to be a nightmare. They wanted to wake up from it, but it was real. Kip's body lay dead in front of them, his blood staining the ground with crimson.

Maniac shouted, "He's dead! We need to go!"

Reluctantly, they piled into the Expedition and sped away, leaving Kip's body behind. They had to leave him. If not, then they were looking at jail time, and there was no way they would be able to avenge his death from behind bars.

THIRTY-FOUR

Kid sprung up suddenly out of his sleep, sweating profusely and breathing hard. It was late, and the room was lifeless and silent. He needed to catch his breath.

He'd had a dream that both he and Kip were in the park playing chess on a sunny day. Kip continually kept knocking over the King piece. Each time Kid picked it up, Kip knocked it back down. Frustrated, Kip wanted to tell Kid something. His mouth kept moving, but Kid couldn't understand what he was trying to say. He couldn't hear him in the dream.

Suddenly, it turned dark with rain clouds. Kid looked past Kip, and several gunmen came out of nowhere and opened fire.

Then the dream took them to a lake. Both he and Kip were young boys in a fishing boat. Kip was smiling and focusing on catching a fish, while Kid was nervous of the vast, deep water. Kip looked up and said something incoherent to his brother.

Next, Kip jumped in the water and continually asked Kid to join him. Kid told his brother he can't swim, and Kip motioned him to come in.

Suddenly Kip began to drown. Kid reached his hand out to save his brother, but he slipped from his grasp and went under.

Kid squirmed toward his chair and slid into it. He felt such sadness inside of him, the tears came soon after.

Before long, there was a knock at the door, and Kid wheeled himself to answer it.

Devon and Papa John walked into the Extended Stay hotel room, but there was no Kip. The two men stared at Kid with forlorn faces, not knowing how to tell him that his only family and caretaker had just been murdered. They stood in front of him looking and feeling guilty.

But Kid already knew. His tears were already pooling down the sides of his face. His pain was showing. He looked at both men gloomily. "He's dead, right?"

Devon and Papa John stood silent for a moment, still unable to answer. The two thugs began to tear up, and for them to cry, especially Devon, the truth was there. Papa John nodded.

"He came to me in my dream. He was trying to tell me something, something he felt I needed to know," Kid told them.

Both men were baffled by his comment. It was the saddest day of their lives.

Kid looked away for a moment and wiped the tears from his eyes. He then collected himself. "Who did it, and why? I want to know everything."

Kid listened intently as Papa John went into detail about everything, first saying to him that it was Maserati Meek who murdered his brother, that there was a shootout and Kip died with a gunshot wound to his neck. He then explained how Kip came up with the idea to rob money from the drop. He talked about Maserati Meek and how he could never be trusted. Papa John brought up Jay P and the failed hit, the murders they did, the money. He didn't hold anything back. He felt that he owed it to Kid to tell the whole truth.

"Kip died in war," Papa John stated.

Kid sat there listening with an expressionless look, taking it all in. His brother lived a thug's life to the fullest. It was no shock to him, though. Kip took plenty of risks, but at the end, it cost him his life.

"We gonna find Maserati Meek, Kid, and we gonna body that nigga. I promise you that," Devon finally spoke. And it was a promise he planned on keeping. "It might take some time, 'cuz that nigga got an army and now he's on point. But sit tight; we got this."

Suddenly, Kid stood up tall and healthy on both his legs, balled his fingers into a tight fist, and slammed it into the wall, creating a gaping hole.

"What the fuck, yo!" they exclaimed together.

Devon asked with bewilderment, "Nigga, you can stand?"

"Kid, what kind of freak shit is this?"

"Kid, you need to tell us somethin'. Start talkin', man, 'cuz"—Devon shook his head quickly—"I'm fuckin' freakin' right now."

"I'll explain later, but now, we hunt down the man that murdered my brother and we make him pay. I want him and everything close to him to suffer," Kid said.

Devon and Papa John stared at him in a trance. Just a moment ago, he was a disabled, chess-playing nerd who read books and played video games. Listening to him talk, they figured his brother's death had momentarily made him go crazy.

"Kid, what are you talkin' 'bout? You ain't built for this shit," Devon said. "Trust me, bruh."

Kid shot back, "Don't tell me what I'm built for, Devon. You have no fuckin' clue who I am and what I'm about."

"We lost Kip. We not tryin' to lose you too," Papa John said.

"Don't worry about me; I know how to handle mine. This entire time y'all thought y'all were looking out for me, I was the one looking out for y'all—especially Kip."

Both men were clueless. He definitely was going crazy. Maybe that's how he was able to walk, by going crazy.

Kid asked, "Y'all remember Uncle Junior and his peoples?"

Devon nodded. "What about them?"

"That's my handiwork."

Suddenly Kid had the attention of Devon and Papa John.

"Uncle Junior was a threat to my brother, and like every other threat before and after him, they needed to go."

"You killed Uncle Junior?" Papa John asked.

"Outside the lobby of his building in Marcy Projects, him and two other niggas," Kid said. "And there was Jay P in Connecticut and many others. I tried my best to protect my brother. This is my fault. I should have bodied Meek a long time ago."

When Devon asked why he remained in the wheelchair, Kid replied, "Because who would ever suspect anyone in a wheelchair?"

Kid had always planned on telling his brother that he could walk, but as time went on, he procrastinated more and more. Kid felt the day of his accident had brought them even closer together, and that Kip enjoyed being his caretaker.

Kid had started walking again five years earlier. The doctors had said his condition was permanent, but they were wrong. He did suffer from a critical spinal injury, but it wasn't damaging enough. Therapy did help some, but his will to walk again helped him even more. Each day was a battle until finally, he could feel his toes, then his feet and shins, and he moved each piece of him slowly but surely.

Kid told Devon and Papa John everything, leaving both men in utter shock. He had been playing possum the entire time.

And with the snap of his fingers, he stepped right into his brother's shoes and became the boss. Papa John and Devon were able to look past the nerd glasses, the wheelchair, and his intelligent speech, and see a cold-blooded, calculating killer who puts in dirty work.

Kid told them, "The moment my brother is buried, the pain will begin."

DIRTY WORK - PART ONE

✳✳✳

The news of Kip's death was crushing and heartrending for Eshon. She didn't want to believe it at first. He couldn't be dead. He had just survived a shooting the other day, they had sex, and he finally said the words *I love you* to her. But when the truth really hit her, hearing the details of his murder, how he was gunned down in the street, she immediately had a panic attack. She couldn't breathe. She couldn't do anything but hyperventilate with her chest feeling like it was about to cave in. She felt faint, sick, and nauseous, trembling uncontrollably. They had to call 911.

Eshon's tears came like a giant flood in her eyes. She couldn't stop crying. She couldn't do anything but grieve. She didn't want to live herself. She couldn't bear living without him, not seeing him ever again. She wanted to marry him and have his kids, but now that dream was destroyed.

✳✳✳

Kip's wake was at Benita's Funeral Home on St. Nicholas Avenue. Many people came to pay their respects and to view his body one last time. He was dressed immaculately in a slim fit, gray virgin wool and silk three-piece suit by Hugo Boss. His body was lying in an ebony black 18-gauge steel casket. There were dozens of flowers surrounding his casket and a picture of Kip three years prior. He was all smiles, wearing a blue Yankees fitted cap and a gold chain, looking like a gangsta.

Kip's funeral was held at Trinity Cemetery on Broadway. It was a warm, sunny Friday in June. Over two dozen people were gathered around the casket at the burial site, including Kid, Devon, Papa John, and Eshon.

Eshon wore a black dress and dark shades. It had been the roughest week of her life, and things were about to get rougher for her. She didn't know if she could go through with seeing him dead in the casket and watching them put his body into the ground, but she had to be there to say goodbye and kiss him one last time.

Brandy stood next to her friend, and though she was in grief too, she was there to console Eshon.

There wasn't a dry eye around. Everyone was grieving and in pain. Though Kip was a thug and gangsta, he was definitely loved.

Each man was dressed in a suit and tie, and they were mournful. Kid hid his tears behind dark sunglasses. He sat in his wheelchair still pretending to be crippled. There was going to be hell to pay for his brother's death.

The preacher said, "Those we love don't go away, they still walk beside us every day, unseen, unheard, but always near, still loved, and still missed, and very dear. But God is here, and our pain will be short-lived. The kingdom of Heaven will forever give peace where we will find comfort in Jesus. Amen."

While the burial was underway, Nana arrived late, looking swanky in a black dress and shoes. She had climbed out the cab and clutched her cane. She frowned at the gate of the cemetery. She didn't want to attend his funeral at all. When she heard the news about Kip, what hurt her most was the loss of financial support.

She had been crying for days, not for Kip but over the breakup. Curtis had left her. Once he had his hands on the $100,000, he was no longer heard from again. He had left town with his younger girlfriend.

Now with no money, no Kip, no Curtis, Nana was worried about her future. What was she going to do? Who would pay her rent? How long would she be able to stay in the retirement community? Nana felt like she was becoming sick for real this time.

She walked into the cemetery and observed everyone from a distance. She could see Kid in his wheelchair, among friends, and grieving by his brother's casket. She had no intention of speaking to him. She had no intention of paying full respect since she had the cab waiting on the street. She showed up just to save face with the brother, and then turned around and left.

Kid noticed her quick arrival and departure. He kept his anger concealed. He would deal with her in due time.

Also missing was Jessica. Kid looked around for her, but she was nowhere in sight. That angered him too. She had made up an excuse not to come. But after everything Kip had done for her, helping her get money, there was no excuse. She should have been at his brother's funeral.

But Jessica was a no-show because she was afraid that Maserati Meek might have eyes on Kip's funeral, and she didn't want to risk being seen there. She didn't want Meek to know that she knew Kip.

When the caretakers started to lower Kip's casket into the ground, Eshon burst out a thunderous cry and screamed. Eshon fell to her knees in heartache and trembled. She wanted to sing at his funeral, but she didn't have the strength or composure. She was a mess. Her tears seemed never-ending, and Brandy did her best to console her.

Papa John and Devon had to help her to her feet and escort her to the car.

Kid shed tears behind his shades. He remained poised, although he felt a mixture of feelings. He took a deep breath, dried away his tears, and kept his eyes on the casket until it was no longer visible.

He tossed a black chess king into the grave, a promise to his brother that his death would be avenged. It was a new day for him and the city. Kid had been reborn. He wasn't a kid anymore—Tragic events had fast-forwarded him into a cold, vengeful man.

THIRTY-FIVE

Though Kid Kane missed Harlem and his home, he felt it wasn't time to go back yet. He felt secure and safe in Mount Vernon at the Extended Stay hotel, the last place he'd seen his brother alive. He had a hundred thousand dollars in cash, thanks to Kip, and he had set up shop there. His days of playing chess in St. Nicholas Park were gone now. He was now the boss. He was smart, and he was provoked into taking Maserati Meek down piece by piece, brick by brick. He had a plan and a crew to help implement his plan.

To everyone else, including Eshon, Brandy, and Jessica, he was still a nerdy cripple—a helpless, grieving little brother. But to Papa John, Devon, Maniac, and other recruits in his growing organization, Kid had transformed into something a lot more sinister.

Devon wanted to take off Maserati Meek's head, but Kid was against it, saying that he wanted to make him suffer. Devon and Papa John didn't see why they should keep him alive, but Kid Kane had the same philosophy as his brother: One way to kill a man and still leave him alive is to take away everything he loves and has. You start by the feet and work your way up to the head, and Meek would see himself falling apart. Kid knew what it felt like to feel crippled and helpless, unable to walk, body falling apart. It was a distressing feeling.

Maserati Meek was about to fight two wars, one with Panamanian Pete and a stealthy war with Kid. And Meek would soon see himself unraveling slowly.

First thing was surveillance, stalking and infiltrating his organization. Information and knowledge were power. Kid wanted to know everything about Meek. He wanted to know what time of the day the man took a shit, where he lay his head, all about his family and any friends, what his favorite food was, what his biggest fears were. Kid wanted to feel attached to Maserati Meek's hip, to think like the man and know his every move before he even thought of it.

Kid sat in his wheelchair in the hotel room. He had transformed the area into a war room, equipped with computers, pictures of foes and territories, maps, battle plans, and ideas and strategies. This was chess in real life. He had moved his pawns forward. He was the king and queen, and he was putting his pieces into play. When it was time for them to move, all hell was going to break loose.

But first, Kid had to handle some personal business and pay someone a visit. It was time, and he couldn't hold in his frustration and anger any longer.

✳✳✳

He arrived in Poughkeepsie early that morning with Maniac. This was going to be his last time in Poughkeepsie and his last visit with Nana. Reluctant previously, this time he was eager to see and speak to the bitch. Alone, he wheeled himself into the building, signed in under a pseudonym, and took the elevator to the second floor. He knocked and waited.

Nana soon answered. She was shocked to see him, but she managed to smile. "Kid, hello. It's great to see you, although this visit is unexpected." She invited him inside. She closed the door, relying on her cane to get around.

It wasn't great to see her. He was there on business. He made his way into the apartment. He looked at her. "I hear you're having trouble paying your rent for this place."

"Since Kip's death, it's been hard for me, Kid." She sighed. "Kip was a great man, and I miss him a l—"

"I'm not here to talk about my brother. He's gone."

"I'm sorry."

"Don't be. I'm here now, Nana."

Nana smiled. She took a seat in a chair, still clutching her cane.

Kid sat in his wheelchair stoic about her condition —if she had one. Now it was time for the truth to come out, and he wasn't leaving until every ounce of her bullshit was revealed.

"Kid, I know you and I have had our differences over the years, but I never stopped loving you like you was my own child. And Kip would have appreciated this."

He gruffly reminded her, "I said I don't want to talk about him."

"Okay, what do you want to talk about?"

"I'm here to talk about you and your cancer. What stage are you again?"

"Stage three."

"What's the name of your doctor that diagnosed you?"

"Doctor Bullard. I can show you papers, Kid. What's wrong? Where is this going?"

"Where I want it to go," he replied harshly.

Suddenly Nana was in the hot seat.

"I know Kip gave you a hundred thousand dollars for chemo and other medical expenses. Where's the money, Nana?"

Nana sat there almost speechless. She wasn't ready for what came her way. How could she tell him that the money was gone? How could she tell him about Curtis, and how he swindled her?

"Kid, the money is going toward my treatment"—A sudden chronic cough interrupted her explanation. Looking short of breath and sickly, she said, "Water. I need some water."

The cough sounded serious. Nana was good, but she wasn't fooling him. He wheeled himself into the kitchenette, opened her fridge, and grabbed bottled water for her.

Nana's coughing continued. She took the water and drank it, trying to placate her cough.

"Shall we continue?" he said coolly. "I have plenty time to talk." He looked at Nana with a hard gaze. She wasn't about to fake her way from the truth. "I found a specialist for you, Nana. I feel you should get a second opinion."

"I don't need a second opinion. Why would I lie about having cancer?"

"I never said you were lying. It's simply a second opinion."

"My doctor is the best. I trust his diagnosis, though I'm scared. And I'm trying to get ahead of this sickness."

Kid grew tired of playing nice. "You're a greedy fuckin' bitch, and you used my brother to get money from him. He did a lot for you when you didn't fuckin' deserve it. He even robbed a drop to help pay for a sickness that you don't have.

"The first day I met you, I knew you were a fake bitch, only looking for cash and handouts. You took advantage of our situation. Nice government checks every month for taking in two ghetto niggas, and giving us the nitty-gritty while you lived in glamor, having nice things. I always saw through you, you bitch!"

"How dare you, Kid! You need to leave now!" she demanded.

"I'm not going anywhere, Nana. We're not done talking."

"You were never him, and you never will be your brother. The only thing you'll be is a crippled fool. You legless, retarded muthafucka! Kip will always be a better man than you, more now that he's dead."

"There she is—the evil bitch I've been looking for. Now that's who I wanted to see come out. It's about time."

"Get out, before I throw your handicapped ass out of my fuckin' house!" Nana lifted to her feet, not needing a cane this time, feeling superior to him. What could he do? What power did he have?

He smirked at her and wasn't intimidated at all. "You know, Nana, we do have one thing in common."

"You think I'm playing with you? We don't have shit in common."

"Oh, but we do. We both know how to play out a sickness very well. In fact, I commend you, because you're a great hustler and a crafty con artist. But you know what? I'm a better hustler and smarter con." He suddenly sprung up from the wheelchair, showing her the miracle. He could stand and walk.

Nana's mouth dropped open in complete shock.

Kid had one last trick up his sleeve. He lunged for Nana, and there was a minor tussle, but he soon overpowered her with a gut punch then wrapped his hands around her neck. He slammed her against the bed and straddled her. He wanted to choke her to death, but he couldn't. He had to do it the right way.

"Sick, my ass!" he said. "You got more strength than a farm mule."

Quickly, he stuck Nana in the back of her neck with a cyanide-loaded syringe. The lethal dose of cyanide started to work in seconds. He stood back and watched the poison do its job. She began to gasp for breath before passing out and suffering cardiac arrest.

Finally, the old bitch was dead, and he felt no remorse.

He wiped away his fingerprints from what he touched, placed the body to make her death look natural, and then sat back in his wheelchair. He rolled out of her apartment feeling he had done everyone a huge justice. He exited the building calmly and had help getting into the van. He felt good.

DIRTY WORK - PART ONE

Kid puffed out with a proud grin and said to Maniac, "Let's get the fuck outta here."

When Kid, as next of kin, was contacted about her death, he refused to pay for her funeral. In people's eyes, it wasn't odd, because he was broke, crippled, and still grieving for his brother.

In the end, Nana's small church raised the money to bury her. Kid didn't bother to show up to her funeral. He wanted her to rot in hell.

***

Kid found it suspicious and disrespectful that Jessica didn't show up to his brother's funeral. Despite Jessica's sudden conflict with Eshon and Brandy, she should have been there. He felt something was odd and wrong, and he planned on getting to the bottom of things.

When he tried to talk to Eshon about Jessica, Eshon was useless, still distraught over Kip's death.

So he went to Brandy and asked questions. Who was this man she was seeing? Where did they meet? Had they ever seen a glimpse of him?

Brandy didn't know the man's name, had never seen his face, and didn't know what his occupation was. The only thing she could tell him was that he had money, and plenty of it, because Jessica had upgraded her wardrobe to Fendi, Prada, and Chanel, she wore expensive jewelry, and she had lots of spending money, sometimes in the thousands.

Kid came to the conclusion that Jessica was trying to hide her man. But why? Who was he?

***

One late night Kid sat parked in a burgundy Honda Odyssey outside Jessica's building and watched the front lobby. He'd changed vehicles because Kip's van was marked and too familiar with people.

As he loitered near the projects, he felt a bit nostalgic but shook off the

224

feeling. This wasn't back in the day. Everything had changed, including him.

Two hours passed, and still no Jessica. Kid sent up a scout to her apartment, a young girl, and had her knock on the door for a hundred dollars. Soon after, she came back to the van.

"Is she in there?"

"No," the girl said.

He nodded. He thanked her, and she left. He started the vehicle and left.

***

Two days later, Kid was back with Maniac, parked by Jessica's building with a clear view of the lobby. He watched everyone coming and going with binoculars. His instincts told him to keep an eye on her and identify the mysterious man that had all of her time and interest.

Tonight, he got lucky. Jessica exited the lobby looking well-dressed and too sexy. She walked toward the Old Broadway.

He was on her, stalking her closely, and he soon observed her climbing into the back seat of an idling Escalade with tinted windows.

Kid had no idea who was inside the vehicle. When it drove off, he followed.

He followed them for over twenty miles into New Jersey, until the Escalade came to a stop at a towering condo in Edgewater, New Jersey.

Jessica got out of the SUV and went into the building, presumably to meet her man inside.

Like a detective, Kid had Maniac take pictures of the vehicle, the plate number, the building, and many of Jessica's coming and goings.

For a week, he followed her, until he finally got what he was looking for—a look at the man she had been secretly meeting with—the man she was fucking. Kid had his cronies everywhere, making Jessica his primary

225

objective. He saw her meet with Maserati Meek at the condo. Jessica hugged him and kissed him and appeared to be in love with him.

Seeing this, Kid flew in a rage. He had to control his impulse because he wanted to kill her right there. He didn't know which hurt more, Jessica being with another guy and never giving him a second look, or the other guy being the man who had killed his brother.

He took pictures of them together on his phone, kissing and hugging. The smile on her face was genuine, and Jessica appeared to be very happy. Maserati Meek would openly grope her in public. Kid couldn't help but feel jealous. So many nights he had dreamed of physically wanting her, and she was sleeping with the enemy. He was going to bring their sexual relationship to an abrupt stop.

He had figured out their routine: She would leave her building and get into a car, usually at night. An escort would drive her to a location to meet with Meek, and the location would vary. One week it was in New Jersey, then Long Island or a place in Queens.

Kid was ready to implement his plan. It was time to make his move on the board. Jessica had no idea that the hammer was about to land down on her hard. Kid was angry with her. She was a traitor, and usually traitors received the death sentence, but for now, he would spare her life.

✳✳✳

Friday night in Harlem the streets were flooded with people enjoying the night and starting their weekend with a bang. Three days from the Fourth of July, fireworks were going off repeatedly around the projects with ball rockets, blockbusters, whistlers, and firecrackers. The skies lit up with an explosion and a colorful display.

Kid Kane and Devon sat in the dark minivan with tinted windows and waited in the Manhattanville projects. There would be no barbecues or cookouts for them, no enjoying fireworks, or mingling with people.

They had a purpose tonight. Kid never got out the car. He had to continue his ruse of being disabled. Devon would be his legs on this mission.

After an hour of waiting, their target finally arrived. The Escalade came to a stop not too far from where they were parked.

Kid and Devon stayed hidden in the shadows of their vehicle and watched everything. The door to the SUV swung open, and Jessica climbed out of the vehicle. She stood upright, looking spectacular in a dress and a pair of wedges. She was dressed for the summer, legs showing, long hair flowing.

Kid fixed his eyes on her and watched her walk to her building. She had just come home from one of her secret excursions with Meek. She looked happy. Kid didn't want her to be happy. He wanted her to feel pain for sleeping with the enemy.

The Escalade drove off.

Kid said to Devon, "You know what to do."

Devon grinned. He removed himself from the minivan with his gun in hand. He approached Jessica with urgency. Before she could reach the building lobby, he called out, "Yo, Jessica!"

She turned, shocked to see Devon. Halfheartedly, she replied, "Hey, what's up, Devon?"

"Yo, let me holla at you fo' a minute, ma," he said.

"About what, homes?" she asked, already looking defensive.

"Just to talk. We missed you at the funeral."

"I've been busy, nigga."

"Yeah, we know, but check this, I ain't asking." He thrust the gun into her side. "We gonna go for a walk and talk, ma, or you know me, bitch—I'll blow your side out right now and won't give a fuck." He pushed her forward, toward the van.

Jessica frowned. She knew he was serious. She had no choice but to go with him. "Did that fuckin' bitch put you up to this?"

Devon didn't answer.

"Kip was her man, not mine."

Their conflict wasn't Devon's concern. He was doing what he was told. But he was furious too that she had been fucking around with Maserati Meek. He felt that she needed to die because of that alone. He continued to coerce her at gunpoint toward the minivan. The side door slid open, and he forcibly pushed her onto the back and closed the door.

Jessica scowled when she saw Kid in the front seat. "Kid, what the fuck is wrong with you, homes? Huh, muthafucka? You lost your mind? This is kidnapping. You think my peoples ain't gonna be lookin' for me?"

"We just need to talk," he said coolly.

"*Cabrón*, we don't have shit to talk about!"

Kid answered, "Yes, we do."

Devon climbed behind the wheel and drove off.

Jessica shouted and cursed at them. She still felt this had something to do with Eshon, but she had no idea.

THIRTY-SIX

Parked in the parking lot of the Extended Stay hotel, Devon got out of the minivan and opened the side door. He dragged Jessica out of the car. She tried to resist, but a gun in her face made her realize it was wise to do what he said. She stood with Devon's gun painfully in her side.

She looked around and found that she was in unfamiliar territory. The hour was late, the place quiet, and it was in the cut.

Kid was still in the front seat. The passenger door opened.

Devon grinned. Jessica had no idea she was about to witness a miracle take place.

Kid turned, and he took his time stepping out of the van, subsequently walking her way with a smirk on his face.

Jessica looked like she had seen a ghost, her mouth gaped open, her eyes wide with bewilderment. "You can walk?"

"I can do a lot of things, sweetheart. Just wait and see."

Consumed by fear, Jessica was about to lose control of her own legs.

Devon grabbed her arm tightly and led her to the hotel, guided her into the room on the first floor. Inside looked like an all-in-one armory and electronic store, with guns everywhere, along with computers, cameras, and surveillance equipment.

"Devon, leave me alone with her for a moment," Kid said.

Devon nodded. He stepped out of the room and closed the door.

"How are you walking?" Jessica asked.

"I'm a miracle. You don't believe in miracles?"

She barked out, "Why am I here?"

"Like I said, to talk. But first things first."

"What?"

"How long you been fuckin' Meek?"

"What? Homes, you can't be serious."

"You think I'm joking with you, Jessica? Answer me!"

Jessica looked blank, shocked that he knew. She had no response.

"Now this is how it's going to go—If you want to live, bitch, then you'll answer all my questions. Did you have anything to do with Kip's murder! Did you know it was going down?"

She stood there for a moment, defiant. "Fuck you!" Jessica spat in his face, incensed.

He didn't respond. His first intention was to kill her, but his heart wouldn't allow it. She had always been his dream girl. He had dreamt about her plenty of nights. What he wanted was intimacy with her, but she was pushing his limits. Evidently, she wanted to die today. Kid wiped the gooey liquid from his face and contained his rage. Jessica was a disrespectful bitch.

Her eyes glared with hatred.

He stepped closer to her and said, "I want you to tell me everything I need to know about Maserati Meek."

"You want me to betray the man I love?"

"*Love*—That's cute, Jessica. We all know the only thing you love is money."

"I do. So what's in it for me? My services aren't for free."

"Besides keeping your life?"

Kid had to respect her game. He wanted to buy her loyalty, but it was only a word to Jessica. The only thing she was loyal to was the highest bidder.

He went into the duffel bag of cash and tossed her ten thousand dollars. "That's a start," he said.

She didn't hesitate to take the money. "A start for what?"

"I want you to work for me, as my snitch."

"Are you serious?"

"Does it look like I'm playing?" he returned seriously.

"Doing what?"

"Don't worry, there's something in it for you. I want you to tell me everything about Maserati Meek. I want to know his locations, his businesses, his trap houses, his comings and goings, his peoples. And for every spot we hit, I'll hit you off with enough cash. You've been with the man for two months now, so I know you know something."

"You gonna kill him?" she asked.

"Nah, I don't wanna kill him, I just want to get rich off of him."

Jessica had money on her mind and her own personal agenda. She nodded. "I'll do it."

Kid smiled. It's what he expected to hear from her. Her greed was her core. She had to look out for herself. Maserati Meek took care of her, but she learned never to put all her eggs in one basket. He was at war, and anything tragic could happen.

Kid stood over her and grabbed her chin with his fingers. He held her face sternly in his hand and looked at her intently. "Listen, you fuck with me on this, and I'll make you feel more hell than you ever felt before. I'm full of surprises, Jessica. Think about it—You thought I couldn't walk, but I can, so imagine what other tricks I have up my sleeve if you cross me, bitch." He released her and then said, "Now get the fuck out."

THIRTY-SEVEN

A white cargo van came to a stop at a red light on Atlantic Avenue and Logan Street in Brooklyn on a calm night. The driver sat smoking his Newport and waiting for the green. He drove conservatively, not wanting to attract attention, especially from the police. He was carrying over fifty kilos of cocaine in the back, smuggled in oil drums. The last thing he needed was an incident, or to have to explain himself to Maserati Meek. The driver's head swiveled left and right, both directions cool and no threat. He had ten miles to go until he reached one of Meek's stash houses with his product.

A panhandler made his way toward the van. His clothes were funky, and his dreads looked like they were filled with lice. "Change, change, spare change, please. All I need is some change," he chanted, carrying a cracked coffee mug. He tapped on the window.

The driver yelled, "Yo, get the fuck away from the van, you bum!"

"Sir, change, change, any spare change, please. All I need is some change."

The driver was losing his patience. He had a load of product to transfer, and it felt like it was taking a lifetime for the red light to change.

While distracted by the panhandler, the bigger threat came from his left with a .50-caliber Desert Eagle.

The window smashed, startling the driver, and when he spun around, the gunman fired two bullets into his head.

The panhandler acted quickly, opening the door, removing the body from the vehicle, dumping him on the street and taking his place behind the wheel. The shooter hurried into the passenger seat, and the van sped away with fifty kilos belonging to Maserati Meek.

***

The house on Grand Avenue in Rockville Centre, Long Island was a quaint, three-bedroom with a two-car garage, manicured lawn, trimmed trees in the front yard, and a porch. The neighborhood resembled Mayberry. The tree-lined streets and affluent homes were a far cry from the projects, but tonight they were about to get a taste of the urban violence.

The three-bedroom home on Grand Avenue was a front; it was one of Maserati Meek's largest stash houses hidden in the outer reaches of a violent society. Here, Meek kept things simple: two people coming and going from the place, a man and a woman who pretended to be married to throw off nosy neighbors and law enforcement but were, in fact, trusted handlers of Meek's product and his money. They drove minivans and SUVs with secret compartments. The garage was attached to the house, giving them privacy when loading and unloading drugs and cash. The house had surveillance and an alarm, and a small arsenal.

Few people knew about the place in Rockville Centre. The man was in his mid-thirties, the woman in her early thirties, and they both played their parts well.

***

At eleven p.m., a black Dodge Caliber with slight tints came to a stop in front of the house. The occupants inside the car gazed at the location with a violent plot to wreak havoc on Meek's organization. For these three men, it was going to be fun. The inside information they were receiving was paying off. They cocked back their pistols and sawed-off shotgun and readied themselves for violence.

Devon took a pull from his cigarette and doused it in the ashtray. He didn't want to risk leaving any DNA behind.

Maniac sat in the backseat with the sawed-off shotgun.

Papa John glanced at the time. "Y'all niggas ready?"

They nodded.

Since Kip's death, these men had been personally at war with Meek. There was no limits, no escape, and they were yearning to destroy everything he had built. With Kid as the brains, they had been many steps ahead of their enemy.

Jessica was helpful with information, along with subtle surveillance of Meek's peoples, and there was help from a city cop Kid had blackmailed. Officer Melton had a gambling problem and a desire for prostitutes. He owed a dangerous man thirty thousand dollars. Kid paid off his debts, and now the cop was indebted to him. To pay off his debts, Officer Melton had to provide Kid with information that wasn't easy to attain.

Kid Kane was building his empire slowly but surely. With what he had accomplished in weeks, it was easy to say who the smarter brother in the streets was.

All three men donned black masks, climbed out of the Caliber, and approached the house heavily armed. They lit two Molotov cocktails and sent them crashing through the front windows of the house. Immediately flames burst open, engulfing the house rapidly, and soon two figures came flying out the front door coughing and scurrying for safety.

Once they had sight of the man and woman, they opened fire.

Bak! Bak! Bak! Bak! Bak!

Boom! Boom! Boom!

Bullets smashed into the fake couple and twisted their bodies, and they fell to their deaths on the front lawn in robes and underwear, bleeding profusely like stuck pigs.

For good measure, Devon stepped to the already dead folks and put a bullet in both their heads.

The violence and gunfire had awoken the neighbors. What they saw was shocking to them. The house was completely in flames, as smoldering fire lifted into the sky. Death and fire were turning their neighborhood upside down.

Devon, Papa John, and Maniac left the money, guns, and drugs inside to burn. It was a message to Maserati Meek—His time was coming, and they knew where to find his shit. The men ran to the car and sped off laughing.

***

Jessica stood, looking dejected, in front of Kid. The other night she had been with Meek sexually. It was all part of the game—using her body for survival—and she figured herself a scheming bitch. She had been playing both sides of the fence, trying to collect enough money from both men to leave town when the opportunity presented itself.

She had given Kid enough information on Meek, risking her life while doing so. She would listen to his phone conversations, eavesdrop, and snoop around his apartment and business. Sometimes she would flirt with one of Meek's lieutenants or soldiers, and they would say something to her that wasn't supposed to be said. Sometimes, after sex with Meek, there was pillow talk, and he found himself confiding in her about certain things.

Jessica did whatever possible to get information for Kid. The espionage business was a scary, but profitable business. She knew if she was caught, Meek would kill her, but the money was good coming from Kid. He kept up his word, giving her a percentage of whatever was taken from Meek's organization, and with incessant gifts and cash coming from Meek's end, she was living the good life.

Kid looked her way and asked, "What you got for me this time?"

She handed him a sheet of paper that listed a few corporations, mostly shell companies, and an offshore account.

"Damn, Jessica! This some heavy shit you got from him. How you get this?"

"I do whatever I need to do."

"I see. He fucked you good last time, huh?" There was jealousy in his voice.

"What?"

"Bitch, you heard me! How he be fuckin' you?"

"Kid, you lost ya mind, homes."

"I didn't lose shit, bitch! Answer the fuckin' question."

"Fuck you!"

He backhanded her, the force sending her crashing to the floor. Her lip was bleeding. It enraged him that she was sleeping with the enemy after Meek had murdered his brother. It also enraged him that he had a huge crush on her and she still looked at him as if he was still a cripple, half a man.

"Fuck you, bitch! You go to him freely, but you ignored me for years!"

Jessica wiped the blood from her mouth and glared at Kid. She saw his jealousy. It was exciting to her, but dangerous too. She didn't have any love for anyone. She had always been about herself. "What's wrong? Mama got Daddy jealous?"

He hit her again.

She laughed from the attack. "Fuck you!" Jessica was tired of his shit. Worn out from playing both sides of the game, she was ready to put a plan of her own into action.

✳✳✳

Kid was smart, but a fool to think Jessica would ever be a one-man whore. He'd given her a task to do with Meek, but it was hard for him to contain his emotions. He saw the way Eshon loved his brother. She would have done anything for Kip, even die for him, and he wanted that same love for himself. But it would never be there with a woman like Jessica. She had no loyalty.

He used her, but he didn't trust her, and unbeknownst to Jessica, he had placed a tracking app on her phone to always locate her.

THIRTY-EIGHT

Maserati Meek just couldn't perform tonight with Jessica. He couldn't get an erection, and he couldn't eat her pussy right. He seemed distracted. He removed himself from the bed, brooding about something.

Jessica sat upright and watched him.

Suddenly he screamed out, "Muthafucka!" and put his fist through the wall then smashed a mirror, and turned over the flat-screen.

Jessica had never seen him so upset. "Baby, what's wrong?" she asked.

"Every fuckin' thing is wrong," he growled. "I'm being attacked!"

She exhaled. There was something special about Meek that made her like him more than the other men in her life. Kid Kane was using her, but Meek was spoiling her rotten with things, and he did care for her.

The betrayal was making her sick, but the money was great. But did she have true feelings for Maserati Meek? With Nia dead, a casualty of the war, she had become his main bitch.

Meek couldn't find a safe place to hide before having to relocate because Kid was always one step ahead of him, and he was trying to figure out why.

"I got a snitch somewhere in my organization," he said. "Someone isn't who they seem to be."

Jessica felt the urge to say something to him. How long could this go on? How long could she be a spy for Kid and be a lover and girlfriend to one of the most dangerous men in the underworld until it all came crashing around her and blowing up in her face? "Baby, we need to talk," she said.

He turned to her. "Talk about what, eh?"

She took a deep breath. "I know something," she started.

Hearing that, he moved closer to her. "You know what?"

"I overheard something from this bitch I know. And word is, it's some crippled *cabrón* from Harlem that's after you for murdering his brother. It's Kip's little brother. His name is Kid."

"He has a little brother, eh. I did not know this."

She nodded.

"My precious jewel, you are." He sat close to her on the bed, looked her in her eyes and asked, "Can you get more intel on this man—this cripple—from this same woman?"

She nodded. "I can."

He smiled.

"Good! You are special to me, Jessica. Very special."

She smiled. Now was the time to implement her plan. She would have her cake and eat it too.

"Now if you excuse me, I need to make a phone call, eh. No more games with these imbeciles! I should show these fools true power."

***

The apology from Jessica to Eshon and Brandy came out of the blue. Jessica had called them up wanting to make amends with them. Eshon's twenty-first birthday was coming up, and to show that her reconciliation and apology were legit, Jessica wanted to throw her an over the top party at a club in the city. Eshon and everyone else was shocked.

"Let's get the E and J Brandy bitches back together," she said to Eshon.

After everything they'd been through, Eshon and the others were down. It was nice of Jessica. Eshon needed something special. After Kip's death, she had been an emotional wreck.

A reunion with Kid, Devon, Papa John, Brandy, and Jessica was the perfect remedy. Jessica would plan it all, and she had picked the place. She would plan a memorial for Kip too. The entire thing would go down in two weeks, exactly on Eshon's birthday.

EPILOGUE

American Airlines Flight 989 from Egypt landed at JFK Airport at eleven a.m. that morning, and three men exited the plane dressed non-descript in shorts, sneakers, and T-shirts. They moved through customs easily and were picked up by a waiting car outside the terminal.

Two hours later, a Delta flight from Egypt landed in LGA Airport, and four men departed the plane dressed unassumingly in shorts, ball caps, loud T-shirts, and sneakers. They were picked up outside the terminal in an SUV after being screened through customs.

Several days later, three more men arrived at JFK Airport from Egypt and were picked up from the terminal. One day later, Flight 989 from Egypt landed at JFK Airport, and two men departed the plane, moved through customs and were picked up outside the terminal by a black SUV.

A dozen Al-Qaeda men were now in New York to meet with Maserati Meek. They came to assist their comrade in the war happening stateside. Their motive was murder, their target, a New York City nightclub.

Maserati Meek stated to them, "Everyone must die!"

THE DIRTY WORK
ISN'T DONE.

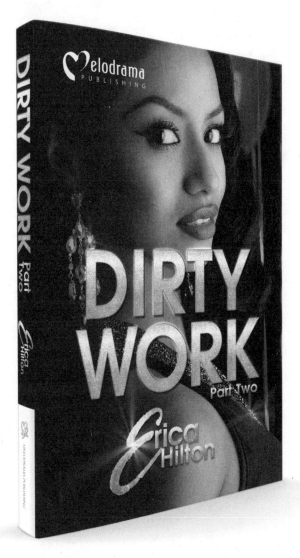

MAFIO$O

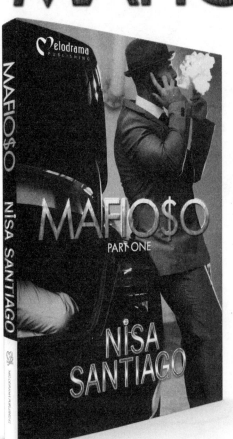

Ambitions as a Mobster

Scott West and his wife Layla have an infatuation with the Mafioso way of life. Armed with what they've learned, they assemble their own family based on the careers of the most successful mobsters and are now in charge of a powerful crime family. Their six children—Meyer, Bugsy, Lucky, Bonnie, Clyde, and Gotti—are all being groomed to manage the family business.

Al Capone's legacy taught Scott to run his drug empire upon fear, helping him prosper as a daunting opponent. When challenged by Deuce, the daring Baltimore crime boss, Scott has to play the game for real as they clash in a mob-style power struggle. When the smoke clears, only one will have a seat at the head of the table.

The enthralling new series by Nisa Santiago

MAFIO$O

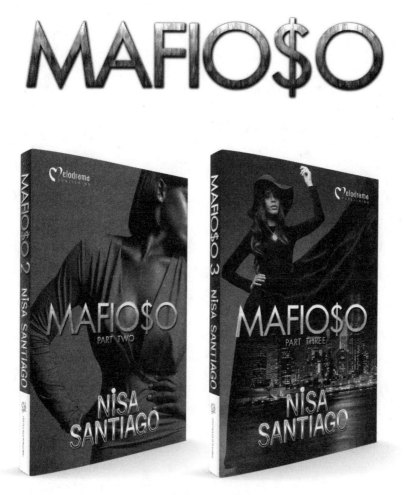

The enthralling new series by Nisa Santiago